THE CLANSMAN

Mary MacGregor shook her head. 'I do not understand you, Rob. *You!* To flee, without a fight? What has come over you, at all? Oh, I know that I said to Greg that it was clear thinking that was needed, not just big words and talk of war. But that was different. Now, the soldiers are at your very doorstep. Even if there are two hundred of them, you could raise men enough to keep them from here, to trap them in the pass up from the loch, to throw them back into the water . . .'

'Aye, I could do that, Mary – nothing simpler. And belike, that is just what Montrose would have me do. But have you considered the cost? I am outlawed now, remember. And all who knowingly will be assisting and supporting an outlaw are liable to outlawry in their turn. Any measures can be taken against outlaws – *any* measures, Mary. If I flee, lass, there will be *one* outlaw only. But if I do rouse the clan, all MacGregors will be outlawed, whatever. How think you of that? All my people, at the mercy of Montrose and those others who do not love us. You – and the young ones. Greg, and his bonny wife and bairns. Your old father at Comer. All – all outside the law. What do you think of that?'

NIGEL TRANTER is the author of many bestselling books about such Scottish heroes as Robert the Bruce, Black Douglas and the Marquis of Montrose, all of which are available as Coronet paperbacks.

The Clansman

Nigel Tranter

CORONET BOOKS
Hodder Paperbacks Ltd., London

Copyright © 1959 by Nigel Tranter

First published 1959 by Hodder and
Stoughton Ltd

Coronet edition 1974
Second impression 1985

Printed and bound in Great Britain for
Hodder and Stoughton Paperbacks, a
division of Hodder and Stoughton Ltd.,
Mill Road, Dunton Green, Sevenoaks,
Kent (Editorial Office: 47 Bedford
Square, London, WC1 3DP) by
Hunt Barnard Printing Ltd.,
Aylesbury, Bucks.

ISBN 0 340 18768 9

PRELUDE

JAMES GRAHAM, first Duke, fourth Marquis and eighth Earl of Montrose, looked down from his window on to the busy London street, and laughed. As a laugh, it scarcely matched the nobility of his Grace's style, background and power. In fact, it might have been described as a girlish giggle in anyone less august.

'I think that we have him, Johnnie,' he said. 'Yes, this time, damme, I think we have – God rot his soul!' And he sniggered again, and lovingly caressed one of the tight black curls of the enormous full-bottomed wig that he affected. His voice was gentle, delicately modulated.

'Aye, your lordship . . . your Grace. I'm glad o' that.' John Graham of Killearn was not yet quite used to his master being a duke. 'No' before time, either.' That was a very different voice, broad, strong, using the unvarnished speech of the Scottish Lowlands. 'We've had him before, mind – but no' to hold. He takes a deal o' holding, does Rob.'

'Think you I don't know that, man! But this time, I'll hold him. I am going to isolate him, knock his damned hairy legs from under him – bare his dirty red backside for all Scotland to gawp at!' The coarseness and indelicacy sounded strange in that fastidious high-pitched voice. The Duke reached into a pocket of his long yellow satin waistcoat for his gold snuff-box, and flicked back the lace from his wrist gracefully. 'Preparatory to the application of a good honest length of rope to his unwashed MacGregor thrapple, 'fore God!'

7

'A bonny day that'll be, aye,' Killearn agreed, but still doubtfully. 'It's maybe a wee thing easier thought on here in London than up on the Hieland Line – as your Grace weel kens. The man's clan are ay thick aboot him as the lice in his ain red fur! And he uses the very land to fight for him, damn him!' Montrose's factor spoke feelingly.

'His clan, and his land! That's the beauty of it, Johnnie. I'm going to make the fellow's very strength work against him.' The Duke turned back from the window to face his companion, laughing again. His voice, now, was seen not to belie him – whatever might be said of his laughter. James Graham, like most of his illustrious family, had extraordinary good looks – even though it might be said that they would better have graced his father's daughter than his son – from his high noble forehead, wide strong arching brows, deep glowing eyes, finely chiselled nose, and small pouting shapely mouth, to the delicately pointed chin. If the effect, enhanced deliberately by the cascading black ringlets of the vast wig and the touches of rouge at the cheeks, was rather more feminine than was everybody's taste, no one who knew him would have therefore read any hint of weakness into the features of Her Majesty's new Lord Keeper of the Privy Seal.

Graham of Killearn, factor of his Grace's great estates in Scotland, where the Lowlands joined the Highlands, certainly had no such illusions. A hard strong man himself, he knew a harder when he saw one.

'It is all most convenient and opportune,' the Duke went on, dabbing at his red lips with a lace-edged handkerchief now; he was always doing something with those slender pointed fingers of his. 'Now that I have the Privy Seal, the Lord Advocate is in my pocket – as, for that matter, is the whole Law of Scotland. Useful, Johnnie – useful. Argyll, who might befriend our Rob, out of unwarranted spite of me, is away in Spain at his ridiculous soldiering. And both Atholl and Breadalbane, poor fools, are in disgrace for being

8

unwise about the Union, of glorious memory!' Montrose himself, of course, had worked hard for the Union of the Parliaments of Scotland and England five years before – hence his dukedom and new-won high office. 'Rob has no one to turn to.'

'Save his own damned MacGregors!' Killearn growled.

'Ha – but they are not his own MacGregors any longer, you fool! His nephew, young Gregor of Glengyle, now no longer needs his uncle to run his people for him. Glengyle is very much the chief, I'm told, with two fine sons of his own. 'Tis said, indeed, that he finds Rob an embarrassment at times – as well he may! Do not think that I have forgotten the barbarous MacGregors, my dear Johnnie.' The Duke was quite capable of naming a man a fool and his dearest Johnnie in the same breath. 'Here is the way of it. It has been a bad year for the cattle trade and the droving, as you know. Prices have never been lower. At the recent trysts at Crieff and Falkirk, Rob Roy has chosen to keep his beasts rather than sell at the prices. That means he has a great many cattle to winter – an expensive business, as we have found to our own cost, eh? He cannot do it in his own Highlands. And it is too late to sell now, with the trysts past. I am told that he is devilish short of silver.'

'Who is not, in Scotland today, my God?' Killearn returned. 'The Union looks like costing us dear. . . .'

'Tush, man – leave that. Do you mind the money I loaned to Rob that time, for the cattle-dealing? Back in '08?'

'I mind the one thousand pounds Scots your Grace invested with Rob Roy, for the supply of beef to King Jamie's army – before we kenned just which way the cat was going to jump,' Killearn admitted cautiously. 'Is that the money you mean?'

'That is something like the sum, yes – less interest accrued. Considerable interest. But I think you both mistake the terms, Johnnie, and put it badly. Badly, yes.' The Duke spoke softly, gently. 'It was a pure loan, to a man in need. And would I, think you, who was Queen Anne's Lord President of the Council in Scotland, have any truck with Her Blessed Majesty's enemies? Would I, oaf? Would I?' Long and hard James Graham looked at John Graham, out of those dark luminous eyes.

The factor cleared his throat, and his own glance fell. 'As your Grace says,' he muttered.

'Exactly, Johnnie, I intend, you see, to demand the repayment of that loan, together with full interest, forthwith. Considerable interest, in view of the unsettled and risky times, as is only just. And, alas – poor Robbie cannot pay! Heigho!'

'Aye. But we tried that before, you'll mind. And Rob claimed you were his partner, and must share losses like you shared profits. He'll claim the same again. . . .'

'Aha – but then I was not Lord Keeper of the Privy Seal, Johnnie, and the Lord Advocate did not have to do what I told him! Rob cannot pay – not till the spring sales. I'll have the Court grant me an immediate citation against him, and have him declared a fraudulent bankrupt. . . .'

'But he still has his lands, y'Grace. He still has Inversnaid and Craigroyston. He can sell you these, and keep out o' bankruptcy. They're worth far more than the debt. . . .'

'But he won't my good clod – he won't. He looks on these as MacGregor lands. Clan land – and he is too fond of his filthy bareshanked clansmen to sell. That's what I meant when I said I'd make his strength fight against him. He'll do many things will Rob Roy MacGregor – but he'll never sell MacGregor land. I want Craigroyston, yes – and I'll have it, too, by God! But not that way. I want it for nothing, you see. And once he's declared bankrupt. . . .'

'But, guidsakes, y'Grace – he'll never attend your Court. Rob'll never put himsel' into your hands. He'll stay snug in his ain Hielands. . . .'

'Of course he will, Johnnie. Whereupon I shall have him

declared outlaw! And, see you, an outlaw's property is forfeit to the Crown. The Crown, Johnnie – and, for the time being, *I* am the Crown, in Scotland! Craigroyston will round off my Buchanan lands nicely, as I think you will agree?'

Killearn blinked small eyes. He was not in the habit of admitting admiration for God nor man, but he could scarce withhold it now. 'Aye,' he said heavily, licking his lips. 'Aye – that's clever. But he'll fight, mind. We'll no' get possession easy.'

'I think we will. Again, he will think of his clan, see you. Any of the lieges who support an outlaw against the Crown become outlaws also, forthwith. Will he turn his beloved Gregor of Glengyle, with his wife and bairns, into outlaws too? And all the rest of his MacGregor rabble? Or will *they* allow it? I think not. Rob has fought us off before, in his damned mountains – yes. But that was in the bad old days before the blessed Union! And it was just our local clod-hoppers and levies that he fought – not the Crown. This time, mark you, it will be Her Majesty's forces. The Army. For, of course, the Crown must protect its own property. I shall see that an adequate force is sent to Craigroyston to take and hold it, in the name of Queen Anne. In fact, it strikes me that it might well be excellent Government policy for a new fort to be built thereabouts, with a permanent garrison – to clip the wings of the deplorable Gregorach for the future. Such a garrison ought to keep Buchanan Castle and the Montrose estates reasonably snug and comfortable, think you not, Johnnie?'

Killearn was now lost in admiration. 'My God,' he said 'you think o' a' things, y'Grace. I cannot see how Rob can win oot o' that tangle.'

The Duke's laugh was positively silvery now. 'Frankly, Johnnie, I cannot see it, myself! So, my good animal, if you can bear to tear yourself away from your sordid lecheries amid the stews of London . . .' The rosebud ducal lips curled in distaste. '. . . and repair forthwith to Scotland, I will have work for you in plenty. Within, I hope, the month. Merry work – work that I think you will enjoy. You have never greatly loved the MacGregors either, have you, Johnnie?'

'No,' the other acceded briefly. He was a curt man, was Killearn. 'Have I your Grace's permission to retire?'

'You have, Johnnie. See that you are posting north by tomorrow. Oh – and for the proper furtherance of Her Majesty's law and order in the good shire of Stirling, I think it would be as well if you were appointed to be a sheriff-substitute of that county! Then you could lead the forfeiting expedition to Craigroyston in person, with all due authority. I will write the Lord Advocate to that effect at once. Authority to take all necessary measures, Johnnie – all necessary measures. You take me?'

John Graham's heavy features creased to a grin. 'Aye, your Grace – I do. Fine, I do.'

CHAPTER ONE

PROVOST DRUMMOND of Crieff looked apprehensively from one visitor to the other, and cleared his throat. 'Did . . . did ye bring many men along wi' you, sirs?' he wondered. 'More than just them, oot there?' And he nodded his greying head towards the knot of red-coated dragoons who stood outside the Tolbooth window.

'There are a dozen stout fellows, there,' Captain Plowden said impatiently. 'Ample, surely, to apprehend one man! Our information is that the fellow rode into Crieff yesterday, alone, and put up at the house of one Lucky MacRae. He is said to have business with a dealer and corn-chandler of the name of Patrick Stewart.'

'Aye – I daresay.' The Provost's grizzled eyebrows rose a little at the accuracy of the Stirling military's information. They must have passing good spies in Crieff town. He wondered how much more they knew? That Rob had business with himself also, as tanner and hide merchant? 'But maybe a bigger troop, see you, would ha' been wise. A kittlish customer, he is. And no' just alone, mind. MacAlastair's wi' him – MacAlastair's ay wi' Rob. . . . '

'Tut, Provost – this is a law-abiding town, isn't it?' the Sheriff Officer interrupted. 'You're no' suggesting that a round dozen o' Her Majesty's sodjers are no' enough to arrest two men in the middle o' the burgh o' Crieff – wi' all your good honest townsfolk at hand to support the Queen's officers?'

The little tanner, who was Crieff's chief magistrate, moistened his lips. 'No, no – never think it, sirs. It's just that ye never ken what Rob'll be up to. And he has a deal o' friends – amongst the baser sort, see you. Rob's ay a great one for the common folk. They like him, some way. I've seen him giving away whole sides o' beef, at the Cross oot there, for the poor. . . .'

'Not good enough friends to make themselves the Queen's enemies, for any nameless MacGregor, I'll warrant!' the Captain snorted. 'You don't foster rebellion in this town of yours, Provost – do you?'

'Guidsakes – no! Och, mercy on us – nothing o' the sort! We're a' right loyal subjects o' Her Majesty. . . .'

'I'm glad of that.'

'You've no MacGregors in the town, to worry you, Provost?' the Sheriff Officer said. 'You're far from the Mac-Gregor country here – twenty good miles and more. There are no MacGregors nearer than Strathyre and Balquhidder. Our word is that Glengyle is away in the south, visiting Arnprior. And Rob Roy's own folk are all out scouring the country for winter fodder for his beasts.'

Again the Provost marvelled at the authorities' informa-MacGregors like hawks. They had waited until he was well outside his own country, and alone, to strike. Biding their time, knowing that come out he must, desperate for winter feed for his swollen herds of cattle. Did they know, too, that Rob was here seeking to barter hundreds of hides to himself, for his tannery, in exchange for great loads of Lowland hay from Patrick Stewart?

'Is that a fact, sirs?' he stalled. 'Och, no doubt you've the rights o' it. There are no MacGregors in town, no. But . . .'

'Devil take it – enough of this!' Captain Plowden cried impatiently. 'We have wasted time enough as it is. I want to be back in Stirling, with our prisoner, before dark. Where is this Lucky MacRae's house, man? Lead us there – in the Queen's name!'

Drummond swallowed. He was not a valiant man. He

had done what he could, put off as much time as possible, kept these officers talking, in order to give opportunity for Rob to slip away, out of town. Whenever they had arrived at the Tolbooth, from Stirling, and sent for him, he had contrived to get a messenger out of the back door, with the word for the MacGregor. He could do no more.

'As ye will, sirs. Lucky's howff is up in the Kirk Wynd. I'll hae the Town Officer to fetch ye there. . . .'

'As well if you came yourself, Provost. As chief magistrate . . .'

The Sheriff Officer paused, listening. Above the stir of the blustery November wind, another sound penetrated, faint but clear, within the massive walls of Crieff's ancient Tolbooth. It was pipe music, thin and high. Not such a strange sound to hear in the streets of the capital of Strathearn, on the very edge of the Highland Line, at some times, no doubt. But strange on a November day in the year 1713, with the Union Government supreme, the Jacobites in eclipse, and the clans in disgrace for having lately preferred James Stewart across the water to Queen Anne in London, and weapons proscribed by law to all but the Queen's forces. Not that bagpipes actually ranked as offensive weapons, of course – but when they played martial music they could be equally dangerous in Scotland, a barbarous challenge to sound order and authority. And the present strains sounded martial enough, in all conscience.

Soldier and Sheriff looked at each other. 'What is that?' the former demanded sternly.

'I . . . I dinna just ken,' the Provost muttered. Which was less than honest. For whether or not these two knew it, he and everyone else in Crieff – except for the dragoons outside, probably – recognised the stirring strains of *My Race is Royal*, the MacGregor march, when they heard it.

'Who would blow the devil-damned pipes in front of Her Majesty's dragoons?' Captain Plowden went on, angrily.

15

'God kens, Captain!' the little man quivered. And again, though undoubtedly true enough, his statement lacked fullest candour.

The soldiers outside had moved forward, to gaze up the climbing High Street of hilly Crieff, pointing and gesticulating. Their commander barked an oath, and turning, stamped out of the room and down the steps to the cobbled street, spurs jingling. After him hurried the soberly-clad Sheriff Officer, clutching his parchments. And, less eagerly, the Provost followed on.

They were not alone in their interest, needless to say. All up and down the street, heads were thrusting out from windows and doors and close-mouths. Many of the good folk of Crieff had already been keeping a discreet eye on the scarlet-coated dragoons, undoubtedly – but this latest development was of the stuff to temper discretion. Miraculously people appeared on every hand, staring.

What they stared at was not, in itself, spectacular. A mere three men – and two of them far from impressive. But people's breath caught in their throats nevertheless – and more than one goodwife hurriedly turned to whisk children and self safely in behind a shut door.

Coming down the very centre of the High Street walked these three men. The first two went side by side, and a comic pair they made; one small, deformed and twisted, with a hunch to his back; the other long and lean and lame; both filthy and unshaven, both clad in tattered rags of tartan so stained as to be unrecognisable, and both puffing away strongly at the bagpipes, hirpling and hobbling. Comic indeed – but no one in all that street so much as smiled. Save one. Obvious to all, they were gangrels, Highland tinks, strolling pipers, routed at a moment's notice out of some back-street den or other, and scarcely sober by the looks of them. But at least they both could play *My Race is Royal*, and approximately in time.

Behind them, a good dozen paces behind, strode another man, alone. And there was nothing comic about this one, save perhaps in his astonishing length of arm, so that his hands hung down to his bare knees – though, again, few would have found that cause for laughter. He was an extraordinary figure of a man, in more than his arms, not seeming so tall as he was in fact, owing to his enormous breadth of shoulder and very slightly bowed legs. But the impact of him had nothing of deformity about it, nothing freakish nor apelike – only strength, a notable and singular impression of personal strength. Those near enough to meet the shock of brilliant pale-blue eyes knew another and still more potent strength, as of a smouldering explosive energy only just held in leash – eyes that many could only look at askance. But they were smiling now, those eyes – for the man was laughing as he walked. His hair a fiery red, the curling hair of his head, of his fierce down-turning moustaches and pointed short beard, the thick furring of wrists and hands and knees, that contrasted so vehemently with those startlingly blue eyes, seemed all part of the latent power of him. A man in his early forties, he was dressed in the full panoply of a Highland gentleman, in great kilt and swathed plaid of red-green MacGregor tartan, a long-skirted doublet of brown-and-white calf-skin, great jewelled clasp at shoulder, silver buttons, otter-skin sporran, woven and diced half-hose, buckled brogues, and sword-belt with basket-hilted claymore. On his head was a bonnet of blue, with a diced band, sporting a sprig of Scots pine, badge of his clan, and a single eagle's feather. Rob Roy MacGregor was always clothes-conscious. He strode down the crown of Crieff's causeway now, alone, apart – but never lonely-seeming – and while it would be unfair to say that he swaggered, his whole bearing and carriage proclaimed a proud and genial satisfaction with the day, the place, the good Lord's providence, and the splendid heartening strains of the Mac-Gregor's march.

Down the street, at his back, but keeping a respectful distance, thronged a growing crowd.

Captain Plowden spluttered his wrath and sense of outrage, incoherent at first from sheer dumbfoundment. He pointed. ' 'Swounds – the damned insolence of the fellow!' he got out, with difficulty. 'It's him – MacGregor! Look at him! *Look* at him . . . !'

The Sheriff Officer was looking, sure enough – and not too happily. But not nearly so unhappily as was Provost Drummond, who was twisting his hands together in major distress, and blinking fast. It was hard, hard on a peaceable man who wished no harm to anybody. Rob had certainly made strange and wicked use of the precious few minutes' grace that he had so generously bought him. 'He . . . he's an awfu' man . . . a right borach!' he stammered. 'Did I no' tell ye – ye never ken what he'll be up to? Och, sirs – this is difficult, difficult, see you . . .'

'Difficult?' the soldier repeated harshly. 'It's a scandal, sir! To add to all his other offences, he's deliberately making a public riot. But at least, we do not need to go find him – he's coming to us! Which will save time.' Plowden raised his voice. 'Sergeant – draw your men across this street. I want that man stopped, held, and taken.'

'Aye, sir.' The sergeant of dragoons ordered his troopers to mount, and after a certain amount of backing and sidling of horses, led his dozen men out into the centre of the street, amidst a clatter of hooves on cobbles. Hands on sheathed sabres, they turned and halted, to form a barrier of scarlet and black across it. The crowd pressed back and out of their way. All eyes turned away towards the single figure that still came striding downhill.

Rob Roy gave no sign that he had noticed the soldiers' manoeuvre. His glance lingered right and left, rather than forward, as he nodded and smiled and raised a hand to townsfolk at door and window.

The pipers, undoubtedly, were less unconcerned. Though

they continued to puff and blow, they were getting very near to the dragoons now, and their heads tended to turn a little, so that *their* glances could flicker backwards towards their temporary employer. Their unease was patent.

The Town Cross of Crieff rose just a few yards uphill of the Tolbooth and Town House, and therefore stood in front of the line of stationary dragoons. As they neared it, Rob Roy barked a word or two in the Gaelic, and with most evident relief his two instrumentalists swung left and right, to turn and face inwards, stationary as the troopers now, but tapping each a foot to the beat of his music.

The red-headed man strolled on, still at one with the world apparently, right up and on to the three steps of the Cross itself. These he climbed, and swung round, presenting a broad back to the soldiers who sat their restive mounts a mere dozen yards further on. The chatter of the crowd had died away altogether.

There was a shouted command from the sergeant. One of the pipers, the hunchback, stopped his blowing, and his instrument hiccuped and wavered sadly. Rob Roy's hand jerked out at once in a peremptory and eloquent gesture that most clearly indicated that a work of the virtue and nobility of *My Race is Royal* was not to be interrupted and cut short in mid-verse under any circumstances. The sergeant bellowed again — but the human voice, however military, is at a distinct disadvantage when in competition with two pairs of bagpipes at close range, and willy-nilly all present must listen to the final triumphant and sustained bars of the MacGregors' march.

Rob Roy, of course, had the advantage of knowing at just what point the recital would end, and it was his great voice therefore that was able neatly to fill the throbbing void the moment that the instrumentalists had bubbled and wailed to an ultimate close, the sergeant being seconds late. His rival did not so much as glance at him, anyway. He was looking towards the Tolbooth doorway.

'Aha, Provost!' he cried gaily. 'I call it civil of you to accord me a civic welcome to your good town. I do so. I pledge you, and Crieff, my thanks.'

The little tanner could not even look at the speaker, in his embarrassment. He mumbled something inaudible.

Captain Plowden did not mumble, by any means. Lifting his voice to its most commanding, he shouted. 'You! MacGregor! Enough of this foolery. Come here.'

Evidently his shouting was not loud enough, for Rob Roy went on talking to the little man. 'If you had told me now, Provost, I'd have brought some of my lads along with me, and made a better showing of it, whatever. Just a private visit it is, you see . . .'

'Silence, mountebank!' the Captain rapped out. 'I spoke to you. I said, come here!' But he started forward himself. Less urgently, his two companions followed.

'Would it be to myself you were after speaking, Captain?' The Highlandman wondered, civilly, still standing on the Cross steps. 'I am thinking you must be having my name wrong, some way. Och, it's easy mistaken, and you an Englishman by your voice. MacGregor it is, see you – MacGregor of Inversnaid and Craigroyston, just.'

'And that is a lie, to start with!' Plowden returned strongly. 'There is no man in this kingdom lawfully bearing that name, today. And the lands that you name are no longer yours, but your creditors'. But enough of this. Give me that sword, fellow – that you are carrying in defiance of the law. I arrest you, in the name of the Queen's Majesty!'

'Och, tut sir – what's this?' the MacGregor protested, but mildly. 'It grieves me sorely to have to controvert a gallant officer of the Queen – but *you* cannot arrest me, Captain. You have not the authority. I am no notary, God knows – but I have enough of the legalities to know that. I am a free citizen of this realm of Scotland – and I know my rights.'

'Fool! Quibbling over words will not serve you now. I

carry you back to Stirling Castle, free citizen or none! But if you must have my authority, sirrah, the Sheriff Officer here will let you have the form of words. Read it to him, sir.'

The Sheriff Officer had stopped quite a few paces further back. He glanced behind him, and over at the substantial line of soldiery, for comfort, unrolled his parchment, and cleared his throat.

' *"To all whom it may concern,"* ' he read out, in something of a hurry. ' *"Proclaimed at Edinburgh, by the Lord Justice General, at the instance of Her Majesty's Lord Advocate for Scotland that:*

' *"Robert Campbell, commonly known by the name of Rob Roy, or Robert MacGregor, or Robert MacGregor Campbell, or otherwise, being lately entrusted by several noblemen and gentlemen with considerable sums for buying cows for them in the Highlands, he did most fraudulently withdraw and flee, without performing anything on his part, and therefore is become unquestionably a notour and fraudulent bankrupt. The said Robert Campbell moreover, being treacherously gone off with the moneys, to the value of £1,000 sterling, which he carries along with him, all magistrates and officers of Her Majesty's forces are entreated to sieze upon the said Robert Campbell and the moneys which he carries. God Save the Queen!"* ' That resounding pronouncement admittedly might have been read with more of a flourish.

There was a silence over the High Street of Crieff, as the Sheriff Officer finished, nevertheless, in which the lowing of cattle from up on the Town Moor could be heard distinctly. Citizens eyed each other askance, and many a head was shaken.

Plowden spoke. 'Are you satisfied, sirrah?'

'Me, Captain?' Rob Roy's voice sounded entirely unconcerned, if a little surprised. 'What is it to me? Who is this Robert Campbell? A terrible man he must be, indeed, to have defrauded all these noblemen. One thousand pounds sterling, was it? A fortune, no less. A strong man he must be, too, to carry it all with him, in gold pieces, whatever! Och, I've heard some queer-like tales of those Campbells in my day, yes – but this beats all. And to buy cows . . . ?'

'Silence!' the Captain cried. 'Such clowning will gain you nothing. I arrest you, now, in the Queen's name.' He turned to his men. 'Sergeant – take him.'

Rob Roy's hand came up, with a swift and strangely authoritative gesture. 'No,' he said. 'That you may not do. It is contrary to the law of this land.'

'What? God in Heaven, man – are you beyond your wits?'

'You stand, Captain, in the town and burgh of Crieff, in the presence of its chief magistrate. No arrest may be made therein, see you, save by the Provost or by his authority – this country not being in a state of war. I call Provost Drummond and the citizens of Crieff to witness! And the Sheriff Officer likewise.'

The soldier took a further pace forward, wrathfully. Then he paused, and shrugged. 'Very well. It matters not who says the words – so long as I take you to Stirling. Provost – arrest me this man. You have heard the proclamation.'

Drummond swallowed, and shifted his feet. 'Aye,' he said thickly. 'Ooh, aye. Dearie me.' He looked from the soldier over to MacGregor, and then to the ranks of his own watching townsfolk. 'I hae no choice. The proclamation speaks plain. . . .'

'Surely, surely, Provost,' Rob acceded readily. But this time his glance was not bent on the speaker but turned up-hill, away up the street that he had recently come down. It would be untrue to say that he peered, but there might have been a hint of urgency in his gaze. 'Do what you must do, friend. But read you the form of words again, Provost, so that all is done right and in order.'

'Nonsense!' Captain Plowden exclaimed. 'What folly is

this? The proclamation has been read, and is clear to all. Have done, Provost.'

'No, sir,' the MacGregor insisted, firmly. 'The law is the law. If the Provost is for making an arrest, he must do so as the law prescribes. Read the proclamation, Provost.'

'Maybe he is right, then,' Drummond said uncertainly. 'Och, no harm in reading it again, to be safe, see you.'

'Lord preserve me from such lawyer's hair-splitting. . . !'

So the proclamation was read once more, even less eloquently than before.

'Thank you, Provost,' Rob acknowledged gravely, at the end. 'But it is as I feared – the thing is faulty, whatever. You cannot arrest a man on false authority.'

'My soul to God!' Plowden choked.

'What . . . what . . . ?' the tanner croaked.

'Your paper is made out against one Robert Campbell. That is not my name, as well you know, Provost.'

'Och, we a' ken that, Rob. But . . .'

'But, nothing. We must be accurate, in matters of law.'

'Damnation – this is beyond belief! None knows better than you, man, that the name of MacGregor has been banished and proscribed by law since, since . . .' The Captain swallowed. 'Well, for years. And that every one of your wretched cut-throat clan has had to take another name. You, who prate of the law, are known as Campbell before the law. Can you deny it?'

'Ha! As Royal's my Race – and there you have it, my friends! I do not deny it. Before the law I may be *known* as Robert Campbell though my name is MacGregor, as were my forebears back to Gregor son of Alpin, King of Scots. But that is not what your paper says, see you. It says Robert Campbell, commonly known as Robert MacGregor. And there is none such in this realm – for no Campbell would ever take the name of MacGregor, for fear of his skin, whatever! The thing is faulty, as I say, and will not serve.' That was declared like a fanfare of trumpets – but, at the

23

same time, the speaker's eyes flickered away momentarily to his right again, up that steeply climbing street.

Plowden actually gobbled in his efforts adequately to express his feelings. Nor was he alone in his incoherent comments. Of all the watchers, only the dozen dragoons sat silent and apparently unmoved. The crowd stirred and buzzed like a bees' bike.

'Silence!' the Captain roared, at length. 'Quiet! You!' He swung on the unhappy Provost. 'Say that you arrest this fool, and be done.'

'You cannot do that, Provost – you would break the law,' Rob Roy's great voice carried clearly, vibrantly. 'The law of which you are a magistrate. You must admit the paper is wrongly worded.'

'Aye – och, maybe. But I canna help that, Rob. What can I do . . . ?'

'You can give the proclamation back to the Sheriff Officer, and tell him to go have it amended. Then he, or the Captain, can come with it to me, any day, at my own house of Inversnaid, and present it again. Lawfully.' Rob Roy smiled. 'They would be warmly received, I promise you!'

'For God's sake! I've heard enough,' the sorely tried Plowden cried. 'Not another word. Forget the proclamation. I am taking this man into custody as a proscribed Mac-Gregor bearing arms contrary to Act of Parliament. On my own authority . . .' He had to keep raising his voice, to be heard.

But it was a losing battle. A louder noise than his authoritative shouting was beginning to fill the air. And to turn all heads – Rob Roy's, the crowd's, even humiliatingly his own dragoons'. Furiously the Captain jabbed an imperious finger first at his sergeant and then over to the MacGregor on the steps of the Cross – a gesture surprisingly clear and eloquent, words or none.

But good soldier as that sergeant might be, he did not obey. In fact, he just was not looking. Not at his officer,

24

anyway. As who was to blame him? He was staring up the street, like everybody else. And what he saw might well have given pause to the boldest of warriors. For coming charging and careering down the hill to them was a great mass of cattle, filling every inch of the street as in the trough of a narrow valley. Tight-packed, heads down and tails up, bellowing their alarm, horns clashing, hooves thundering, they came in crazy stampede under a cloud of steam, the half-wild, shaggy, long-horned cattle of the hills. Behind them, the flicker and smoke of brandished bog-pine torches was just discernible through the dust and reek.

As though by witchcraft the street cleared before them – since nothing would withstand or survive the impetus of that cataract of beef. There might have been anything up to a couple of hundred of the brutes, rounded up from the near end of the Town Moor, not a few of them Rob Roy's own beasts, brought in the night before to sacrifice to the tan-yard as hides to buy fodder for thousands more. Like rabbits into their burrows the townsfolk disappeared into doors and closes, none being hindmost.

The MacGregor was laughing now, in his relief, a changed man. It was not the first time that he had had re-course to this trick – though the first time in a town's streets. He roared his mirth as his two decrepit pipers went running and stumbling for shelter to the nearest close-mouth, and then turned, still standing on the Cross, to stare directly at the row of dragoons. He was all there was now, between them and the oncoming stampede.

No soldier's eye met his own. They had other things to look at. Already some of the horses were rearing and back-ing, whites of eyes showing in fear. Troopers' glances swivelled between the menace in front, the sergeant and their commander. The Provost and the Sheriff Officer were already scuttling to the Tolbooth doorway. Captain Plow-den, more courageous, lingered a few seconds longer. Then he began to back, then to turn and stalk with such dignity as he could muster, in the same direction, and finally to break into a run.

At that the sergeant hesitated no longer. Pulling his mount's head round, he waved his hand in a round-about motion which clearly meant scatter – and more than one of his troopers were already anticipating the order. Unfortunately, mounted men could not just disappear into houses and entries – and in the narrow confines of the street scattering was a manoeuvre more readily ordered than carried out. The dragoons interpreted the command in the only way possible; they turned and fled in a ragged straggle of scarlet and black, down the High Street, their chargers' hooves striking sparks from the cobblestones. Rob Roy MacGregor's great laughter followed them, though unheard.

The Town Cross of Crieff was the usual stone column, standing in the middle of the street, raised on three or four steps so that pronouncements and public statements could be proclaimed from its platform. Even so, its top step was not more than three feet or so above the cobbles – but fortunately for Rob the shaft of the Cross rose out of a sort of plinth of its own. Eschewing any flight or scuttling, the MacGregor climbed up on to this, one arm round the column, and so gained a further eighteen inches. There, like a mariner clinging to the mast of a wreck, he stood.

He was only just in time. In a surging red and brown tide the cattle swept round him, a sea of heaving shaggy bodies, snorting nostrils, tossing horns and rolling eyes. The man all but choked with the stench and stour of them. On and on the brutes pounded and plunged. The street shook to their weight. Wide horns came perilously near to the man's legs. The drooling slavers of foaming mouths splashed his colourful finery. But the splayed steps saved him, and the herd thundered past.

Behind them, the group of nondescript youths and boys, discarding smoking torches, had halted and were in process of melting away discreetly. Only one man came on, a dark-haired, dark-avised unsmiling gillie, dressed in short kilt and plaid of stained MacGregor tartan and little else, sitting a shaggy Highland garron and leading another. Close in the wake of the streaming cattle this man rode, to pull up beside the Cross.

'*Dia*, man MacAlastair – the time you have been!' Rob Roy cried, in the Gaelic, but cheerfully. 'I was thinking you would never come. Were you after milking the cows first, or what? I near talked my tongue out of my head!' Leaping down from his stance, he vaulted on to the back of the second pony, in a flurry of limbs and tartan.

'The torches, it was,' the gillie mentioned, shrugging. 'Finding the torches.' A man of few words, he sat his mount calmly, unmoved and unmoving.

His master turned to face the Tolbooth. He bowed from the waist, and sketched a graceful salute with his hand – for his bonnet was to be raised to no man save his chief and perhaps James Stewart in France. And slapping his short-legged garron's rump, brogues almost trailing on the cobbles, he set off at a trot uphill, his attendant at his heels. He did not forget to bow right and left either, as he went – as he had done on the way down, of course.

Only a pair of flattened and ragged bagpipes remained to show for it all in the town centre of Crieff.

CHAPTER TWO

THE barking of the deerhounds caught Rob's ear, and he set down his two-year-old second son Ranald, and stepped over to the window.

'It is Greg,' he reported. 'And in a hurry, as ever.'

Up the side of the headlong Snaid Burn rode a splendid figure, a young giant of a man on a big black horse – no stocky Highland garron, but a handsome Barbary charger. Even so, the horseman's long tartan-clad legs trailed low, for he rode without stirrups, in the Highland fashion. His plaid streamed out behind him in the wind, and two tall eagle's feathers thrust proudly above his bonnet. At his back loped two running gillies, deep-breathing but light of foot still, plaids wrapped around their middles, though it was November, leaving their muscular torsos bare. And behind them three graceful deerhounds bounded, baying in answer to the yelped welcome of Rob's own dogs.

'Alone? From down the glen? From Arklet, not Glen Gyle?' Mary MacGregor asked.

'Aye. And bravely dressed. For visiting, surely.' Rob gently pushed the little boy away. 'To your mother, my cock ptarmigan. Run, you.' And turning, he strode to the door, and out.

Inversnaid House stood on a grassy terrace above a bend in the stream, within the open mouth of the lovely green and secluded glen of the Snaid Burn, near to where it joined the wider and greater Glen Arklet. The waters of long Loch Lomond lay only a mile away to the west, but unseen and many hundreds of feet lower. It was a comparatively modest house of two storeys, reed-straw thatched, that Rob had enlarged from a mere farmhouse to bring his bride to when they were married. It was no fortified strength or castle, for your Highland laird was apt to rely for security on walls more potent than stone and lime – the inaccessible mountain fastnesses, and the loyalty of the clan's folk in whose midst he dwelt. Outside his ever-open door, now, Rob Roy stood, in his oldest tartans and worn leather doublet. His voice rose in shouted welcome to his nephew, pupil, friend and chieftain, to wake new echoes alongside those of the hounds, from all the tall and mighty hills that hemmed them in.

Gregor MacGregor of Glengyle came clattering up from the waterside in fine style, to leap down lithely, for all his size, and toss his charger's reins to a gillie.

'Ha, Rob!' he cried. 'As well that I find you at home. I have come hot-foot from the Clachan of Aberfoyle. . . .'

'Aye, Greg – and when did you ever come cold-foot from anywhere?'

'*You* to talk!' Gregor Black-Knee of Glengyle, chieftain of the Clan Dougal Ciar branch of the Gregorach, snorted. He was an open-faced yellow-headed young man – an unusual combination in his race – and notably good-looking in a vigorous and gallant fashion. Clad today all in tartan, but with long and almost skin-tight trews instead of the kilt, cut on the cross and hugging an excellent leg lovingly down to the ankle, he made almost as eye-catching a figure as his uncle – almost, but not quite. Of a cheerful, uncomplicated and laughter-loving habit, he was, at twenty-four, almost seventeen years younger than Rob – but a mere babe nevertheless, if compared with the complex character of his famous relative and guide. And, for once, there was no laughter showing about his eyes and mouth.

'It is crazy-mad! Beyond all belief,' he said, the words tumbling from his lips. 'But you are put to the horn, Rob – outlawed! They have proclaimed you outlaw!'

'What! *Outlaw*, did you say?' That was a woman's voice. Mary MacGregor stood in the doorway behind her husband, the little boy in her arms. 'It . . . it cannot be!'

'True it is. I saw the paper, myself. Some misbegotten Lowland scum had dared to nail it up outside the inn, during the night. Our people tore it down, of course – but the dominie has it. He showed it to me. I was on my way to visit Buchanan of Arnprior – but I came back here, right away. I saw the paper. It said that you had put yourself outside the law, failed to submit yourself to justice, and a deal more. Aye, and that you, by open fraud and violence, had embezzled much money. And kept a guard or company of armed men, in defiance of the Crown. *Dia* – the insolence of it! You, Rob – Captain of Clan Alpine, Captain of the Highland Watch, descendant of kings . . .'

'. . . and stumbling-block in the path of James Graham!' his uncle finished for him. 'So-o-o! It has come to this, has it? I did not think that he would dare so far.' His voice was even, deliberate, with none of the violent outburst that Gregor had expected. Rob Roy raised those piercing pale blue eyes to the lofty summit of Beinn a Choin, the Mountain of Weeping, that soared to the north between his own fair valley and that of Glen Gyle, and stroked his pointed red beard.

'If Montrose has dared so far, he has dared too much, 'fore God!' Gregor cried, the more strongly for the other's unlikely restraint. 'Does he think, because the woman Anne in London has named him duke, that the Gregorach will bow the knee to a Graham, and do his bidding?'

'Hush, you,' his uncle mentioned, and jerked his head to the side. A boy had appeared from around the gable-end of the house, a lad of ten or eleven, bright-eyed and eager, who was darting his glance between his elders and the handsome fidgeting charger, obviously torn between interest in what was being said and admiration for the horse. It was Coll,

30

Rob's eldest son. 'I'm thinking we might continue this discussion indoors.'

'The Gregorach bow the knee only to God, don't they? Though they'll touch their bonnets to King Jamie across the sea,' the boy's voice came, high-pitched and earnest. And then, equally fervent, 'Can I have a ride on Barb, Cousin Greg? Please! I will be very careful.'

'A short one then, Coll – for I must be off again, to Arnprior. Down to the Arklet and back – no more.'

'I wish that I could vault right up on to Barb's back – the way you did when you stole it from the dragoon officer, Cousin Greg. I wish . . .'

'Stole?' Gregor repeated sternly. 'Watch your words, young Coll. Glengyle does not steal. He takes!'

'That is an old story, boy – and better forgotten perhaps.' his father observed, smiling. 'Your cousin is now a respectable married man. Like your father. And does not harry the Queen's officers! *Maxima debetur puero reverentia!*' Rob always had a weakness for Latin tags. He led the way indoors.

Mary MacGregor was waiting for them. She had passed the toddler on to one of her house-women. 'What does it mean, Rob? Outlawry? How much will it harm you?' she asked, directly. 'And us?'

'It will not harm *you*, my love,' her husband said, quietly. 'That I shall ensure. Never fear.'

'What harm could be in it, for anyone – here in our own country?' Gregor declared. 'Montrose's writ stops short at Drymen and Balmaha and Aberfoyle. So long as Rob stops within our own country, the word means nothing. There is no *harm* in it – only insult and offence that cries to high heaven! And, by God's shadow, insult that Montrose shall rue! The man who slights Rob, slights all our race, all Clan Alpine – and shall pay for it. The Gregorach will teach such folk a lesson. . . .'

'Wheesht, Greg! A truce to your great swelling words,'

Mary MacGregor interposed, but not unkindly. 'A clear head is what is needed now, I think.'

Gregor looked abashed. As ever, this woman who was his aunt could silence and confound him – as to some extent she could her puissant husband also. Not by her words so much as by her sheer calm and unruffled beauty, some steadfast inner quality of mind and spirit of which her extraordinary loveliness of face and figure was but the outer symbol and sign. Gregor had a comely wife of his own at Glengyle House, another Mary, and fair indeed; but familiarity with her good looks left him none the less in awe of this prouder, classic, almost tragic beauty of his dark-haired aunt, however close a relative. For Rob, of course, had married his own cousin, daughter of MacGregor of Comar, from under Beinn Lomond.

Her husband nodded. Undoubtedly his nephew's news had made him more than usually thoughtful. 'Mary is right, Greg,' he said, now. 'This calls for more than slogan-shouting. Outlawry means more than just cocking my bonnet at Montrose. He has the power of the State behind him now, see you. And these are changed days in Scotland, since the Union. The power of the central government has waxed greatly. We are not so far from Stirling or Dumbarton or even Edinburgh as we were a few years back, lad.'

'But, *Dia* – you do not mean that you will submit to this thing? That you will not fight. . . !'

'Rob will fight, of course,' the woman said, level-voiced. 'Could he do otherwise, and remain himself? But there are more ways of fighting a mad bull than by butting it with your head!' She gave the glimmer of a smile. 'As *you* ought to know, Gregor Tarbh Ban.'

But no answering smiles were aroused by this reference to her nephew's famed exploit with the White Bull of Gallangad that had marked his entry into man's estate.

'Aye,' Rob said, a little heavily for him. 'Just that.'

Gregor looked from his uncle to his aunt doubtfully.

'Myself, I think that you are taking this a deal too seriously,' he maintained stubbornly.

'How legal is it, Rob?' Mary asked. 'How far will the law support this outlawry?'

'Does that matter, my dear – so long as the Advocate and the Justice-General support it? And Montrose has them both in his pouch, it seems. But I daresay that it could be made to stand in law, whatever. They will have it that, since I am not paying Montrose what he demands, I am bankrupt. And since I have not attended their court in Edinburgh, to be thrown into a debtor's cell, I am outside the law. Outlawed. Och, it fits nicely enough, I grant you.'

'It stinks to heaven!' the younger man cried. 'It is a dastard's trick! In the first place, Montrose has no claim on the money. He *invested* it with you, as he had been doing for years. He shared the profits – he must needs share the losses likewise. That is but business. And the man has more than doubled the sum, for interest, the thieving huckster! In the second place, how can you be bankrupt – you, with five thousand cattle to your name, and all the lands of Inversnaid and Craigroyston?'

The other shrugged his great shoulders. 'James Graham knows well the state of the market, the bad prices, and the cost of winter feed. He knows my difficulties – and he knows too that I would not pay his damned blackmail even if I could!' Rob Roy's voice vibrated there with a hint of its accustomed vigour.

'Aye, then. What will you do, then, Rob? My sword – every claymore in Clan Dougal Ciar – is at your service!'

'My thanks, fire-eater.' His uncle smiled a little. 'Can it be that you are tiring of wedded bliss, maybe? What of your bonny Mary? And of the two little small fellows? How will they take to your swording, Greg?'

Gregor frowned. 'Mary has them still with their Aunt Meg at Arnprior. I was on my way to bring them home, just. They will be fine at Glen Gyle. With the honour of the

33

Gregorach at stake, I . . .' The young man's eyes caught those of his aunt, and he coughed, and let the important matter of the MacGregors' honour lie for the moment. 'What are we to do then, Rob?' he asked again.

'You – get you to Arnprior and bring your Mary home, lad. For me, I have a letter or two to write, I think.'

'*Letters!*' Gregor all but choked on the word. 'Is it pen-and-ink you would be at, in this pass! *Dia* – I'd have thought that Rob Roy MacGregor would have answered louder than with a pen's scratchings!'

'There are times when a whisper can reach as far as a shout, Greg.'

'Is it to Argyll you will write?' Mary MacGregor asked.

'No – the pity of it. He is still in Spain, I hear. It must be to Atholl. Set one duke against another. And maybe Breadalbane. . . .'

'That knave! That traitor! That broken reed!' Gregor cried. 'A mercy – if that is the way of it, then I'll leave you to your scratchings, and be back on my road to Arnprior!'

'Do that, Greg,' Rob Roy agreed, gently. 'My respects to Robert Buchanan. And when you have Mary and the lads safely home to Glen Gyle, we'll be over to see them. In a day or two.'

'Greet her warmly for us, Gregor,' his aunt added. 'But, think you that she might not be better staying at Arnprior, for a while? Safe in that great Whiggamore house of Buchanan's?'

'No. Not so,' the other said definitely, slapping his bonnet on his yellow head – though automatically adjusting it so that the eagle's feathers stood up tall and proud. 'In troubled times, the place for Glengyle's wife and bairns is in Glen Gyle. God keep you, both!' And swinging about, he went marching outside.

They watched him go long-strided down to the burnside, a gallant figure, his huge voice raised in bellowed commands for Coll, his horse, and his gillies.

'Heigh-ho,' Rob Roy declared ruefully, shaking his head. 'The lad's sore disappointed with me, I doubt. He judges me as failing him and his notion of the Gregorach. Aye – and that notion *I* instilled into him, whatever!'

'Does that count – so long as you do not fail your own self, Rob?' the woman asked quietly.

'Aye. As ever, you have the rights of it, Mary my dark love. Fetch me the quill and the paper, will you?' But the man sighed as he said it.

*   *   *

'*. . . his Grace of Montrose thought fit to procure an order from the Queen's Advocate to secure me, and had a party of men to put this order in execution against me. This is a most ridiculous way for any nobleman to treat any man after this manner. God knows but there is a vast differ between Dukes! Blessed be God for that it's not the Atholl men that is after me! If your Grace would speak to the Advocate to countermand his order, since it's contrary to Law, it would ease me very much of my troubles. . . .*'

Rob was reading over what he had penned, quill poised in a great hairy hand that seemed wholly unlikely to have formed the neat and indeed stylish writing before him – for however contrary to his reputation he was a man of education and culture – when he raised his head to the sound of a commotion outside. A man's voice, breathless and hoarse, was demanding to see Himself. Himself still meant Rob Roy to most of Clan Gregor, even though he was not their chief, nor even, like Glengyle, chieftain of a sept. He rose.

Mary showed a panting dishevelled gillie into the room. 'News, Rob,' she announced. 'For your own ear.' She would have retired, but her husband stayed her with a gesture.

'Ha, Murdo,' he greeted the ragged-garbed but lusty newcomer. 'What sets you running, this time? Has Cailness fallen into the loch again? Or is it your own wife chased you out of the house?'

'Boats, it is,' the other panted, briefly. 'Many boats.'

'Eh?' Not only Rob's voice but his whole posture and bearing changed, tensed. Abruptly he was a different man. 'Boats? On Loch Lomond? As far up as Cailness? Tell me, man.'

'No. Not so far – yet. But coming, see you. Ian Beg saw them. From Rowchoish. He came running up to Cailness. Cailness sent me to warn you. Myself, I saw them from the high ground as I came. A score of boats, at the least. Och, maybe more. They were creeping up the near side of the loch see you, and hard to count. . . .'

'*Diabhol* – a score, you say! That could make two hundred men!' Rob Roy's glance lifted, to meet that of his wife. 'Here is an expedition, whatever!'

'Yes, then. And Ian Beg said that he was after seeing red coats in the boats.'

'So-o-o!'

'They . . . they are coming here, Rob?' Mary asked.

'Where else – if they have got as far up the loch as that? And who else would they send hundreds of men for, up Loch Lomond, but Rob Roy MacGregor?' A keen ear might have detected just a hint of pride in that. 'From Dumbarton Castle they are, for sure.' He swung back on the messenger. 'Creeping up close to the loch-shore, you said, Murdo? This side? That means that they are not wanting to be seen, at all. A surprise it was to be. At this time of day, that can only mean a night arrival.' It was mid-afternoon, and the unseen November sun would be setting behind the great hills to the west in just over an hour. 'They want cover of darkness, then – so it is no peaceable visit!'

'Aye. So Cailness reckoned it. I was to say, Rob, that he was for gathering all the men that he could, whatever, and bringing them to you.'

'M'mmm. I see.' Rob Roy looked out of the window, stroking his pointed beard. 'How long have we got? Of a mercy, the wind is from the east. It will not speed the red-coats' rowing. And if they are for hugging the shore, they will take the longer.'

'They were large and heavy boats, and going but slowly. . . .'

'Aye. If they were south of Cailness when you saw them, Murdo, I'd say that they would not reach Inverarklet for over an hour yet. Two hours before they come knocking at my door here, eh?'

The other nodded an unkempt head.

Rob drew himself up. 'To the kitchen with you, then, Murdo – and get you a bit and a dram. You will be needing it.'

'No need. Will I not be after running to warn others? Corrarklet? And Corrheichen? And Comar, and the rest? You will be needing all your gillies to rouse the clan.'

'No, no. Leave that to me, Murdo. Go you, now.'

When the man had gone, Rob looked at his wife. 'So James Graham has not let the grass grow under his ducal feet!' he said. 'I had not thought that he would act so fast. He must have had this planned for long enough, the man. I am sorry, my dear.'

'Rob – this is a great evil that has come to us,' Mary MacGregor said. 'I . . . I could wish it otherwise, indeed. At this time – with the children. . . . But what is to be, will be. At least, your conscience is clear.' Her lovely eyes gleamed to the suspicion of a smile. 'Clearer than sometimes, perhaps!'

The man grinned. 'Aye – and much good *that* will be doing me! Still, it is a change, is it not?' Then he was grave again, swiftly. 'This may well be an ill business for you, Mary. And the boys. As well perhaps that you should be off to Comar. To your father. You would be safe up there.'

'No, Rob. My place is here. I cannot whisk away two babes, into the hills, at an hour's cry. I will stay. You will not be fighting them round the house itself?'

'No,' he answered her, flatly.'

'But do not waste time on me, Rob. I will do finely. You will be needing to rouse the glens, to get the gillies running to Corraklet and Glen Gyle and Stronachlacher and . . .'

'No,' her husband said again, as flatly.

She stared at him, eyes widening, at the note in his voice. 'No . . . ?'

'No, Mary. No gillies. No rousing of the glens. Not this time.'

'But, Rob . . . ?'

'Flight, it must be this time, *a graidh* – not fight! For me. They will not catch me – but I will not fight them. They will come here and find me gone.'

Mary MacGregor shook her head. 'I do not understand you, Rob. *You!* To flee, without a fight? What has come over you, at all? Oh, I know that I said to Greg that it was clear thinking that was needed, not just big words and talk of war. But that was different. Now, the soldiers are at your very doorstep. Even if there are two hundred of them, you could raise men enough to keep them from here, to trap them in the pass up from the loch, to throw them back into the water . . .'

'Aye, I could do that, Mary – nothing simpler. And, belike, that is just what Montrose would have me do. But have you considered the cost? I am outlawed now, remember. And all who knowingly will be assisting and supporting an outlaw are liable to outlawry in their turn. Any measures can be taken against outlaws – *any* measures, Mary. If I flee, lass, there will be *one* outlaw only. But if I do rouse the clan, all MacGregors will be outlawed, whatever. How think you of that? All my people, at the mercy of Montrose and those others who do not love us. You – and the young ones. Greg, and his bonny wife and bairns. Your old father, at Comar. All – all outside the law. What do you think of that?'

'But . . . ?' She shook her head once more, dark eyes tragic indeed.

'No, lass,' he went on. 'The Gregorach have suffered enough. Already they are proscribed and denied their name, a by-word. I will not put them outside the law as well, my God! Not in the present state of Scotland. Not for *my* sake. Nothing would better suit James Graham, I think. And there is something else, see you. An outlaw's lands and property can be forfeit to the Crown. Inversnaid and Craig-royston are mine, yes – but MacGregors are living on them. They are the clan's lands, too. Make those clansmen outlaws also, and they can be swept off the lands and all property confiscate. But let them remain law-abiding subjects, tenants and tacksmen, and it will be a deal more difficult to dispossess them and take over the land. Do you not see it, Mary?'

'I do not know. I see Rob Roy MacGregor talking like any Lowland lawyer. Talking – not acting. You have ay been wont to act, Rob – not talk. I do not know, at all . . .'

'Where is the clear thinking now, then? Tell me lass – would you see Greg and his Mary and their boys in the heather, outlawed, hunted and homeless, because of what I have done, or have not done? Tell me!'

'So!' Almost shrilly for her, with her deep quiet voice of calm, his wife cried. 'It is your beloved Greg that you are thinking of! That is the way of it. Always Greg. You are not Tutor of Glengyle any longer, remember. . . .'

'I name him and his, because I esteem it little use naming you and yours, woman!'

For moments they looked at each other, the big powerful-seeming man and the beautiful woman, so contrasting yet somehow so complementary, strong characters both. Then Mary sighed.

'I do not know, Rob. You will do what you must,' she said. 'Always you have gone your own road – and will go it to the end, I do not doubt. If this is it, then you must take it – quickly. God grant that it is the right one!'

'Yes. The responsibility is mine, and I must carry it. I must have time, you see. Time for Atholl and Breadalbane to get my letters. Time for my friends to do something – for I have friends still, mind. More important – time for the winter snows to fill the passes and keep the red-coats out of MacGregor country. Give me a month, and Montrose will be baulked till the snows melt. After that – who knows? Argyll will be home from Spain, likely. And there will be a market for cattle again. . . .' He shrugged, as though putting all such considerations finally aside. 'Now – get me food, lass. For two. I will take only MacAlastair. Have him told. I will finish this letter, and be gone.'

Nodding, wordless, she left him.

Some twenty minutes later, the Captain of Clan Alpine, Captain of the Glengyle Highland Watch, famed warrior of the fierce Gregorach, and Laird of Inversnaid and Craig-royston, buckled his sword-belt over his broad shoulder, and turned from the two garrons and the impassive Mac-Alastair back to his waiting family. He gripped young Coll's shoulder and shook it gently, telling the boy to look after his mother and see that he was not too hard on everybody while he was master of Inversnaid. He picked up the two-year-old Ranald, tickled him, and chucked the baby James under the chin. Then he enfolded wife and child together in his long arms, and kissed the woman on hair and brow and lips.

'Do not fear for anything, *a graidh*,' he said. 'This is the best way. I will come to you, or send for you, as soon as I may. God remain with you.'

'Yes, Rob. But I would have preferred that you remained with me, also!'

Long and sombrely he looked into those great eyes, before shaking his head. Then he turned to the garrons. He mounted, but without his usual vigorous vault, raised a hand, and flung the ends of his oldest plaid across his shoulders. Mac-

Alastair mounted, without word or gesture, at his back. And waving away his deerhounds not to follow him, he pulled the pony's head round northwards. Quietly, with no single backward glance, the two men slipped away up the green Snaid valley and into the already shadowy hills.

From many a cot-house door, as well as his own threshold, eyes watched him go, doubtful, perplexed, uncomprehending.

CHAPTER THREE

IT was later than might have been expected before the visitors announced themselves by a great and imperative banging on the front door of Inversnaid House. It had been dark for fully two hours. The callers had been very careful, taken every precaution. Mary MacGregor had been kept informed of their progress, of course, by fleet and silent-footed gillies, all the way from the landing at Inverarklet, up the steep pass that climbed through the woods for four hundred feet above the loch, to the entrance of the hanging valley of the Snaid. She had heard how there were scouts out before and to the flank, and how soldiers stepped softly with arms muffled and to whispered commands; how, where Snaid joined Arklet, there had been a halt and conference, while men, many men, had been sent off in parties into the night, right and left, obviously to surround the house and its vicinity. Knowing that the ring of armed men now wholly encompassed and enclosed her home, in the darkness, she had waited, with her children, the house-women and a couple of gillies. Rob's word that there was to be no fighting, no resistance, no gathering, had been obeyed. Rob was always obeyed.

The door was not locked, and without waiting for any sort of answer to the summons, it was thrown open, and men streamed in. First, a group of red-coated soldiers clearing a way for an Officer of Foot; then John Graham of Killearn followed by a rabble of civilians – bailiffs, constables, sheriff officers and Montrose hirelings.

It was as though a storm had hit that house in the green

glen, a violent uncontrolled cataclysm of insensate nature, rather than an entry of an official party or disciplined men. Without request or enquiry or even pause, men swept and stamped and surged through the building, shouting, swearing and knocking over furnishings. Mary MacGregor was flung roughly aside, and one of the gillies who sought to aid her was felled to the floor – but otherwise the occupants were for the moment ignored. Into every room and cupboard and cranny, upstairs and down, the tide of violent men poured, swords and bayonets drawn and sticks brandished, to swipe and prod and slash in a fury of destructive search. The house resounded and shook to the crash of broken glass and china-ware, the banging of doors and the splintering of woodwork. From outside came a corresponding din, as the outbuildings, stables and byres were similarly ransacked – and through the windows the ominous red glare of fire began to flicker, as thatched roofs were lit.

There was utter pandemonium for a while. But not for long, for Inversnaid was not a large house and its search no major task. The savage tide turned and ebbed, and men went streaming outside again in angry chorus. But not all of them. John Graham of Killearn, the officer in charge of the troops, and sundry others came stamping back to where the mistress of the house stood pressed back against the hallway wall, biting her lip, the baby James at her breast and clutching the sobbing Ranald to her thigh. Young Coll, nose bleeding from a swipe he had received when rushing to his mother's defence, stood close by, lower lip trembling, and striving hard to blink back unmanly tears. The gillies were gone, and of the women only the oldest remained, an apron thrown over her grey head and keening shrilly – though her cries did not wholly drown the screaming and the sobbing pleas of the other younger women from the kitchen quarters.

'Where is he?' Killearn demanded, halting in front of Mary MacGregor. He had to shout to make himself heard.

'Where's he hiding, the cowardly red-headed stot?'

Head up, white-faced, burning-eyed, she stared back at him, unspeaking.

'Answer me, woman — or by God it will be the worse for you!' Graham roared. 'We'll find him in the end, never fear — wherever he's skulking. *You* can't save him. Better look to yourself.'

From tight lips Mary spoke. 'Think you, if Rob was here, he would suffer you to insult his wife, ruffian!'

'Watch your words, woman! Where is he?' The man took a pace nearer.

'Think you, even if I knew, that I would tell *you*? Montrose's jackal?'

Killearn's open hand shot out to hit the woman hard across the alabaster white of her lovely face. 'Bitch!' he jerked.

The baby, struck by the heavy braided cuff of the man's coat, wailed. Young Ranald buried his face against his mother's side, screaming. And Coll launched himself bodily at Killearn, small fists clenched and beating — to be hurled aside by the factor's back-handed swipe. One of the Montrose servants grabbed him, flung him into the nearest room, and held the door shut on him.

The officer, a major of The Buffs, looked a little uncomfortable. 'There is no profit in this, Mr Graham,' he said. 'He is not here, clearly. He's been warned, and bolted.'

'He won't be far away,' Killearn grated. 'And this bitch will ken where he is, I'll wager.'

'If she does, it seems that she will not tell. . . .'

'She'll tell, all right, before I'm done wi' her!' the other snarled. 'Get your men outside, Major, searching these animals' cabins and hovels. Leave me to see whether or no' I can make this woman talk!'

The officer hesitated — but only for a moment. Probably he was glad to go, and to be spared responsibility in the business; and of course he and his men were there only in support of the Sheriff-Substitute's civil activities, so that to that extent he was under Killearn's orders. With just a flickering glance at Mary MacGregor, the pallor of her face now marred and barred with a scarlet band, he turned and strode outside, calling the few remaining soldiers after him. From out there, the angry baying of a deerhound suddenly ended in an agonised choking yelp.

The feel of his hand against the woman's face seemed somehow to have affected John Graham, to have changed his attitude. He was actually smiling now, and gently rubbing that hand with the other, eyes narrowed but fixed on her features. Closely, comprehensively, he considered her – and the tip of his tongue emerged to moisten his lips in one or two places. 'Aye,' he said, on an exhalation of breath. Undoubtedly there was satisfaction in the sigh. He continued to rub his hand.

Mary met his gaze unflinchingly, her dark eyes blazing – though she could not wholly control the tumult of her bosom, against which she clutched the six-months-old James. Perhaps it was the baby's motion that spurred Killearn on.

'Take the brats – both o' them,' he barked.

There was some competition amongst his henchmen to obey – especially to grab the baby in arms. Two or three hands reached for it – and in the process of detaching it from the clutch of its mother, her gown was somehow torn down the front. She fought to retain the child, fiercely, silently, and the tearing went on. By the time that she was flung back against the wall, panting, her full breasts were uncovered heaving as though with their own life.

For a moment there was the silence of involuntary admiration. Then comment broke out, loud and appreciative.

'Dirty bitch!' Graham mumbled, peculiarly – but with no indication of revulsion.

Mary MacGregor was no shrinking maidenly girl, but a mature, beautiful and spirited woman – and a MacGregor born as well as wed. Her arms came up, not to cover her body but to reach out still for her tiny son, in an instinctive gesture at once proud and pleading.

Killearn gestured, too. He jabbed a finger in the direction of the door behind which young Coll was already hidden. 'Put the bairn in there,' he rasped. 'This other one, too.' Again his finger stabbed, towards the open door of another room, the principal front chamber of the house. 'Tam! Wattie! In there wi' her. Take the woman in. God's sake – let's have a mite o' privacy, eh!' And he laughed.

Two of his own men, in the Montrose livery, grabbed Mary each by an arm, and knocking roughly aside the little yelling Ranald, half-pushed, half-carried her into the room. Graham came striding in after them, and slammed the door shut behind him.

It would have been dark in that large apartment had it not been for the red glare of the flaming roofs outside. In the baleful uncertain light the three men and the woman stood – and there was nothing kindly in the half-dark to offer cloak for her shame. For a little only the sound of panted breathing competed with the din outside. Nor was Mary MacGregor's breathing the loudest.

'Well – where is he?' Killearn asked, at length. He said it levelly. It was not a question at all, but only a necessary form of words.

She did not speak.

'A-a-aye!' Again that gusty sigh of satisfaction. 'All right, lads,' he said. 'I'll wager you can make the bitch give tongue! She's yours!'

For just a moment the two men stared at him, questioningly, in the flickering firelight.

Graham motioned with his hand, a gesture eloquent as it was obscene. And he barked a throaty laugh.

His henchmen required no further encouragement. They leapt on the woman, hands clawing. Rending and tearing at her garments, they forced her back and back to the wall.

46

Like wolves they worried at her, wrenching and pawing. She fought back, twisting, struggling, scratching, till a fierce buffet to the side of her head left her dazed and reeling against the wall. Merciless hands ripped the pathetic remnants of her clothing from her, till she stood naked amidst the fallen ruin of it.

The men drew back for a moment, gulping and gasping.

Even then she did not cringe nor huddle nor plead. Nor did she speak, at all. Swaying and dizzy as she was, she stood up straight, defiant, proud even, all her outraged loveliness erubescent in the leaping glow and shadows of the flames. The hand that lifted to her head was not to clutch her bruised temple nor to cover her blazing eyes, but to finally tug loose the fillet which still partially held up the coils of her dark hair. With a toss of the head that spoke louder than any words that she could have used, she shook down the long heavy tresses about her shoulders.

'Ha So there we have it, eh?' the factor said thickly. He had moved over to the side, the better to see and so as not to obstruct any of the firelight from the window. 'No' bad! Och, no' bad! I've seen worse, aye – dammit I have!' His voice rose. 'But the bitch's no' yelping yet, lads. Ye're ower gentle, I doubt. Is that the best ye can do, damn you? *You*, Tam!'

Again the men launched themselves upon their victim. This time it was not at clothing that they pawed. Savagely they wrestled with her, forcing her over towards a great wooden chest. Fiercely she fought back, using her nails, even her teeth. Her attackers were shouting now, though the woman said never a word. Suddenly the man called Wattie yelled with pain, as Mary MacGregor's teeth sank into his wrist. Wrenching his arm free, he swung his clenched fist to the side of her head, in his fury. She sagged limply to the vicious blow, and her struggles became feeble, semi-involuntary.

'Man, Wattie – you're no' up to your usual, the night!'

Killearn reproved, but jovially. 'Och, a bit spirit's ay as good as a sauce, man. Ye should ken that.'

Cursing and stumbling, the two of them as good as carried the swooning woman to the chest. And there, gripping her by the coils of her hair and her arms, they had their brutal way with her, one holding her down for the other. As well that she was only semiconscious. But before they were finished with her, she was struggling and twisting again, to the men's inevitable discomfiture – and to Killearn's evident glee.

Graham, a man with a distinct preference for the supervisory role in most affairs, was offering further practical and amusing advice, when the door burst open, and a sheriff officer's head thrust round.

'Maister Graham!' he cried. 'Maister Graham – you'll hae to come oot o' there. . . .'

'Devil roast ye, man – what's the meaning o' this? Did I no' say I was no' to be disturbed?' the factor roared. 'Get out – and shut that door!'

'But Maister, Graham – your pardon, sir. But, och – the hoose is afire! *This* hoose! The roof's catched alight, frae the others. D'ye no' smell the smoke? D'ye no' *see* it?'

'God's curse on it!' Killearn had been vaguely aware of the smell of burning for some time, of course – but had assumed that it was coming in from the blazing outhouses. And the illumination in that room was not such as to show up curling tendrils of smoke. Now, through the open doorway, it could be seen against the torchlight, billowing down the hallway. Anathematising all and sundry, and ordering his two panting henchmen to have done, to leave the filthy shrew, to put themselves to rights and get out of this, the new sheriff-substitute and county court judge of Stirlingshire stamped out of that ravaged room without another glance at its prostrate mistress.

Muttering, blaspheming, and already beginning to cough with the acrid fumes, his two minions disentangled themselves and went stumbling after him.

In only a comparatively few seconds there was not an intruder left in Inversnaid House. Only the crackle of flames, the wailing of women and the screaming of children resounded.

Mary MacGregor did not add to the din. After a moment she dragged herself upright to stare around her, wild-eyed. For a little she stood there, swaying, but otherwise unmoving. Then, as her mother's consciousness, despite all else, distinguished her Ranald's yelling amongst the rest, and the baby's feebler plaint, she tottered over to where the ruins of her clothing lay, and dazedly sought to cover herself to some extent with what had survived those rending hands. Back at the same chest that had supported her shame, she opened the lid and drew out a couple of large tartan plaids. In one she wrapped herself, and taking the other with her she staggered out of the room.

Young Coll and his two small brothers were locked into the apartment opposite. Their mother opened the door and ran to her children, picking up the baby James from the floor. She clutched them all to her, dry-eyed, wordless. Then, coughing from the now thickly rolling smoke, she put the baby into Coll's arms, with the other plaid wrapped round it, and took up his two-year-old brother herself, to lead the way out, through the kitchen and rear quarters.

The upper floor of the house was now a blazing inferno, fanned by a wintry east wind. Mary MacGregor led her brood, around the stair-foot and down the passage, as though sleep-walking, without expression or any comment. About the back door were grouped hysterical women in various stages of undress, a gillie lying with a broken head, and two dead deerhounds. At sight of their mistress the women's screams rose afresh, declaring their rape, their agony, and their ruination.

Mary MacGregor spoke to none of them, looked at none of them. Straight ahead of her she walked, past them all, through the trampled kitchen-garden and orchard towards the birchwood behind, out of the red ruin and the grim radiance of its blaze, holding her children close, her head high. Darkness, blackness, anonymity, she sought fiercely. And her lovely eyes were wild, wild.

*　　　*　　　*

Up on the open hillside, about half a mile above the house, was a sort of cave contrived out of a great outcrop of rock that had split down the middle, with a narrow opening and lined with pulled heather – a favourite haunt from which young Coll MacGregor was wont to sally forth to do battle with the champions of all the lesser clans of Scotland. For this shelter his mother made, in the darkness, sure of foot as of direction. And in its draughty sanctuary, huddled close together under the two plaids for warmth, the wife and children of the famed and dreaded Captain of Clan Alpine passed that November night, while below them, on the low ground, the red glow of fires died away and the shouts of men faded. Not once did the woman close her eyes throughout.

At first light, on a grey chill morning of thin driving rain, Mary MacGregor sent Coll downhill, with specific instructions. He went, bent low, dodging, skulking, darting from cover to cover, as his father had taught him in stalking the deer, screening himself amongst the great numbers of somnolent cud-chewing cattle with which that green valley was filled. An hour or so later he was back, leading a couple of garrons. The sun still had not risen behind the mist-shrouded hills to the east.

On his mother's instructions he had avoided the smoking ruins of his home, just as he had avoided contact with any of their people. Except for Old Seana that had been his nurse, as she had been his father's before him. To her black-house of stone and turf he had made his inconspicuous way, collecting the two ponies from one of the in-fields. An old and bent crone, Seana had escaped molestation at the hands of the intruders – though most of her chickens were missing. From her the boy had brought a bag of oatmeal, some cold meat and one or two old pieces of women's wear for his mother. Also the news that the invaders had retired back to their boats at Loch Lomond, in the darkness, no doubt fearful of reprisals from the clan. No soldiers remained around Inversnaid meantime. He had spoken to none other, and, tight-lipped and great-eyed, he did not expiate on what he had seen.

Mary MacGregor asked no questions. Indeed she said but little, at all. Something seemed to have dried up within her. Anonymity she craved still, within herself almost, and certainly from her fellow men and women.

Presently, wrapped in a plaid against the chilly rain, the baby in her arms, and seated on one of the placid and sure-footed garrons, she led the way out from their shelter, Coll, with Ranald before him, riding at her back. She turned the beast's head northwards, keeping to the high ground. Well up on the side of the long ridge that separated the Snaid valley from that of Loch Lomond, she rode, heading into the wilderness of empty mountains between Glen Falloch and Glen Dochart. And not once did she glance down towards the scattered houses in the floor of the glen, nor backwards towards Glen Arklet, where help and comfort and sympathy were there for the asking, or over to Comar, her childhood's home under Beinn Lomond. Not even half-right towards Glen Gyle, where the Lady Christian, Gregor's mother, would have cherished her. Unspeaking, straight-backed, expressionless, she gazed directly ahead of her, from eyes that glowed with a strange smouldering fire.

The long-maned, long-tailed garrons paced deliberately, picking their way through stones and heather.

Rob Roy had a house at Corrycharmaig near the west end of Glen Dochart, on the fringe of the safe Campbell country of Breadalbane.

CHAPTER FOUR

IT was four days later before Rob Roy himself came riding down Glen Dochart to Corrycharmaig, MacAlastair at his back, with no hurry on him and all the time in the world to play with, a man philosophically seeking to enjoy the freedom of outlawry. Intent on involving no others, save MacAlastair, this shadow of his, in the displeasure of the authorities, he had lain up, the day following his departure from Inversnaid, snug on Eilean Dhu, a tiny island in the middle of Loch Katrine, waiting for nightfall before moving on again. Avoiding all contact with men – for he was too well known and eye-catching a figure to remain unrecognised anywhere in the Highlands – he had made his way north by east by the head of Balquhidder and Glen Ogle to the great strath of Tay, heading for the castle of Finlarig, seat of his own mother's cousin, *Mac Cailein Mhic Donnachaidh*, John, first Earl of Breadalbane, chief of the Glenorchy Campbells. He had decided to deliver his letter to Breadalbane in person. Not that he had any love for the man, nor even respect – save perhaps for his undoubted shrewdness and cunning – knowing that he would betray friend, ally and country whenever it suited his interests so to do; nevertheless, besides being undisputed lord of some hundreds of square miles of the Central Highlands, a powerful figure, and undeniably the cleverest rogue in all Scotland, he hated Montrose. In the circumstances, that was of vital importance. So Rob had gone to see Breadalbane, and for the very reasons that he sought to avoid and not involve other men in his outlawry he had come to Finlarig openly and with almost a flourish. As far as John Campbell was concerned he recognised no duty, no conscience; he would involve him if he could. How much good his visit to that wily and slippery customer might have done him, remained to be seen.

So now, Rob rode down Glen Dochart in the thin wintry sunlight, to his house of Corrycharmaig under the towering mass of snow-capped Beinn More. He was surprised to see, rising from one of its chimneys, a drift of woodsmoke, blue against the rich sepia of the old heather that soared beyond. He had not expected the house to be occupied – but perhaps some of his folk in the two or three cot-houses near by had installed therein some traveller of quality in need of shelter? Highland hospitality could demand more than that.

None of his people emerged to offer him warning of any hostile presence in the house, so Rob did not hesitate to ride right up to the door. His surprise grew still further as he saw a boy at play with a puppy up at the edge of the pine wood behind the house, a boy whom he suddenly realised was his own son Coll. Nor did his wonder abate anything when the lad, after staring at him fixedly, not only failed to answer his wave of greeting, but abruptly turned away and went slowly but deliberately into the darkness of the trees.

Fingering his beard perplexedly, Rob jumped down. Though the garrons' approach must have been audible, nobody was waiting in the doorway to greet him. He strode into the lobby – and all but tripped over young Ranald, who was crawling about the floor. At sight of him the child jumped up and ran screaming into the kitchen.

'Ho ho, small fellow, little frog-in-the-bog! What sort of welcome is this for your sire?' the father demanded, great voiced. But he prevailed nothing against the bawling.

Corrycharmaig was not a large house – for Rob had no use for large houses, being essentially a man of the open air, of movement, whom no hearthstone could bind. Three or four paces took him into the kitchen. And there he found his wife.

She stood facing him from the far end of the room, almost as though she had retreated there at the sound of him. But there was no expression of fear of an unknown intruder about her – nor of welcome or relief either, for that matter. No expression of any sort, indeed. Her proudly beautiful features were calm, still, almost impassive, as though wiped clean of expression. She did not smile to him. She did not speak. Her hands were folded in front of her. She did not move. Only those great eyes glowed. And the light in them was distinctly peculiar.

'Mary, my dear, my heart's love!' the man cried. 'Here is a great surprise.' Long-strided he came across the room to her, to enfold her in his arms, to swing and lift her right off her feet, to hold her aloft. 'What brings you here? What means this move? Did you . . . ? But, no – do not tell me! It is plain – och, you just cannot be doing without your husband, woman!' And setting her down, he kissed her.

The woman's lips did not stir under his. Her body did not stir within his arms. No word came from her.

Concerned, the man drew back from her. Holding her from him, his hands on her shoulders, he peered into those eyes – and somewhere near the base of his neck an incipient shiver was born at what he saw therein.

'What is it, Mary *a graidh*?' he demanded. 'What ails you, my heart?'

Slowly her dark head shook.

'Come, my dear,' Rob insisted, frowning. 'Is it ill you are? Or what, then?'

Almost as though it was a physical effort, her lips moved slowly. 'What . . . is that . . . to you?' she whispered.

Astounded, her husband stared. 'Dear God,' he besought. 'What has got into you, woman?'

54

'*That* you may well ask!' The first hint of emotion, that of bitterness, was there. 'What, indeed!'

Rob tossed his bonnet on to the table, and ran a hand through the curling thatch of his red hair. 'I do not understand,' he declared. 'For God's sake, Mary, tell me what this means! Tell me what sort of a woman you have become, to speak so!'

'Tell me, rather, what sort of a man *you* are, Robert MacGregor, to have turned your back on your wife and children, to have failed me as surely as you have failed your honour and your clan?' That was said levelly, without evident passion or anger, and was the more wounding therefore. 'You threw me to the dogs and rode away – you, the hero of men! You said that it was the best way, that I was not to fear anything. You preferred that God should remain with me, in the crutch of trouble – not yourself. And God did not do so. God turned His back on me, as did yourself. God and you, both, Robert MacGregor.'

He shook his head, wordless.

She went on evenly, as though reciting something that she had learned by heart. ' "The responsibility is mine," you said, and you must carry it. "I must have time," you said – and you bought the time with me! You said . . .'

'Stop it, Mary – stop it! What are you trying to tell me, at all . . . ?' That was little more than a whisper, but a fierce one.

'Little enough to you, perhaps, who have your mind on greater things. Only that your home is in ashes, your glen savaged, your children abused, and your wife shamed!'

'Wha-a-at!' The huge hands came out to grip her shoulders again – and though he scarcely knew it, they shook her bodily.

'But, you – *you* won clear. And the clan did not rise. So it may be that you are satisfied, whatever!'

'Be quiet, woman! Enough of that,' the man said roughly. 'Tell me what . . . ?'

'I have told you. They burned down your house and all within it. They abused your women. Your children they struck, and tore from my arms . . .'

'And you? They did not strike *you*, my God?'

'Me! Aye, Rob – they struck me! Would God that it had been with the sword, and that I had died at the first stroke!'

'Mary!'

She winced involuntarily with the pain of his grip. 'I would have done what little they left undone . . . with a dirk in my own heart . . . had it not been for the children. Jamie needed me. And Ranald. They need me yet. For a little time yet. Then, pray God, the grave will hide my shame at last! Though,' she paused, seeming to gaze through and past him to horror indescribable, 'my mother's bones will shrink aside in their grave when mine are laid beside them!'

'Merciful Lord!' her husband cried. 'What . . . I cannot . . . are you . . . ?' He gulped. 'By the Powers of Heaven – what have they done to you? What hellish thing is this?'

She shook her head, impassive again, but otherwise did not answer him.

'Mary, my love, my heart's desire – what have they done? What have *I* done to you? What? What, I say!' And at her blank stare, he abruptly all but flung her from him, and went off storming round the room, the extremity of his emotion exploding into compulsive physical action. Fists clenched and shaking, he stamped and strode and swore, cursing heaven and hell and men, tossing the heavy table out of his way as though it had been a toy, the room itself seeming to quiver to the vibration of his own fierce urgency. The woman herself shrank back instinctively, for Rob Roy MacGregor in the grip of passion was an unnerving sight. So much power and energy racking a human frame was something to be eyed askance. Men who did not love him had suggested that he was devil-possessed; others, rather that he had the spirit of the ancient heroes within him.

At length, with a tremendous and very evident effort, the man controlled himself. 'The soldiers did this – the damned red-coats?' he demanded, his voice trembling. 'I would not have believed it possible. Not at this day.'

'No? Have you forgotten Glen Coe and the MacIans? What they did there?'

'That was twenty years ago. In the aftermath of war. This is peace. The crime that I am outlawed for is that I have not surrendered to a charge of bankruptcy! A mere civil offence. And, for this . . .!' He swallowed, almost choked.

'It was not the soldiers,' she sad. 'It was . . . it was . . .' Almost it seemed as though she could not bring herself to speak the name. 'It was Graham. John Graham of Killearn.'

'*Killearn*? The factor?' The Blazing-eyed he strode up to her again. 'That . . . that oaf! That bullock of Montrose's! He it was that . . . that struck you?'

She nodded.

'Then . . .' Rob Roy drew a great shuddering breath. 'Then, as Royal's my Race – he shall pay for it! Pay in full. Pay for it with his wretched life! Before the throne of God Almighty I swear it – John Graham shall die!'

Coldly the woman nodded. 'Aye, he will die. Sooner or later he will die. But not as I died four nights agone. Would that he could!'

'I shall make him suffer first, Mary, I promise you . . .'

'Will you?'

'Yes, then. On my soul I swear it!'

'What will you give him to suffer? What that will recompense? A little pain, before the end? A little fear? What is that? Think you that will serve, Robert MacGregor?' The woman's eyes glowed again.

Rob's own brilliant eyes blinked a little at the intensity of feeling that he saw in them. He was a Celt himself, and well knew the black fire of hatred that humbled and slighted pride could engender in his race. But he had never before seen it in Mary, a calm, serene woman, however strong-minded. But she was a MacGregor, of course. . . .

'Aye,' he said slowly. 'Rest assured, it will be sufficient.'

She said no more – but the man turned away at the blaze of something like contempt, mockery, in her glance.

After a moment, he said, 'Tell me how it was, Mary – the things that were done.'

'No,' she answered. 'The things that were done that night are not to be told. Not ever. Enough, and more than enough, that they happened. They cannot be undone. I cannot seek my grave yet awhile, as I would – but at the least the words can be buried!'

'But . . . och, Good Lord, woman . . . !' Helplessly Rob shook his head. 'Would you have me ignorant of the facts – myself, who must avenge what was done? Your own husband . . . ?'

'You will never avenge what was done. And what husband are you to me, who turned your back and left me? You chose ignorance when you rode away. Keep it. I have nothing for you, now – and want nothing from you. Save peace. Go, now.'

'But, Mary . . . !' Perplexed and uncertain as he had never been before, in all his life, Rob Roy spread his hands wide. 'What am I to do with you? How may I help you, my dear?'

'You cannot. Save perhaps in one thing. Find me another place to hide in. A secret place, deep in the mountains. Far from all men's eyes. Where I may hide myself and my children. That is all that I ask of you, Robert MacGregor.'

He sighed. 'As you will, *a graidh*. That I can do, yes. But is that all that I mean to you, now – after all our years together, lass?'

'Our years together ended four nights aback. You it was who ended them. Now go, please. That you can do for me, as well. . . .'

Rob picked up his bonnet. He looked at her, steadfastly

58

and sadly – and never had he seen her more beautiful. Deranged she might be, beside herself, a stranger almost – but she was still the most lovely woman on whom his eyes had ever rested. With a hand raised in salute, he turned and went.

*　　　*　　　*

He did not go right away and leave her, there and then, of course. Abruptly waving away MacAlastair and the ponies, he went striding savagely off up the hill behind the house, on and on, climbing ever higher up the steep side of Beinn More, as though he would leave below him in the valley all the heartache and ruin of his life there represented. To the very summit of the mountain he went, tireless, like a man possessed, there to sit in brooding stillness, unmindful of the chill that grew on him, eyeing without seeing all the far-flung vista of mountain and valley, and fighting his own battle with himself. It was almost dark before he came down, heavy-footed, to Corrycharmaig.

He found the situation as he had left it, as far as his wife was concerned. With young Ranald he managed to re-establish relations, but Coll remained distant and wary, despite all his father's efforts. It seemed that, in the boy's eyes, he was a shattered idol. From him, however, Rob learned, by questioning, what had happened at Inversnaid House four nights before up till the time when the children had been locked away in the inner room.

That night the master of the house slept, wrapped in his plaid, on the kitchen floor, excluded from Mary's room.

The day following he hung about the house and its vicinity, seeking to maintain a surface illusion of normality – with scant success. Mary fed him, replied after a fashion when he spoke to her, looked through him rather than at him, and made it obvious that she wished him away. He tried to break through this armour of reserve, tried honeyed words, pleading words, angry words, and no words at all.

59

But all was of no avail. And to a man of Rob's urgent and vigorous temperament and active habit, this state of affairs was more than trying. One day was as much of it as he could stand. Moreover, the fever for vengeance was burning within him like a searing flame.

At sunrise next morning then, he flung out of the house, shouting for MacAlastair and the garrons. They rode into a grey sombre morning, with mist low on the hills, everything dripping moisture, and Loch Iubhair below the house leaden as Rob's heart. Westwards they went, fording the Dochart to avoid the clachan of Crainlarich and the need to be civil to any man, and on up Strathfillan. At Tyndrum they swung right, to commence the long climb to the watershed of Scotland, high birthplace of rivers that ran east to the North Sea and west to the Atlantic, using the old zigzagging drove road that was Rob's favourite route for bringing down herds of cattle from all the north and west. The summit of the wild and lonely pass was thick in mist, but beyond the watershed, as often happens, the weather changed. Through a break in the clouds a few miles away the noble peak of Beinn Dorain frowned down on all that barren wilderness. Barren, that is, save for a single fertile island of green that crouched right below the savage mountain, a green startling and lovely as it was unexpected in all the waste of rock and heather, tucked into the mouth of a steep glen. And amidst the green haughland and watermeadows, a single small house stood, the only habitation of man as far as eye could see. It was the place of Auchinchisallan, or more commonly, just Auch. The men rode down towards it.

This was all Breadalbane country, and for a consideration its lord leased Auchinchisallan to Rob Roy, who found its extraordinarily rich pastures and fine shelter uncommonly useful for the assembling, sustenance and strengthening of his cattle droves, weak and hungry after long travelling, before they faced the final trial across the watershed. Moreover, the place was strategically situated – always an important consideration with the Mac-Gregor – guarding the back door into Glen Lyon and covering the flank of Glen Orchy. He had found it a useful investment in the past.

All winter, with the droving season over, the little house was apt to stand empty. Now the two men set about putting it to rights and making it a reasonably comfortable place of refuge for Mary MacGregor and the children. Though a mere dozen miles, as the eagle might fly, from Corrycharmaig, Auch was more than twice that far as men must travel, and hidden deep enough in the wilderness for any would-be anchorite. A couple of days' work, and Rob was satisfied. Leaving MacAlastair to finish certain improvements, he rode back to Corrycharmaig, and the next day brought back a little procession consisting of his wife and children, a couple of elderly but trusty gillies with their unmarried sister, a number of garrons, four milk cows, and some poultry slung in wickerwork panniers. It was not a cheerful journey, even allowing for its slowness and the effect of driving rain.

Two mornings later, Rob made his farewells. Mary did not ask him where he was going, and he did not volunteer the information. She suffered him to kiss the alabaster-white of her brow – and in doing so he perceived silver hairs, amongst the raven-black, that he had not seen before. But she made no gesture towards him, did not unbend her stiffness, did not even come to the door to see him go.

Heavy-hearted, he turned his horse's head southwards towards the pass once more, MacAlastair silent as ever at his heels. When he looked back, only Coll and the gillies stood there. At least the boy raised a hand in valedictory salute.

CHAPTER FIVE

HIDDEN amongst boulders on the high ridge of Creag an Fhithich, the Raven's Crag, with long Loch Lomond far below at his back, Rob Roy MacGregor looked down into his own fair and grassy glen of Inversnaid – and his mood was savage. He could see the blackened ruins of his house. He could see that many of the other habitations of the glen, the cot-houses and cabins of his people, were roofless and abandoned. Though it was drawing towards evening, he could see no blue columns of smoke from evening fires arising from any of them. Many of his cattle still grazed placidly on the valley sides, and especially around the little sheet of green water, Lochan Uaine, in mid-glen – but then, cattle were a drug on the market meantime. He could not see any of his large herd of horses, save for a scattered beast or two fairly high up amongst the cattle.

Not that he was looking for them with any urgency. The man's attention was concentrated on a spot within the very mouth of the glen, down where it opened into the wider and deeper Glen Arklet. Here, as distinct from elsewhere, was life, movement, activity – and colour. The colour, how-ever, was rather noticeably scarlet. Though there *was* the blue of woodsmoke at the lowermost end of it. The move-ment was concentrated in three fairly closely linked areas – two in the valley floor, near the burnside down there, and the third a little way up the hillside near by, around a rocky projecting bluff in the very jaws of the valley. That bluff, Tom na Bairlinn, the Knoll of Warning, had long been used as a platform for a beacon-fire, since it commanded wide views up Glen Arklet to the east and out across Loch Lomond to the west. The activity seemed to be greatest at this point and at the higher of the two by the riverside – that only a short way below the ruins of Rob's own house – but the scarlet colour was confined to the group lower down, where the valley opened wider and it seemed that tents were pitched.

'What think you of it?' Rob jerked to MacAlastair, pointing. 'What are they at, down there, think you – damn them?'

That taciturn man shook his dark head. 'Busy, they are. At what, I cannot see. We could be going nearer.'

His master nodded. By keeping well over on the west side of their ridge, they could move down, unseen from Inversnaid, for another mile almost. Nor might they be spotted from Loch Lomond-side because of the steep overhanging woods of oak and ash that clothed the entire escarpment on that side. And there was no one to observe them from out on the surface of the loch.

The early November dusk was settling on the hills before the two men reached their final vantage-point, a little birchwooded hill that rose directly across from the rocky knoll aforementioned and a mere four or five hundred yards from it. The dusk helped to hide them, but it did not improve their vision – nor did the smirr of rain that was drifting between. Still, the situation was fairly obvious now, as from amongst the silver and shadow of the birches they peered.

'*Dia*! They are building,' Rob exclaimed. 'See – walls are going up. There. And there. And, look you – they are quarrying into the side of Tom na Bairlinn. They are winning the stone from there. See the men busy like ants at it, whatever!'

'Aye,' his companion agreed, briefly.

'Damnation! See you what it is – what it must be? Those walls are to be thick, strong, my goodness. It is a castle that they are making. A fort. As Royal's my Race –

they are for building a fort on *my* land! Mine, devil take them!'

There could be little doubt that such was the case. On a grassy terrace or shelf where the Snaid Burn made a loop before plunging over in a series of little cataracts in its descent into Glen Arklet, masons were active in erecting stout walls of the reddish stone that others were quarrying from the base of the rocky knoll behind. Those walls were of little height as yet – but clearly they were going to be both wide and substantial and of greater extent than any mere house. Rob saw where some of his horses had gone; many of them were being used to carry and haul the stone from the knoll to the terrace. The men involved were all dully-clad labourers; the colour came from further down, below the cataracts, where there was room for a small military camp, and where, amongst the tents and cooking-fires a company of scarlet-coated soldiers lounged – guards for the masons and quarrymen presumably, and too fine to be demeaned with manual labour.

The site selected for the building gave fine views in most directions and an excellent field of fire – almost as good as on the top of the nearby Knoll of Warning – with the added advantage that drinking-water could be gained without deep well-drilling through rock, which no doubt always was a preoccupation with fort-builders who had to visualise siege conditions. Nevertheless, Rob himself would have built that fort on the summit of Tom na Bairlinn. Not that he did not recognise the advantages of the chosen site; had it not been his intention, years before, to build his own new house exactly there, instead of merely enlarging the existing farmhouse a little further up?

'So – we are to be permanently occupied, are we!' he said, in a tense whisper. 'As God's my witness, we shall see about that!'

As daylight faded, the busy men down there knocked off work, and went straggling away in groups and parties, some on the ponies, but most walking, by the steep track through the little pass that led down to Loch Lomond. Presumably the contractors for the work were not disposed to permit their unarmed hirelings to stay overnight up there in the open, surrounded by MacGregors, even under guard of the military. Only the red-coats in their camp remained. It would be chilly weather for camping, too.

When it was quite dusk, Rob and his attendant shadow slipped back out of the wood, leading their garrons and moving silently. Up the glen-side again they went, amongst the cud-chewing cattle, till it was safe to mount and ride once more. Then they turned downwards, crossed the Snaid Burn just below Lochan Uaine, and set their beasts to climb the steep hillside beyond that enclosed the glen on the east. This was a much higher ridge than that to the west, but the sure-footed ponies picked their way unerringly and tirelessly through grass, dying bracken and short heather till presently they were over the summit and slanting down into the pit of the valley beyond. This was Corrie Arklet, a parallel but shorter and less fertile glen than that of the Snaid, a couple of miles to the east. Down the track that followed its central burn the travellers rode, with the lights of Corraklet House gleaming ahead of them in the mouth of it.

But though the master of that house was Rob's own distant cousin, John MacGregor – and Mary's uncle into the bargain – they did not present themselves at its hospitable door. Skirting its many cot-houses – for Corraklet was the major centre of population for all the area – Rob took up his position amongst a group of boulders and thorn trees on the hillside above, and then sent MacAlastair on foot down to the lamp-lit house below, his instructions definite. The gillie melted into the blue of the night without a sound.

It was some time before the sound of heavier footsteps and still heavier breathing proclaimed the arrival of someone other than MacAlastair. Rob waited until he could just distinguish the blur of movement in the darkness before he raised his voice, from behind a great boulder.

'Wait you there, now,' he called, quietly. 'Greetings, John *mo charaid*.'

'Och, is that yourself, man Rob?' a panting voice replied. John MacGregor was getting to be an elderly man now, and heavy for hurried climbing. 'What sort of nonsense is this, at all . . . ?'

'Wait where you are, John, I say,' the younger man repeated, as the other continued to come up. 'And put you your plaid over your head, see you.'

'Och, for the Lord's sake, Rob – what ails you, man? Have you lost your wits . . . ?'

'No, Cousin – other things I have lost, but not my wits maybe. Hold him, MacAlastair. 'Tis for your own good, John – for the clan's sake. Tomorrow, I want you to be able to say, on your oath, that you have not seen me, that I have not been to your house. Otherwise, you may well find yourself outlawed likewise, for aiding and abetting myself. And you have seen what outlawry means, in this year of our Lord, seventeen and thirteen!'

'*Dia* – so that's it! Think you that I am afraid of them, Rob? That I am afraid to acknowledge you? Think you that I fear the dirty, skulking, burning women-fighters? Think you that I cannot take to the heather, yet, with fifty good claymores with me, and teach this Sassunach scum what it means to insult a MacGregor! I tell you . . .'

'Aye, John – aye,' Rob interrupted heavily. 'I could have done that same, too – with three hundred blades instead of fifty. And written the final death-sentence on our clan! Should I have done that, John? Should I, man?'

'Hech – what way is that to be speaking, Rob? The Gregorach are not so easily disposed of, my God! We have had them hounding us before, and thrown them back. In the old days . . .'

'Aye – but these are not the old days, *mo charaid*. These

66

are the new days, in Scotland. London rules now, in Scotland – and the nominees of London. Our true king twiddles his thumbs in France. Scotland is at peace – and the Government has many soldiers, and little for them to be doing. I could have thrown this parcel of ruffians back into Loch Lomond, yes – but only with the help of the clan. And with what result? The Government, with no one else stirring against them in all the land, could have sent their hundreds, their thousands of soldiers against this corner of the Highlands, to wipe our houses and our families off the face of the land – however snug we fine sworders might be in the heather! Was that the price that I should have paid? We know that many in high places, and one James Graham in especial, just wait their opportunity to destroy, once and for all, the very name and memory of MacGregor. *Dia* – of all the wide lands that once were ours, Glen Orchy, Glen Strae, Glen Lyon and Glen Lochay, Strathfillan, Glen Falloch, Glen Dochart, Glen Ogle . . .' The man's deep voice quivered as he named them, like the proudest notes of a lament. 'All these, and more, are gone. Only this little corner – Glen Gyle and Glen Arklet, Inversnaid and Craigroyston, are left to us. We have clung to these, though hated and proscribed, through all. They would have been the price of my swording, John. Would it have been worth it? Even at the cost I have had to pay? And nothing, I wager, would better have pleased the man who sent those soldiers – James Graham of Montrose.'

Save for a long exhalation of breath, the older man was silent.

It was a strange interview, up there on the bare hillside in the darkness, with the curlews calling and calling wearily around them and no other sound to the night but the sigh of the wind over heather – one cousin hidden behind great rocks, the other with his plaid-end tossed across his face, and MacAlastair standing by, silent, expressionless.

There came a pleading note into Rob Roy's voice, such

as few men could have heard before. 'You understand why I did it, John?'

'Aye. Aye – it could be that you are right. But . . . my God, it is an ill day for the Gregorach when Rob Roy MacGregor turns the other cheek for the Sasunnach to spit upon!'

Beyond a sharp intake of breath, the younger man answered nothing to that.

'Are we then to swallow their spittle? Do we stand by and bow our heads, man?' Corrarklet went on. 'We have done as you bade us. We have not risen. We have not touched a hair of a soldier's head. It has been hard to do, as Heaven's my witness – but we have done it. I do not know if I can be holding our people in much longer. . . .'

'You must, John. You must. What of Gregor – what of Glengyle? How does he take it?'

'Och, he is away yet. He is not back from Arnprior. Had you not heard? His wife is sick, and he waits with Buchanan of Arnprior. By the Powers – if Gregor Black-Knee had been home, no red-coat would be remaining in these glens!'

Again Rob was silent.

The older man wagged his head, so that the plaid dropped. 'And you, Rob?' he demanded. 'You, of all men! Do you accept it all, just? They name you outlaw, and burn your house, insult your wife – even strike her, it is said, my God – and turn her and your boys out of doors! Is that nothing to you . . . ?'

'Fool! Fool!' The sudden violence and fury of that eruption from behind the boulder made even the speaker take an involuntary backward step, so fierce and unexpected was it. 'Damn you – think you that I am a crawling reptile! A cold-blooded worm and no man! As Royal's my Race – I'll make them pay for what they have done! Montrose and Killearn shall rue the day that they did this thing. Before the throne of Almighty God, I swear it! They shall pay, pay, pay . . . !' There was anguish and pride and

68

hate and a savage determination in that throbbing rising voice. But by an effort that must have been tremendous, the mounting wrath was checked, disciplined, and the voice steadied. 'But I myself shall pay my debts, see you. Not the clan,' Rob went on. 'What has been done has been done to *me*. What is done in return shall be done by me! They can do no more to me, now, save take my life. But I can do a deal for *them*, before that day! Fear not that they shall not pay, John *mo charaid*. Only, *I* shall set the price, and no other. Is that understood, Cousin?'

'Aye, Rob. Aye – if that is your wish.' Corrarklet's enunciation of the words was thick. Any man who had abruptly borne the full impact of Rob Roy MacGregor's unleashed anger was apt to be dry-mouthed for a little. 'What . . . what would you have us do, then?'

'Two things, John. Keep the clan quiet – and keep me informed. I want information all the time. I shall need it, whatever. Our folk must not raise their hands – but their eyes and their ears must be mine.'

'They will know that you are fighting back, Rob? That your pride – and theirs – is not lost on you?'

'They will know, by Heaven! But they must help me in the way that I say.'

'And Glengyle . . . ?'

'I will attend to Gregor. Now, John – I want information from yourself, here and now. Tell me how the soldiers are placed, just? What are their numbers? How goes it down at Loch Lomond-side?'

'Aye, then. This is the way of it, Rob . . .'

*   *   *

By the dark waters of Lochan Uaine Rob halted, and dismounted. MacAlastair was still his sole companion, but they had three ponies now, the third one fairly heavily laden. Away to the south, in the mouth of the glen, they could see the red glow of a single large fire; evidently the soldiers had let their numerous cooking-fires die out, but kept one blaze going, no doubt equally for its light and for the comfort of unfortunate sentries. Apart from that red gleam of light, the night was black. It was after midnight, starless, and with a drift of fine rain in the cold air.

They had halted at the lower end of the lochan. The water was high, after days of rain, lipping over the dam that Rob had built a few years before. Always there had been a natural pond there, a mere widening of the burn in a hollow, more reeds than water at the height of summer; Rob, as the cattle-droving business expanded, had found it expedient to dam up this lochan, as he had done with others elsewhere, to provide storage reservoirs for watering large numbers of beasts in dry weather.

While MacAlastair unloaded the pack-pony, Rob ferreted about at the lower side of the dam, peering and feeling and testing. Since it was he who had erected it, he knew the construction and points of weakness therein; but it was difficult to trace the exact conformation in the darkness, and to find or contrive the cavities and corners that he required. He had never looked upon himself as an expert in demolition.

They had appropriated the major part of the Gregorach's cherished store of gunpowder. MacAlastair was unpacking it slowly, handling the stuff gingerly, much less sure of himself than usual. It was a pity about the threatening rain, since they must keep the powder dry.

In order to create a cavity large enough to be effective, and placed so as to give maximum disruption, the two men had to labour long and uncomfortably, in a cramped position, digging with dirks and bare fingers, loosening, prising and extracting stones and rubble and soil. It seemed to be an extraordinary expenditure of effort when explosive was supposed to be doing the work – in fact, Rob more than once snorted that they might as well forget the gunpowder and pull the thing to pieces by hand. But at length they had a hole large enough and deep enough to accommodate their supply of powder. To keep it dry from trickling water, they lined the cavity with an old dear-hide rug from Corrarklet House, and thereafter filled in the explosive. This had all to be packed in again securely with replaced stones and turfs, to conserve the force of the blast – but a small gap had to be left, through which the igniting charge could be led. The total toil was considerable, and it was a couple of hours before Rob was satisfied.

He sent MacAlastair off, then, to try to drive away out of the floor of the glen any cattle that might be passing the night therein. Cattle represented life to the MacGregors. Meanwhile Rob had to lay his detonating contrivance. This was a problem, for he had no slow-burning fuse, nor anything which he could produce at short notice which would serve with any certainty. The only thing for it was to lay a line of gunpowder itself to a sufficient distance for his own safety, and in due course ignite this. And it would not do for such a train of powder to get wet, in the interim.

While giving MacAlastair the time he needed, Rob prospected as best he could an unimpeded and sheltered route for his fuse-line – with a view to his own hasty retreat once it was lit. Just how fast the flame would run, he had small idea. So he plotted his own line of flight with fair thoroughness also.

At length he decided that MacAlastair had had long enough – he was not to go too far down the glen anyway, for fear of alarming the soldiers' camp. Rob laid his trail of black powder – difficult to do evenly in the darkness – hastily reassured himself as to his line of flight, and got out his flint and tinder from his sporran. Striking sparks into the tinder, he blew on it, saw it flare up, and tossed the little blaze on to the gunpowder line.

He turned and ran.

He did not run far. There was a large rock-fall about thirty yards back and uphill, behind which he had intended to hide himself. But he had gone barely half as far before he felt the ground convulse beneath his feet. Without a moment's hesitation he flung himself flat, to join that heaving earth. It seemed to co-operate, as though it rose up to meet him. Indeed, the unanimity appeared to be almost too urgent, all but knocking the breath out of the man – though possibly that was the effect of blast. Curiously enough, Rob was aware of no great uproar, no huge explosion of sound. Probably that also was the effect of blast on his eardrums. Gasping for breath and clawing instinctively at the ground for some sort of security, the first sounds of which he was aware, after a period of seeming suspended sensation, were the thud and clump and patter of things, large and small, raining down around him and upon him – stones, sods, gravel, water. But this was quickly drowned under a much more potent volume of sound, an uproar now, authentic enough if delayed, and rising mightily – the swelling irresistible voice of pent waters released. From a drumming rumble it rose to a thunderous roar, and the ground beneath the sprawling man, that had been heaving, now began to quiver and tremble. Somehow he managed to drag himself to his feet, and went stumbling and staggering on, higher, out of reach of the clutching tearing flood that he had unchained.

Behind the rock-fall that he had selected as refuge, Rob turned and gazed back. Dark as it was, there was no difficulty in seeing the result of his handiwork, for the waters were black no longer, but foaming white, leaping and spouting in a wide and headlong cataract. On and on they poured, completely overwhelming and submerging the modest bed of the burn. It seemed astonishing that so comparatively small a lochan could have contained so great a volume of water.

Rob stood watching, bemused, fascinated by the violence of the power that he had unleashed, even a little abashed.

At length, with the noise beginning to abate and the level

of the torrent manifestly dropping, he climbed up to where the garrons still stood, restive. He soothed them with a word or two, mounted his own beast, and leading the two others, set off down the glen, keeping his distance well above the valley floor. He passed the sites of three of his people's cot-houses. They had had their thatches burned by the soldiers, and had been deserted – and now no trace of any of them remained, that Rob could see.

Presently a dark figure materialised from behind a whin-bush. It was MacAlastair. Wordless he took his place behind his master.

Rob turned. 'Well, man – what of it?' he demanded, a little testily perhaps, for him. 'You saw? You had time enough – for the cattle? What think you of it?'

'It was an ill thing, that,' the other returned, flatly. 'You were after washing away every last stone of the house where I was born. And others too, whatever.'

'Aye, maybe. But maybe also I washed away more than that! Maybe I washed some little of the defilement from this glen, see you.' That was sombrely said. 'Come.'

As they neared the mouth of the valley, they dismounted and left the ponies, to proceed cautiously on foot. No red glow of camp-fire now beckoned them on. No sound other than the rush of the swollen stream and the sigh of the wind came to them.

From the shadow of Tom na Bairlinn they peered downwards, right and left.

MacAlastair spoke – and it was not often that he initiated any discussion. 'Think you that they are all drowned dead?' he wondered.

Rob shook his head. 'No. They would be hearing the noise of it, for sure. They would have the time to get out. Their sentries would wake the camp. And the glen widens there, below the falls. Och, some of them might be caught, yes – but the most of them would get out of it.'

'Your own house, too? It will be gone, like the rest? I

cannot see that far, in the dark . . .'

'Maybe – what was left of it.' Rob shrugged. But it was not upstream that he peered, to where the blackened walls of Inversnaid House had stood above a bend of the burn, but directly below, to that other shelf where the fort-building operations had been in progress. 'But what matter – so long as these other walls are down? Their castle. Their fort. Can you see them? See if they still stand? Or is the water still covering them?'

'I cannot see, no. But . . . can that be? Those walls they were building were thick. Strong. No house walls.'

'Aye. But the mortar is new. And better than that – that site is bad, see you, though it looks the best place in the glen, I grant you. It is undercut by the burn. A shelf of rock there is, yes – but underneath it is sand. That is why I did not build my house there. I started it, you will mind – but changed. After two days of rain, I saw the cracks appearing, whatever. So I moved away. Come – we will see.'

Cautiously they climbed down the steep and slippery slope, past the gaping hole of the new quarry and over towards that shelf above the stream. They had to pick their way amongst a litter of stones and boulders that had not been there previously, and their feet sank into gritty mud and sodden ground indicating that the flood had reached as high as this.

They did not require to go searching for what might be left of those new-built walls. The entire shelf, they found, had sagged and collapsed and side-slipped drunkenly into the deeper rock-bed of the stream. Whether or not the fresh mortar had held was now of no consequence, for most of that stone terrace was now merely a series of slantwise foam-forming obstructions in the snarling waters. And much of the bank behind, no longer supported, seemed to have come down in the form of a landslide, to complete the chaos. No fort would arise on *that* site, to tame wild MacGregors.

Grimly Rob Roy nodded. 'It is well,' he said. 'Very well. The first instalment of my debt paid, whatever. As Royal's my Race – Montrose will find that MacGregor is not quite bankrupt yet! I warrant he . . . Hist! Did you hear aught there, MacAlastair? Did I hear men shout? From down yonder?'

The gillie shook his head. To hear anything over and above the noise of rushing tortured waters, here in the gut of the glen, was asking too much.

Rob looked about him, seeking something – something close at hand, and not the source of distant voices. He found it, in the shape of a tall birch trunk, uprooted and brought down by the flood, and now securely wedged between two boulders at the upper end of the broken terrace. It was as near to the site of the projected fort as might be achieved. Reaching into his sporran, the man drew out a folded paper. He smoothed it out with a cut and muddied hand, and whipping out a small *sgian dubh*, or dirk, from his hose top, he skewered this firmly to the tree-trunk, adding a stone on top for further security. In the darkness he could not read again what he had earlier written thereon – but it would serve.

With a jerked word to his companion, Rob turned away and went climbing back whence they had come. Above the quarry he paused for a moment and faced back southwards, to raise his great fist, clenched above his head, and shake it, silently fiercely, with a world of menace, into the gloom, before slipping off up the glen towards the horses.

That gesture he left behind him – with a ruined site, a wrecked camp, sundry drowned and missing men, and a spreading desolation. Also a paper inscribed thus:

To All Whom it May Concern

No man builds stone upon stone in Inversnaid without my permission. What I have, I hold. I alone have done this. None other dweller in these glens has art or part of it. Any reprisal towards others I will avenge ten-fold. All men take note. In especial James Graham of Montrose, and John Graham of Killearn. These two have cost me dear. The first shall support me and mine hereafter, in return. The second shall die. This I swear, as my Race is Royal.

Robert MacGregor of Inversnaid and Craigroyston.

CHAPTER SIX

ROB ROY lay sprawled at ease on a couch of pulled heather, in the mouth of his cave. The aromatic smoke from his fire of resinous knots of bog-pine was drawn back over his head, deep into the cave, by the draught from a multi-mouthed chimney contrived with much care amongst the cracks and crevices of the roof. Neither smoke nor soot, nor the dispersed openings themselves, would reveal that refuge to the keenest eye. Not that the bog-pine, jagged stumps of the giant primeval conifers that once had covered all Highland Scotland to the summits of the highest hills, made a smoky fuel; impregnated with turpentine, it burned with a clear and intense orange flame that was fiercely hot.

And its heat was more than welcome, up there, high above the present tree-level, that late-November morning. Of sanctuaries innumerable that he might have selected, Rob had chosen this eyrie as his temporary headquarters, at the lofty head of the long smiling valley of Balquhidder. Tucked into a shallow corrie of broken rocky hillside, only a hundred feet or so beneath the summit of Cruach Tuirc, the Hill of the Boar, it held many advantages beside its wide prospect. It was not on his own land, not even on actual Gregorach territory – which was important; yet it was readily accessible – for the sure-footed and the stout-hearted – from all parts of the MacGregor country. Rob could turn downhill in three distinct directions; east into Balquhidder itself, a happy no-man's-land of broken clans and independent characters, where no authority ruled save a sense of humour, a fleet foot and an agile wrist; south into Gregor's

Glen Gyle, Loch Katrine-side, and beyond to Snaid and Arklet; and west into Glen Falloch and the head of Loch Lomond. Moreover, this Hill of the Boar rose out of a veritable moat of black and treacherous peat-hags, which only the initiated would cross save at their peril. Nothing less than an army – and an exceedingly well-informed and fast-moving army at that – could hope to corner Rob up here, much less to extract him.

One of Cousin John's gillies from Corrarklet, Finlay Broken-Nose by name, squatted before him at the fire, gnawing at a foreleg of cold roe venison. MacAlastair kept watch on the further, western, side of the hill.

Rob was pondering the information that Finlay had brought. Two days had passed since the shattering of Lochan Uaine and the projected fort. The soldiers, it seemed, had arrested Donald, Corrarklet's younger son, charging him with complicity in the outrage. Apparently he had been encountered by the alarmed red-coats as they fled before the devouring flood-waters. What Donald Mac-Gregor had been doing in the vicinity of the camp at that hour of the night, the gillie had not specified – but Rob had a fairly shrewd idea; Donald was something of a gallant, and though suitably married and with a fine son of his own, had not shown himself to be wholly insensitive to the charms of other ladies – in particular one, the generous and conveniently placed daughter of Malcolm the Mill, Seana by name, who lived at the mill-house in the pass between Inversnaid and Loch Lomond. The chances were that he had been on his belated way home from a nocturnal assignation when, all unwitting, he had blundered into the after-effects of Rob's explosion – and thereby presented himself as a most opportune scapegoat. At any rate, he had been accused of being an accessory, had been unable or un-willing to explain his presence on the scene of disaster, and was to be sent to Dumbarton Castle for trial. Moreover, it transpired that, later, his poor wife and child had also been taken into custody, as hostages to ensure non-interference by the MacGregors.

Rob Roy was concerned. He felt responsible. Though it might be that young Donald deserved a lesson, he surely had not earned the kind of justice that he would be apt to get at Dumbarton. Moreover, the older man had a soft spot in his heart for the unfortunate wife, Marsala, a gentle doe-eyed creature, who again was a far-out relative of his own. The MacGregors had never concerned themselves about the inter-marriage of cousins. In the circumstances, it was obvious to Rob that he would have to do something about it. Perhaps it was significant that the military had considered hostages to be necessary.

'You say that the red-coats are now all camped down at Loch Lomond-side, at their boats?' he asked. 'They hold their prisoners there?'

Finlay Broken-Nose nodded. 'That is the way of it, yes. But there are no boats in it,' he amended. 'The boats all are gone. Och, they were after sending all the masons and the building-men back to Glasgow in them – for there is no work for them at all, any more. All the boats were needed, and they have no boats left – some of our own people's boats they were after taking, indeed. They cannot be sending Donald Beg down to Dumbarton until the boats come back.'

'I see,' Rob sounded thoughtful.

The other leaned forward. 'Och, yes. This is what I was to tell you. It is a great chance, see you. Corrarklet says it.' Finlay gestured with his roe's leg to emphasise his point. 'If the clan was to be raised now, we could come down on those soldiers like the hammers of hell and drive them into the loch, whatever, and make an end of them! Before their boats are back. They could not be getting away from us. None would win back to Dumbarton, at all. Strike, it is – before the boats get back.'

'Aye,' Rob nodded slowly. 'Maybe, Finlay. Strike – but

not that way, I think. Those soldiers the clan might drive into the loch, yes. But there would plenty more come up in their boats from Dumbarton to avenge them – and all Glen Arklet and Glen Gyle would burn and die. No – there is a better way than that. The clan shall *not* rise – tell you John of Corrarklet that, from me! I will save his son for him, from Dumbarton Castle, never fear – but in my own way. When are they expecting the boats to be back?'

'Today. Before night. That is why I am here early. That is what the soldiers say. They are not happy, those ones, without their boats – God's curse on them!'

'Aye. I'ph'mm. They have twenty miles down the loch and ten more beyond, by the river, to Dumbarton. It makes a deal of rowing, for heavy boats, How many boats have they? Who have they at the rowing? Not red-coats?'

'Och, no. No work for soldiers, that. Some of the masons rowed, and they took some of our own folk. About ten of them. Near a score of boats, there were.'

'So! The masons will not be there to row back. They will be short of oarsmen – so they will have to be towing the empty boats. Time, that will take. Did many red-coats go with them?'

'The officer only – the major-man, Selby, who commands them all – and four others. Two of them hurt in the flood.'

'The major – this Selby – has gone, himself? For instructions, no doubt – about the fort, likely. The question is – will he be bringing back reinforcements?' Rob's query was put to himself. 'I think not. He has most of a company there – and only the two men to fight. The clan has not risen – he scarce can ask for more soldiers. Not yet, with not a shot fired! No . . . I think maybe that I see my way through this tangle, Finlay. Not just clearly yet, mind you – but it comes, it comes! Now – back with you to Corrarklet, man, and tell you my good and warlike cousin to be patient. Patient, just – no more is asked of him.'

The other, rising to his feet, grimaced. 'Patience, it is?

Be Patient, it seems, has become the motto of our clan, whatever! One time it was E'en Do and Spare Nocht!'

Rob's startlingly blue eyes narrowed as they met the other's wry glance. Not the most patient of men himself, words surged to the tip of his tongue. But he choked them back. He nodded curtly. 'Off with you,' he said.

He watched the gillie go, for a little, dark-browed. Then, rising, he extinguished the fire, and went in search of Mac-Alastair.

*   *   *

It was past noon when Rob and MacAlastair parted company, on the steep tree-clad hillside high above Loch Lomond, a good five miles south of their eyrie on Cruach Tuirc. Away below them, glimpsed through the hanging woods of oak and ash and hazel that were steadily losing their shrivelled leaves to a gusty wind, was the deep defile by which the brief River Arklet, reinforced by the Snaid Burn, made its abrupt descent of four hundred feet from its own loch to the great Loch Lomond. Down there, beside the little harbour near the final waterfall, were the few huddled houses of Inverarklet and the many scattered tents of the military. From so high above, all seemed remarkably peaceful and inoffensive.

'See you now – do not be killing anybody,' Rob instructed finally. 'That would only bring down reprisals on our people. Give the man this receipt for what you take – tell him, if you can keep him conscious, that it is for the use of Rob Roy MacGregor only. Then come you as fast as you may to the big bluff beyond Rowchoish. Four miles it is, from here, so you do not have over-long for it. I will be awaiting you there. Is it understood?'

His uncommunicative henchman nodded, and slanted off downhill through the scattered trees and the withering bracken.

Keeping to the high ground, Rob continued on his way

southwards, parallel with the loch. For this expedition the garrons had been left behind, as too conspicuous. He held to the uppermost limits of the trees, the best part of a thousand feet above the water, for he was almost as anxious to avoid the notice of his own people as that of the military – and Gregorach crofts and holdings dotted the area along the loch-shore for miles. This was his own domain of Craig-royston, comprising a dozen miles of steep forested hillside and rock and heather, flanking Lomond's eastern shore and extending right down to Montrose's northernmost property of Rowardennan. It might seem a somewhat rough and barren area to be the prime object of ducal covetousness, but looked at from another angle it certainly made a distinctly thrusting salient into the Grahams' more settled territory – and MacGregors could be restless neighbours.

Scrambling amongst the rocks, threading the tall crackling bracken, leaping burns innumerable, and seeking not to disturb noticeably the cattle that clung to even this precarious pasture, Rob nevertheless covered the difficult terrain at an impressive speed. He boasted, of course, that there was no man in all Scotland – save perhaps MacAlastair – who could keep up with him on the hill. It was no idle boast. Even tall Gregor of Glengyle, younger and with longer legs, was apt to be left behind.

Above Cailness, the home of another of his many far-out cousins, Rob began to dip down, discreetly. There were clearings and open meadows in the woods here, steeply slant-wise but fair, with much stock. To avoid them, the man, for much of the way down, crept actually in the rocky scrub-lined channel of the tumbling Cailness Burn – that was indeed more waterfall than anything else. He was wet – but he might well be wetter. Presently the grey-stone house of Simon of Cailness lay below him, with the usual scattering of cot-houses and cabins around it. Folk were moving about – but Rob had little fear of attracting their attention; it was the dogs, and to a lesser extent the children, that he had to watch for. Cailness himself, of course, like every soul there, would have been only too eager to hail and aid the fugitive. But he was determined that it should be otherwise; his fondness for these folk demanded more of him than sociable greetings and calls for assistance.

Making a wide detour, he approached the little bay below the houses, unobserved. Three boats lay on the shingle, at the water's edge. The smaller one would serve him finely. But extracting it unseen was going to be a little difficult. . . .

Moving away again, inland a little and to the south, Rob selected a small glade in the woods, with care. Through the trees he could still see the houses, a mere three hundred yards away. The wind was south-west as usual, gusty and sufficient. And there was ample dead bracken in the clearing. Quietly gathering some armfuls of the stuff, and adding some dry sticks for substance, he got out his tinder and flint and struck a light. In less time than it takes to tell, he had three well-doing fires blazing, spaced out and setting alight the standing bracken. As billowing clouds of acrid smoke rolled up, and, fanned by the breeze, bore down through the trees towards the homestead, Rob turned and slipped away in the other direction, satisfied. There was no hurry, for a little while.

He heard the shouts and cries of alarm before ever he reached the vicinity of the tiny bay. Give them a little while, and no man, woman, nor child would be left around the Cailness houses – for a forest fire was a most urgent challenge and had to be confined and beaten out immediately, or pasture and stock would suffer. Not that they would have much trouble in defeating this blaze; Rob had chosen this area carefully, anxious that it should not spread but only provide a diversion. In twenty minutes or so it should all be over – but meantime there would be much confusion and excitement.

His fire served him well. Not only did it distract the attention of all – including, very clearly from the noise, the dogs and children — but it sent down such a thick and choking curtain of brown smoke on the south-west wind as effectually to screen the shore from any eyes not already preoccupied with the threatening conflagration. Moreover, if Rob's own tears were anything to go by, no eyes were likely to be very efficient anyway, in the circumstances.

With only a gesture at hiding, then, he made his way round and down to the shingle of the little beach. The oars had been left in the boats, and all that was needed was for Rob to set his wide shoulder to the stern of the smallest craft, push it a yard or so down into the water, and jump in. No more than a minute of strong pulling, and he was out of the bay, and its little headland to the south intervened to hide him finally from Cailness.

Rob turned to stare southwards. As yet he could see no other boat on all the wide slate-grey spread of water. But Loch Lomond was long, over twenty miles long, with innumerable headlands and bays and inlets, to say nothing of its islands. The fact that the man could see no craft from where he was did not mean necessarily that he had unlimited time to spare. He recommended his rowing, pulling with long and powerful strokes that sent the little tubby vessel squattering forward at a great pace. He hugged the wooded shore closely.

There were other MacGregor cottages and cabins down that lochside — but not many, for the hillside was now merely the foot of mighty Beinn Lomond itself, and becoming increasingly steep, riven and barren. When Rob approached the vicinity of any such house, he pulled further out into the loch and covered his flaming head of red hair with his plaid; hunched and seated thus, he might just possibly escape identification, should he be seen — always a problem with that conspicuously made man.

Rounding the great headland of Rowchoish, he pulled on for a further mile and more, till he came to a small and narrow inlet, barely to be distinguished amongst the overhanging trees, and tumbled massive rocks. Into the mouth of this he rowed his borrowed boat.

It was a strange haven that he had chosen. A few yards in from its rocky constricted jaws, it turned sharply to the right around a steep soaring bluff, and then unexpectedly opened out into a wholly landlocked little lagoon, hemmed in by the hanging woods. It was all the work of a headlong turbulent stream that came in here, and, after carving through the solid rock at the lochside, had cut back and back through softer material behind to form this secret pool, into which the loch's waters had followed. Cascading down in a sizeable waterfall at the far end, the burn was still busy at its enlargement – and no doubt would be so until the end of time. It had proved a useful corner for Rob Roy Mac-Gregor ere this.

Tying his boat to a rowan sapling, he clambered out and went hastening up the hillside above, climbing at his fastest. He was heading for a tall and bare shoulder of the hill, where, unhampered by trees, he could gain a clear view for many miles down the loch.

He did not have to attain his vantage-point. Before he was half-way there he perceived the boats. Perhaps three miles away yet, these were not hugging the shore. In three distinct strings they came, a number of craft, perhaps half a dozen, to each string. From this distance it was impossible to count men – but the chances were that only the foremost boats would be manned, the remainder being roped together and towed behind.

Rob frowned. Even though progress was bound to be slow and the rowers would be tired, less than an hour would see those boats level with Cala nan Uamh, the Haven of the Cave, his hidden lagoon. They had the wind behind them.

It all depended on MacAlastair, now. If he was late, all was in vain. But how soon could he be expected? The gillie's task might well have proved more difficult than his own –

though it was MacAlastair's own choice.

Rob hurried back to his haven. He had work to do. From the top of the little bluff round which the entrance to the creek bent, he surveyed the possibilities. Quickly he saw the tree that he wanted – for there were many to select from, overhanging the narrow channel. His choice was a twisted red-barked Scots pine, growing at the edge of the rocky entrance passage near the bend, its sinuous roots gripping into the seams and fissures of the stone. A pine's roots are shallow.

Hastening round to this tree, he went to work. He had no axe available, and must just use his dirk, inadequate tool though it made. One after another he tackled the spreading roots of that pine, hacking, sawing, digging, severing. It was difficult, knuckle-barking labour, and frequently he used the enormous strength of those long arms and great shoulders to pull up roots by main force rather than cut them through. The rocky nature of the ground was a help, in that it kept the roots high and exposed – but it took the man all of half an hour before he was satisfied. Only two or three slender roots then held the tree, and it swayed ominously to the push. Propping some large stones against the trunk, to leeward, in case the gusty wind should bring it down before its time, Rob left it and returned to his bluff.

No sign of the boats yet. Time passed. He waited, but could not sit still. Soon he was pacing the limited area of his rock-platform like a caged thing. Where was MacAlastair?

It was the little armada that came into view first. Cursing, the waiting man eyed it. He could not have more than fifteen or twenty minutes left, now. What in Heaven's name was MacAlastair doing . . . ?'

In a few further precious minutes it occurred to Rob, ruefully, that he would be better employed in trying to think out some alternative course of action than in anathematising his faithful attendant. But nothing of the sort came to his impatient mind, rack his brains as he would. With only the two of them, the situaion was difficult indeed. Not that his present project was likely to work out simply, to be foolproof or assured of success. But at least it would give them a chance. . . .

Then, suddenly, MacAlastair was standing below him, at the edge of the lagoon, quietly waiting as though he had been there for hours. The fellow had an infuriating facility for giving that sort of impression. Rob went hurrying down to him.

'*Dia* – but you have taken your own time, man!' he cried, in greeting. 'The boats are out there, just. We have not a minute to spare. You got it – what was necessary?'

For answer the taciturn MacAlastair merely nodded, and unrolled the plaid that he carried bundled up under his arm. From its folds fell a scarlet brass-buttoned coat with buff facings, black breeches, three-cornered hat, bandoliers – in fact, the entire uniform and equipment of a private soldier in Her Majesty's East Kent Regiment of Foot, The Buffs.

'Good,' his master commended. 'Quick, then – get into the things, man. You chose somebody of your own size? You did not have to kill the fellow . . . ?'

'A sore head he will be having – that is all,' the other informed, shrugging. He was discarding his sword-belt, ragged kilt, and rawhide brogans, and with every appearance of distaste began to don the royal uniform. With urgent impatient hands Rob helped him on with the long heavy coat and clapped the three-cornered hat askew on the other's shaggy black locks.

'No musket?' he demanded, as he fitted the crossed bandoliers in position over the other's chest.

'They do not carry the muskets to relieve themselves behind a bush,' the gillie mentioned heavily.

'Aye. Well, maybe not. Come, then – or it will be too late, whatever.'

They bundled into the boat, MacAlastair taking up pride of place in the bows, Rob handling the oars and pushing off.

He had doffed his own bonnet with the single eagle's feather, and put on his gillie's plain one, pulling it down hard over his head to hide as much of his ruddy locks as possible. He kept his plaid around his shoulders, too, to seek to hide his outline. At the entrance to their hidden harbour he turned to stare out over the loch.

The three strings of boats were now in full view, the foremost no more than five hundred yards or so away. It was as Rob had anticipated. Only the first vessel of each string was occupied, four men rowing in each of the three leading craft. These weary-looking oarsmen were clearly Highlandmen, bare to the waist. But in each of these same boats also sat one scarlet-coated soldier. Fifteen men in all.

'Aye,' Rob nodded. 'Just so. The fine fellow in that first boat there, with all the gold braid and the epaulettes, will be this Major Selby, no doubt. He has no reinforcements – or if he is to get them, he has not brought them with him, Heaven be praised! Now – listen you to me, MacAlastair.'

As Rob dug in his oars and pulled out towards that leading boat, he told his companion just what he was to do, very precisely. He was to screen Rob's person with his scarlet uniform, and he was to wave. But he was not to speak, or even to hail. Rob would do that himself – for he did not trust MacAlastair's English to be such as would deceive Major Selby, even at a distance. MacAlastair was to open his mouth and seem to be shouting – but the words would be Rob's. He would see that they did not come near enough to the other boat for the deception to become evident. And when he had to turn this craft round, to face the other way, the gillie was to transfer himself quickly to the stern, so as to continue to come between his master's noteworthy frame and the Major. There was more – but that was enough for the moment.

At Rob's word, MacAlastair, standing up in the bows, began to wave towards the other boats almost at once. Rob raised a halloo or two, to draw attention to the fact. He was approaching the advancing boats' course at a tangent – and crouching as low he might and still be able to row.

Promptly enough they received an answering wave from the foremost boat, and as Rob continued to halloo, the Major turned his craft a few points to starboard, towards them. So far, so good.

Carefully, his head turned back over his shoulder most of the time, Rob watched that decreasing stretch of water between them and the flotilla. To turn away too soon would look suspicious – but to get too close was to put too much of a strain on MacAlastair's disguise, however vivid his red coat, and to risk a recognition of his own person. It had to be nicely judged. Two hundred yards was as near as he dare allow – at this stage, at any rate.

When he reckoned that they were less than three hundred yards apart, Rob told his companion to put a hand to the side of his mouth, and seem to shout. Then behind him, he raised his own voice.

'Hi, sir! Major Selby, sir!' he cried, seeking to make his voice as like that of an uncultured southern Englishman as he knew how. 'Cap'n Taylor's compliments, sir. Will you come ashore, sir, he says? Follow us in? Cap'n's got that ruffiian Rob Roy MacGregor cornered, sir. In the woods, here. You ahearing me, sir?' He was hailing into the wind, and was uncertain how his words would carry.

'Aye, aye. You've got Rob Roy, you say?' a thin high voice came clearly across the water to them. 'Where, man? Where is Captain Taylor?'

'Just in here, sir.' In a very different tone, Rob jerked to his gillie, 'Point, MacAlastair. Point towards the *cala*.' And raising his voice again, 'There's a creek, Major. Hidden. Follow us in, sir. Cap'n Taylor needs your help. In the woods. . . .'

'Very well,' the officer called back. He turned, and started to call and signal towards the other leading boats of his flotilla.

Rob decided that they were close enough. Throwing a command to MacAlastair to change positions, he swung the little boat round swiftly, rowing one oar and backing with the other, and commenced to pull for the shore again. Necessarily he was facing the little fleet now, but the gillie's person still screened him.

Soon they heard the Major shouting to them once more, asking for details of what was going on ashore. Rob affected not to hear him at first, for answering in the assumed English voice was a strain to him, and he did not want to risk more of it than was essential. But when the questions were repeated more loudly, he had to answer – hoping that Mac-Alastair's mouthings would still seem authentic at this closer range.

'Cap'n Taylor has him caught, sir,' he called, extemporising urgency. 'Has him in a cave. But Cap'n has few men with him. Dare not take him back to camp through the woods, sir. They might rescue him. Too many MacGregors about. We saw your boats. Cap'n Taylor reckoned safer to carry him back by boat. . . .'

'Aye, aye. Very good.' The Major obviously accepted all that.

Rob's boat drew ahead on the pull shoreward, being light and unencumbered. He was thankful to be spared more of difficult long-range explanations. He headed directly for the barely visible entrance to the little haven.

As they approached the rocky jaws of the place, Rob shouted his last instructions. 'In here, sir. Follow me in. There's a bend. Plenty of room round that.' The Major's boat, with its string of towed craft, was roughly two hundred and fifty yards behind him.

And now he was giving urgent directions to MacAlastair, in his own language. What happened thereafter must happen fast, and with all too many opportunities for mishap.

As the boat rounded the tight bend in the entrance channel, Rob tossed the oars to his companion, and leapt lightly ashore, leaving MacAlastair to row on up to the head of the little enclosed lagoon. He clambered swiftly up the steep side of the rocky bluff that towered over the bend. He did not allow himself to be seen on the top of it, keeping well back till opposite his propped-up tree. Then he threw himself flat, to peer over cautiously.

Major Selby's craft was just entering the outer channel, still with its towed tail astern. The leading boat of the next string was just behind, with a sergeant and four Highland oarsmen. The third group, necessarily, were some distance further off.

Rob had to calculate quickly. Obviously they could not all get round the bend and into the net of the lagoon in time. He would have to do the best that he could. He glanced behind him. MacAlastair, his boat now just below the waterfall at the head of the inlet, was jumping ashore.

Selby rounded that tight bend in the channel. He was delayed a little in getting his empty boats after him, so that the sergeant's craft drew level with the last of them. They were close under Rob's bluff now, so that he could edge much further forward without being seen. The third soldier, out on the loch with the last string, might spot him – but the fellow seemed to be concentrating on what his superiors were doing.

Rob waited, tense. Selby was well round the corner now, out of sight. The sergeant was about to negotiate the bend. MacAlastair was disappearing into the trees, climbing up-hill, shouting vaguely and waving the Major on.

He heard a different kind of shouting from Selby then, with question and alarm in it. And promptly Rob acted. Leaping up he flung himself at that undermined tree, kicking away the supporting stones, and pushed with all his great strength. Slowly, majestically, the pine swayed and toppled, creaking, the remaining roots snapping like musket-shots. With a resounding crash it fell over and down. Right on top of the second boat behind that of the sergeant it pitched, shattering it with the impact and sinking the next behind it also by the spread of its branches. A vast spout of water rose up, drenching even Rob, and when it settled, there was the tree half-submerged and wholly blocking the narrow channel, two empty boats sunk and a third slowly filling. Major Selby's and the sergeant's craft, with seven or eight others, were securely bottled up within the lagoon.

The creator of the havoc delayed not a moment. As the babel of cries and curses uprose, he leapt across the top of the bluff to the far side, whipping the heavy cavalry pistol out of his belt as he went with one hand, and a wicked little dirk from his gartered hose-top with the other. Without waiting to charge or prime the former, he halted wide-legged above the little lagoon. From their boats thirty feet or so below, men stared up at him in alarm.

Rob's voice rang out, as he jabbed the pistol first towards the agitated Major Selby and then at the sergeant. 'Is it a ball in your chests, or your throats cut, at all?' he demanded ferociously. 'Say the word, make a move – and it will be your last, I tell you! I am Robert MacGregor of Inversnaid and Craigroyston – and I do not start what I cannot finish!'

There was a choking angry expostulation from the officer, and a stream of curses from the sergeant. Also some comment from the Highland oarsmen, mainly to the accompaniment of wide grins; most of them were MacGregors.

Rob cut it all short. 'Enough!' he cried. 'Silence! Mac-Alastair – come you and relieve these gentry of their weapons. You are my prisoner, Major. And you too, Sergeant. Or would you rather be dead men, whatever?'

There was no answer to that. MacAlastair, the scarlet coat discarded, materialised out of the trees, a pistol in his hand also. Major Selby wore a sword but apparently carried no firearms. The sergeant's musket lay on the floorboards of his boat.

Rob spoke tersely, in the Gaelic, to the oarsmen, while

his companion disarmed the two soldiers, telling them to come ashore but to take no part against the red-coats. There must be no suggestion that they were in league with himself, or the whole clan would suffer.

In only a minute or so it was all over, with Selby and the sergeant standing unhappily on the grass, disarmed, staring into the muzzle of MacAlastair's pistol, and the oarsmen in a whispering group a little way apart.

Leaving them for the moment, Rob turned back, on his bluff-top, to see what the remaining soldier was doing. He found that that perplexed individual had halted his rowers just off-shore, and was waiting events with every appearance of uncertainty. As well he might; he must have seen the tree crash down and could not have failed to hear the subsequent shouting – but what went on round the bend in the channel he would be at a loss to know. A mere private soldier, he obviously was in a quandary. He had picked up his musket, but held it without any confidence in its worth.

Rob ran back and began to climb down towards the sergeant's boat. 'Throw me up that musket there, Mac-Alastair,' he directed.

Taking the sergeant's weapon, he clambered back to a position of vantage on the bluff. The third boat, with its satellites in tow, still lay motionless, no more than seventy yards away. Rob rose to his full height, the matchlock aimed from his shoulder directly at the sitting soldier.

'Drop that musket, man – or die!' he shouted. 'Quickly, now – for I am an impatient man, by name Rob Roy MacGregor! Your major and sergeant have chosen to live, as my prisoners. Do you choose different?' He hoped that the fellow would not prove stubborn or stupid, for the weapon in his hands was not primed. To help the other's decision along, he spoke to the oarsmen. 'You at the oars – row you in here. Up to this sunken tree, see you. Quickly.' He repeated that in the Gaelic, adding that they were to do only and exactly what he told them.

The rowers did not require further invitation, and the bewildered infantryman, however heroic he may have desired to be, apparently perceived no advantage in opposing the very definite trend of events. He laid down his musket and sat his thwart glumly as he was rowed into the mouth of the inlet.

Rob ordered the rowers to jump ashore at the other side of the channel, where the rock walls were sufficiently broken to be climbable – and the soldier to follow them, leaving his musket in the boat. In a few moments they were reunited with the rest of the expedition.

Now that the pressure of events was eased, Rob allowed himself to relax – though MacAlastair still stood by, pistol cocked and pointing unfalteringly – and addressed himself to Selby, civilly.

'My regrets to so rudely inconvenience you, Major, and interrupt your journey,' he apologised. 'But you see how it is? Just the two of us there are in it – MacAlastair and myself – so that we could not be so gentle as we would have wished. Och, pointing pistols and the like is no way to be dealing with problems between gentlemen.'

'A rope round your neck, MacGregor, will mark the end of *your* problems, never fear,' the officer said tensely.

'May be, Major – but not this afternoon, I'm thinking. Time enough for your ropes when I am *your* guest, and not you mine. I have better hospitality to offer you than that – a snug cave for shelter, good heather for your couch, a sufficiency of meats, and a dram to drink. Och, you will do fine, man – just fine. And the sergeant too, of course. Though likely enough you will not be with me that long, at all. . . .'

'A truce to your chatter, man! You will suffer for this outrage against an officer of the Queen, I promise you. What you expect to gain by it, God knows!'

'That is easy. Your Captain Taylor has taken into his custody a friend of mine, one Donald MacGregor, an inoffensive lad. Moreover, he is holding his wife Marsala and his baby son as hostages. So now I have taken hostages too, Major. It is entirely simple. You and the sergeant, here, in exchange for Donald and his wife – och, and the Queen in London getting the best of the bargain whatever, as I think you will agree?'

'Ruffian! Do you think that I will agree to any such shameful transaction. . . . ?'

'I care not whether you agree or no, Major. It is Captain Taylor who will agree, I'll wager. The poor man can do no other.'

'He will lead a punitive expedition against you, forthwith. . . .'

'How will he be doing that? I shall sink every one of these boats in the loch – so that he cannot move from Inverarklet save through my heather. And think you that any Southron soldier could catch Rob Roy in his own heather? He cannot take Donald MacGregor to Dumbarton without boats – that I can promise you. I'm thinking that your captain will be happy to get his senior officer back at so small a price!'

The other stared at the MacGregor, biting his lip.

'Aye, then – here is the way of it,' Rob went on. He pointed at the private soldier. 'This bold fellow shall carry my message to Captain Taylor – and yours. These rowing men – who, you will note, have no part in this business – shall take him up through the woods to Inverarklet. It is five rough miles, so they will not be there till night. MacAlastair shall go with them, and wait at a suitable distance from your camp, for the Captain's answer. Tomorrow, I am hoping that you will be exchanged. Till then, sir, such poor hospitality as is left to me is at your disposal. Not the hospitality that I could have offered you under my own roof. But then . . .' Rob paused significantly. '. . . you burned that, did you not? My wife . . .'

Selby swallowed, and hastily looked away. 'That was

95

none of my doing,' he assured urgently. ' 'Pon my soul, that was Graham's work. Killearn's. The Sheriff. I had no hand in that. . . .'

'Aye,' the other said, softly. 'Just so. Graham's work!'

The Major began to speak quickly about what message should be sent to Inverarklet.

A little later, with the grey dusk already beginning to settle on the land, MacAlastair, with the private soldier, and all the Highland oarsmen in attendance, set off on the difficult walk northwards through the steep hanging woodlands. The gillie had his instructions. The two other soldiers, their hands tied behind their backs with rope from the boats, went with Rob in the opposite direction. There were many caves and crannies in the rocks in that country, and Rob Roy knew them all. The one that he was making for might not be so secure and lofty a refuge as was his sanctuary on Cruach Tuirc, and moreover might be a little damp – but it would serve admirably as a prison for gentry who thought house roofs were for burning.

CHAPTER SEVEN

MAJOR SELBY and the sergeant were exchanged for Donald MacGregor and his wife and child the following day, in an early flurry of the winter's snows. The transfer of hostages took place in a wooded glade about a mile from Inverarklet, with elaborate precautions on both sides against trickery or bad faith. Rob Roy did not appear in person, any more than did Captain Taylor – though undoubtedly one was no further off than was the other. The MacGregor, after parting from Selby with unreturned if marked courtesy, the sergeant's loaded musket retained in his hands, watched from a rocky hidingplace as MacAlastair led forward their two prisoners to the rendezvous, pistol cocked and prominent. After only a brief delay, the figures of Donald and his wife Marsala, the child in her arms, appeared, escorted only by the same private soldier who had acted messenger before. How many more of the military might be hidden in the background could not be known. There were no formalities, no sort of ceremony. The two parties to the exchange merely stalked up to each other, and passed, with scarcely a pause or a gesture, while the escorts took over their new charges with no more civilities than would pass between a pair of stiff-legged suspicious dogs. MacAlastair came all the way back to Rob's cover, walking sideways, eyes trained whence he came, pistol still at the ready. He was a distrustful man by nature.

Rob did not delay their retiral by any prolonged welcome for the rescued. A brief word to young Donald, and a warm squeeze of the girl's shoulder, and he took the little boy within his own arms and forthwith set off up-hill, long strided. The others followed on, with MacAlastair acting as watchful rearguard.

If there was any sort of pursuit or trailing, the fugitives saw nothing of it. Presently, Marsala breathless and distressed but holding them back only a little, they reached ground sufficiently high and broken to satisfy Rob that they were safe, for the meantime. They rested, to decide upon their further programme.

In fact, of course, there was little choice open to them. Donald MacGregor, now a marked man, and rescued thus, could not go back to his normal life and his father's house. Nothing was surer than that the military would seek to avenge their humiliation upon him, if they could lay hands on him again. He must either leave the district, then, or join Rob Roy in his defiance of the Government. Donald chose the latter course, without hesitation. And though Rob was by no means anxious to recruit any tail of supporters, he had to admit that there might well be occasions when he could use an extra pair of hands and perhaps an extra broadsword. Moreover, despite all his undeniable excellences, MacAlastair was not the most lively of companions, and Donald, a cheerful, ebullient and handsome young man, if somewhat headstrong and lacking in responsibility, was excellent company. As for his wife, the best arrangement was for her to go Auchinchisallan, where she could live with Mary. She was a gentle loving creature, and a closer relative to Mary than she was to Rob.

So it was decided. Rob was glad enough of the excuse to return to his wife with some token of vengeance taken. They would escort Marsala and the child to Auch forthwith, and give the turmoil here at Inversnaid an opportunity to settle down.

By devious hidden ways, around the head of Loch Arklet, they went, picking up their ponies *en route*, and leaving a message for the clan at the remote house of old MacGregor of Comar, Mary's father — at the same time borrowing two more garrons for Donald and Marsala. By evening they were at the head of Balquhidder and able to pass a cold night in Rob's cave under Cruach Tuirc. In the morning, with a thin covering of snow on the ground, they made their inconspicuous way northwards into Breadalbane. They came to Auch, in a blizzard, at dusk. It seemed a haven indeed.

But there is an inclemancy of climate that can chill even the warmest and snuggest haven. If Rob, not looking to be received exactly with open arms, at least had expected his wife to rejoice in some measure at the recital of his reprisals upon the forces of her hated enemies, he was disappointed. Mary, though she welcomed and accepted Marsala and the child with warm sympathy, greeted her husband with no more rapture than she did Donald or MacAlastair. His accounts of his exploits, even though they lost nothing in the telling — for Rob was no more inhibited as a story-teller than as a man of action — produced surprisingly little enthusiasm, or indeed reaction of any evident sort. Mary listened to what he had to say dutifully enough, but made only the one comment — to ask if Graham of Killearn had been involved. On learning that he had not, she betrayed no further interest. Rob was crestfallen as he was perplexed.

The weather was severe for the time of the year, with heavy and continuous snowfalls that tended to box the men up in the little house. And despite its warmth and comfort, Rob Roy at least, as the days and the nights passed, came to recognise that he would have been happier in his cave on Cruach Tuirc. It seemed to him that he just did not know this woman to whom he had been married for so many years. Had he never really known her? Or had she changed so entirely into a quite different person? Was that possible? She looked the same. Her beauty was no less, the near-perfection of her eyes and features and figure, tantalising him so that he ached for its solace in his body, and grieved and resented his loss in his mind. She was a passionate woman – or had been – a true MacGregor; but now she seemed to be not so much empty or frozen as encased in a hard shell, an armour of reserve. Was that it? Was the real Mary still there, hidden away and cowering? But Mary never hid or cowered; she was not that sort. And why cower from *him*, her husband and protector, her Rob?

If it was a shell that Mary had assumed, the man did all in his not inconsiderable power to pierce it. He coaxed and wheedled, he pleaded, he stormed and commanded, he wooed her again, using every art and stratagem and expedient within an imaginative man's ken – in so far as she permitted and the crowded little house allowed – but to no avail. Mary remained encased, inviolate, unmoved.

His children, to some extent, he managed to win back to him – but that only seemed to underline his failure with his wife.

By the time that the weather cleared, a week later, Rob had had as much as he could stand – more especially in view of young Donald's all too evident enjoyment of *his* wife's favours. It was the heather for him again, he decided – and therefore for Donald and MacAlastair too.

Donald at least was accorded an affectionate, even tearful farewell.

CHAPTER EIGHT

ONCE again Rob Roy was ensconced amongst the rocks and thorn trees of the hillside above Corrarklet House, in the darkness of the December night, talking with the laird thereof. This time they sat, huddled in their plaids against the chill, and spoke face to face, for John MacGregor had refused to continue to talk with his unseen cousin from behind a boulder, asserting strongly that any lies that he might feel bound to tell to the accursed military were his own responsibility. Not that the soldiers were bothering the district much; they had come to Corrarklet, making enquiries and searching the place, after Donald's rescue, but had not since made themselves too objectionable. Rob, however, refused the older man's urgings to come down to the comforts of Corrarklet House, insisting that, in this area, it was best that he darkened no MacGregor doorway. Young Donald, however, had gone down to greet his mother.

John of Corrarklet's news of the local situation was not dramatic. After an initial and more or less token search of the vicinity for the fugitives, the red-coats had lain rather low, down at Loch Lomond-side. There had been no reprisals on the local MacGregors, nor on the oarsmen from the illfated flotilla. Almost certainly Selby was somewhat fearful about their security, and not anxious at the moment to provoke the clan into rising against them. This was hardly to be wondered at, in the circumstances. Rob had sunk their entire supply of boats – and left word for any loch-side MacGregors to scuttle or hide any odd boats of their own that still might have remained unrequisitioned; in consequence the soldiers' link with their base by water was cut, and any communications must be by the lengthy and highly precarious overland route through the mountains to Aberfoyle, by a series of passes that provided innumerable opportunities for ambush, and thence across the quaking wastes of the vast Flanders Moss where a dozen bold men could trap and drown hundreds. By this roundabout and dangerous route Dumbarton Castle was fifty difficult miles away, and Stirling Castle more than forty. There was no road down the precipitous east side of Loch Lomond, and anyhow, the Pass of Rowardennan could be made impassable by a couple of determined men. This was why the Gregorach had managed to remain uncontrolled, though proscribed and anathematised, for so long. Only by water were their fastnesses vulnerable. Again, the winter was no time for campaigning in the Highlands, and the low-country soldiers were at every sort of disadvantage.

So Major Selby was being cautious. He had issued sundry proclamations, to tuck of drum – one of them declaring Donald MacGregor to be considered an outlaw for having consorted and concerted with Rob Roy; another announcing that every boat whatsoever in the area was herewith requisitioned in the name of Her Majesty; and a third to the effect that anyone found abroad during the hours of darkness would be treated as an enemy of the Queen. But all this was largely face-saving, since he confined his men strictly to Inverarklet itself, down at the loch-shore. Tents made inadequate quarters in this weather, and the troops had moved into all available shelter – but this was scanty, houses being few, and overcrowding and discomfort was considerable. It might well be, Corrarklet thought, that the Major would soon recognise that the situation was unprofitable, and seek to advise his superiors to withdraw the expedition until more propitious conditions might prevail – if boats could be found to take his men south. Meantime, presumably on instructions that Selby had brought back from Dumbarton, a start had been made, in a tentative sort of way, at building the projected fort on a new site – on top of Tom na Bairlinn, the Knoll of Warning, where no floods could reach it. But this was mainly at the clearing and planning stage, for it was not the season for successful masonwork, and the soldiers were no builders.

All this gave the listener a modified satisfaction, since it indicated that for the time-being the tide was flowing his way. Montrose would gain considerably less satisfaction out of it all – which was good, so far as it went. But that was by no means far enough for Rob Roy. Somebody else was very much on his mind.

'And Killearn?' he demanded. 'John Graham – what of him? Has he been back – God's everlasting curse upon him!'

'No. No, I think not, Rob,' the other answered. 'I have seen and heard nothing more of the man. He keeps his distance, I trow. Unless . . . unless it could have been him at Glen Gyle? Och, but no – it would not have been him, whatever. Gregor would have said, for sure. . . .'

'What is this, man? What of Glengyle?'

'I was coming to that, Rob. Gregor sent me the word two days back that he had had a visitor at Glen Gyle in whom *you* would be very interested. He named no names, but said that when next I heard of you, to let you know. You were to go to him, there. It was important, he said. Gregor was not long back home, his own self, from Arnprior . . .'

'Important, he said? And secret, it seems? Two days back? Is this man, this visitor, still at Glen Gyle, then think you?'

'I do not know, Rob. I know no more than I have told you. But I think I would have heard, whatever, had it been John Graham of Killearn. . . .'

'Nevertheless, I shall go see. Right away,' Rob told him, grimly, rising up as he spoke. '*There* could be an appointment, John man, that could not wait! Tell Donald to be at the cave on Cruach Tuirc by morning. I shall be there, if you have further word for me.'

'As you will, Rob. But it is no weather for the caves. Bide you the night under my roof, man, in warmth. . . .'

'I have the wherewithal to keep me warm, Cousin,' Rob interrupted harshly. 'Hatred! Warm stuff – as good as any bed of blankets! Never fear that I shall suffer cold or discomfort while John Graham still breathes! Good-night to you.'

As he turned away downhill, and the shadow that was MacAlastair slipped past him, after his master, the older man thanked God that he was not John Graham of Killearn.

*　　　*　　　*

An hour or so later, but still on the right side of midnight, Rob Roy sat on another hillside, waiting, in a very similar situation. But this time the glen below him was wider and deeper and more populous, and many lights shone from the windows of the fairly large house within its sheltering screen of trees, while away to the east an emptiness seemed to yawn, that was the great nightbound expanse of Loch Katrine.

Presently he heard the faint swish of rawhide brogans in the deer-hair grass, and the deep breathing of climbing men, and he stood up. 'Well met, Greg,' he greeted. 'You were not abed?'

The towering figure of young Glengyle came striding up. '*Well* met, is it, Rob – and you skulking up here in the heather when my house and all within it is yours to command!' his nephew cried warmly. '*Ill* met, I call it! By God's shadow – what way is this to come to Glen Gyle? I near sent MacAlastair back to you with the word that if you wanted to see me, you could honour my house with your presence, whatever!'

'Hush you, Greg – if you do not want all Strath Gartney to know our business!' his uncle reproved – but not unkindly. 'What a terror you have become for the words, man! I'm hoping . . .'

'More than words I have for you!' the younger man interrupted, breathy as he was from his climbing. 'My sword and all I have is at your service, Rob. I will not be mewed up and confined any more, like some child. I am chieftain of Clan Dougal Ciar, and have suffered as much of the insults and presence of insolent soldiery as I intend to do. I have done as you ordered, hitherto, and acted the craven and the sluggard, raising no hand to protect my own honour or yours. But, as Royal's my Race, I've had sufficient of that! From now onwards . . .'

'Lord ha' mercy – the madcap! The drawcansir! Spare us, Greg, or you'll have me deafened! Was it thus I taught you, when I was Tutor of Glengyle?'

'You taught me that MacGregor bows the knee to no man, and doffs his bonnet only to his true and lawful king!'

'Aye. But not that MacGregor cuts his own throat when his true and lawful king happens to be interested in somebody else! Man Greg, the clan is more important than you or me, and honour an expensive commodity when it must be bought with other folk's lives.'

'Is that what you said when they burned your house, abused your wife, and drove your children into the night?' Gregor demanded sombrely.

'God's curse! You . . . you . . .' Rob's powerful voice deepened and vibrated like some great bass viol, so that even the young giant opposite took an involuntary pace backwards. 'What you your words, boy – or . . . or . . .' The older man controlled himself with obvious effort. 'This visitor,' he said abruptly changing the subject. 'This man you sent word of to Corrarklet. Is he still here? Is it Graham of Killearn?'

'Graham? No. Why should Graham come here? I'm thinking that cur will not dare show his snout in these parts again for a long time, my God! No – my visitor was another altogether. A friend of yours.'

'A friend? Why so secret, then?'

'Because of his errand, just. It was Colonel Hooke!'

'Lord – Hooke again! Does that cock still crow? Do not tell me, Greg, that it is the old story once more? Errand, you said? Not the old business over again?'

'It is, yes. The King is minded to try again, it seems. Nathaniel Hooke is spying out the land, once more. Making enquiries. He cannot travel the Highlands in this weather – but he made his way here, disguised as a packman. To see *us*. He was sore disappointed not to see you, Rob.'

'He is gone, then?'

'Aye. He went the night after he came. He could not wait for you. There is to be a meeting, see you, in a few days time – two days it is now, just – at the house of Harry Maule of Kelly, in Angus, brother to my lord of Panmure. Hooke had to be back for it. He left the word for you to join him there – in the name of His Majesty!'

'*Dia* – he did, did he! Across the breadth of Scotland! The man has not changed, I see! Here is folly, to be sure. . . .'

'Think you so? Such negotiations are needful, are they not, if the King is to be restored to his own again? Information he must have. . . .'

'Aye. But information from *Scotland* is the least of it, lad. Information from his own France is what will count. Here we will do our duty, yes. But, over there . . . ! I wager it's the King's own character that is the problem, and the delicate stomachs of his advisers in France that will decide the issue – not the loyalty of Scotland!'

Somewhat shocked, Gregor considered his uncle, peering at him in the darkness. 'But . . . but do not say that His Majesty should not try to regain his throne, surely?'

'Far from it. But after the last two fiascos I say that it is our own selves that will require information from Hooke –

not him from us! We have been made fools enough, already.'

'But it may be that Hooke *has* this information for us – the assurance you seek,' the younger man urged. 'That will be what the meeting is for, belike. He said that it was important that you should be there.'

'May be, Greg – may be so. Perhaps I judge over-fast. But the price – the price good men paid for folly, four years back – was costly. As you well know.'

Rob Roy drummed fingers on his bare knee. Five years before, Colonel Nathaniel Hooke, Irish emissary and spy of the exiled James Stewart in France, had arrived secretly in Scotland to plot and plan an armed uprising that would coincide with the signing of the unpopular Treaty of Union between England and Scotland. Rob, and to a lesser extent his nephew, had taken up the enterprise heart and soul, acting as Hooke's principal couriers and go-betweens to the clan chiefs of the Highland North and West. But when all was ready, the clans mustered, and the hour struck, King James took the measles at Dunkirk and turned back. The rising was postponed, the armies melted away, the clans returned to their glens, and London's hand clamped down heavier than ever. Then, a year later, Hooke returned. Scotland was now seething over the first effects of an incorporating Union, and a second attempt was made. This time James sailed, with a French fleet and troops in support. But with Queen Anne's ministers and generals packing their bags and preparing to change sides, and all Scotland ready to fall like a ripe plum, the French admiral had suddenly taken fright and turned back at the very mouth of the Firth of Forth, despite James's entreaties, carrying the young king with him. And the rising was off once more, leaving the relieved Government of Queen Anne to take reprisals consistent with the scare it had received.

Now Hooke was back again.

'It is a devilish nuisance,' Rob declared, out of his cogi-

107

tation. 'I have more to be doing than traipsing across Scotland chasing a political rainbow. I have to . . .'

'But you *will* go?' Gregor put in, eagerly. To add, in a rush, 'I said that you would be there, whatever – and my own self with you!'

'You did, then!'

'Och yes, Rob – the honour of the Gregorach demanded. . . .' Glengyle coughed. 'In the King's name it was, see you. It is an appointment that is not to be rejected. . . .'

'I have another appointment that is not to be rejected, either,' the older man asserted grimly. 'With John Graham of Killearn!'

The other nodded. 'Aye – 'fore God, you have! We all have. But that is not yet. That one will not step north of our Highland Line for long enough, I think.'

'Then I will step south of it!'

'Och, but man, man – you cannot do that! Not far enough south. Not to Killearn and the Lennox. You would have no chance, at all.'

'I have stepped further south than that, in my day, and returned. Into England itself. . . .'

'Aye. But then you were not known as you are known today, Rob. *Dia* – everyone in the kingdom knows the name and fame, and what is more, the *looks*, of Rob Roy MacGregor. With the shape of you, and the hair of you . . . and now you are outlawed with a price on your head . . . och, man – it is not to be thought of. That is, unless you are for taking a couple of score of good Gregorach broadswords south with you! Then we might achieve something. . . .'

'No. Alone I would go. This is my own business. The clan's name is proscribed already – I will not have it outlawed, on my account, likewise.'

'Then, even if you reached as far as Killearn, you would never win back home, Rob,' Gregor said earnestly. 'That is certain-sure. Surely you see it?'

'So long as I settle my account with John Graham, the

winning back here is of secondary importance,' his uncle told him, sombrely. 'You prate of honour, Greg – you will know that there are debts that must be paid whatever the price?'

'May be. But . . .' Gregor shifted his stance. '. . . you spoke of the clan's needs. The price that you would pay must be your own, you say – not the clan's. And yet your death would be the clan's price. Too great a price. We need you. You are the Captain of Clan Alpine. Lacking a High Chief, as we do, you are our war leader. And if Colonel Hooke speaks true, it looks like war again. No man north of the Highland Line is so potent and well-versed in war as is Rob Roy. The clan needs you. The King needs you. Would you be throwing all away for John Graham? Killearn will keep, Rob. He is better keeping. And if Scotland rises for King James – then you may travel where you will, and Killearn cannot escape you. Let him sweat in his fear till then – but come you to this meeting in Angus.'

'A-a-aye!' Rob sighed, raising and sinking great shoulders – but eyeing his erstwhile pupil with a strange mixture of exasperation, affection and admiration. 'Words and more words, Greg! Slay me – but you near drown me in the flood of them. Must I needs wrap myself in silk, for the clan's sake? And scurry across Scotland for the King's sake? And heed humbly to damnably lengthy sermons for *your* sake. . . . ?'

But the battle was won, and Gregor knew it. 'You come with me to Kelly Castle, then?'

'What says your Mary to this?' his uncle countered, gruffly. 'She will not smile at Hooke's name again, I'll wager! She'll not be for you meddling in such matters, and leaving her. . . .'

'Mary is a good wife, and accepts what her husband decides is best . . . mostly,' the bold Gregor asserted. 'I . . . er . . . she need not know where we are going, whatever. How soon can you start?'

'When I have filled my belly. I have not eaten since morning. We shall have to travel by night, and if the meeting is in two days just, the sooner we are on our way the better. But we can eat as we ride.'

Gregor MacGregor threw back his yellow head, and laughed into the December night. 'There speaks my laggard and reluctant uncle!' he cried. 'Come you down, and we shall see what Mary's larder can do for you.'

CHAPTER NINE

In a couple of hours the two men were on their way. Mac-Alastair was left behind, at the cave on Cruach Tuirc, to keep an eye on the military – and also on the impetuous Donald MacGregor. Where the two travellers were going, Highlandmen would look conspicuous – which, for once, was the last thing that these proud sons of the royal race of MacAlpine wanted – so that they went clad in a strange and ragged assortment of ill-fitting Lowland apparel, with only their oldest plaids wrapped around them against the rigours of the winter's night. They rode their garrons, and each led another laden pony behind, to give the impression that they were travelling packmen – though unlikely packmen they must seem indeed, if anyone was to examine them closely in a good light, the gigantic blondly handsome Gregor and his enormously broad, long-armed and red-haired uncle, each with an inborn swagger of carriage and assurance of expression that no amount of play-acting would hide for long.

Rob did not cross the threshold of Glengyle House, despite his nephew's near-offence, and so did not witness Gregor's leave-taking of his bonny Lowland wife, nor hear what story he spun to her. Mary Hamilton in all probability was not deceived, anyway; she had been married to her Gregor for five years, and undoubtedly could read his not very subtle character like a book.

After crossing over the steep and rocky Bealach na Choin, the Pass of Weeping, difficult going even in daylight, but familiar to those two as the backs of their hands, they came down into the long and pleasant valley of Balquhidder and a beaten track for the ponies' hooves. From now on they maintained the tireless swaying trot that is the sturdy garron's unexciting but most profitable pace, eating up the long dark miles. For they had many, many miles to cover. All told, it would be fully one hundred miles to the Angus seaboard and Kelly Castle, near Arbroath, and roundabout routes and diversions might well be necessary.

Three times they were challenged, late as it was, down the length of Balquhidder – for this glen of broken clans, professional drovers more often named cattle-thieves, and confirmed individualists all, was as chancy a place for strangers as any in all the broad Highlands. But a brief word from Rob promptly cleared their passage. His name meant more in Balquhidder than that of any man alive or dead – some said than that of the Deity Himself; here, at Monachyle, Rob had had his first independent farmery and had started his unorthodox but lucrative career as a cattle-dealer.

Two hours after leaving Glen Gyle, they were at the mouth of Balquhidder and the head of Strathyre. By then it was nearly four o'clock, with sunrise still four hours ahead. Those four hours carried them along the south shore of Loch Earn, up Strathearn to Crieff – where Rob had embarrassed the little Provost – and over the hill to Glen Almond, out of the Highlands. They could have reached further by daylight, but preferred to lie up for the day, before reaching the more populous country of the Tay valley above Perth. In the chilly rain, they halted in dripping woodland on high ground above Logiealmond. The chances of being disturbed, up here, on a December day, were negligible. Hobbling their garrons, they found a cavity under the spreading roots of a wind-fall tree, wrapped themselves more tightly in their plaids, and lay down to sleep. They had covered some forty-five miles.

The early darkness saw them on the move again,

cramped and chilled but sustained from a leathern bottle of whisky, and chewing at forelegs of venison as they rode. They came down to the broad Tay in the vicinity of Redgorton. Crossing the great river, which was bridgeless and too deep to ford presented a problem, but there were ferries dotted along its course and nothing was simpler than for Rob quietly to slip down to the one below Redgorton, purloin the flat-bottomed scow without arousing the ferryman in his house, let it drift silently downstream to where Gregor waited with the horses, and so cross to the other side in comfort. Rob, being a man of sensibility, left a silver piece in the abandoned boat for the ferryman, Lowlander as he might be.

Thereafter they followed the Tay northwards through the flat cattle-dotted haughlands. They took its tributary, the Isla, when it led away to the east through the great vale of Strathmore, avoiding Coupar Angus and Meigle, nearly to Glamis, leaving it to strike seawards through the Sidlaw foothills to Inverarity and Carmylie. Long before dawn the fresh east wind had the tang of salt in it, and daybreak found them on Kelly Moor, near the little village of Arbirlot, with the grey North Sea fretting and sighing in front of them on a savage coastline. Many dogs had barked at them and some had even chased them – but never a man had they set eyes upon throughout. The canny Lowlander, it seemed, kept indoors after dark of a winter's night, and did not waste money on illuminations.

The travellers did not have to ask the whereabouts of Harry Maule's house, for the old grey tower of Kelly Castle thrust up above wind-twisted trees clear for all to see. The two Highlanders presented themselves at its heraldically decorated doorway in excellent time for breakfast – whereupon followed a somewhat undignified scene with the place's graceless servants before the visitors could vindicate their right to use the front entrance of the establishment. This at least had the effect of drawing the attention of all to the entry of two Highland gentlemen, as was only suitable.

Harry Maule, younger brother of James, fourth Earl of Panmure, was a quiet and capable man and no political firebrand – though possibly a more worthwhile adherent to the Jacobite cause than many who shouted a deal louder. His house had been chosen for this secret meeting, by his brother, as less conspicuous than the Earl's own castle of Brechin. It was his lordship, however who presided at the gathering.

Rob and Gregor, in the event, were welcomed with open arms – for they were the only true Highlanders present, and as such represented the most important source of actual manpower for any rising, however much of rank and title and wealth might be manifested otherwise. The remainder of the company, numbering perhaps a score, included the Earls of Southesk, Carnwath and Linlithgow, the Lords Kilsyth, Kenmure, Rollo, Duffus, Drummond, Strathallan and Ogilvy, Sir Patrick Murray of Auchtertyre, Sir Hugh Patterson of Bannockburn, Sir John Preston of Preston-hall, and other similarly resounding names. And, of course, Colonel Nathaniel Hooke, who was responsible for it all.

Hooke, an unlikely Irishman, grave, unsmiling and a Puritan, greeted Rob with as much enthusiasm as his nature would allow – and no doubt perceived a still more notable lack of the quality in the MacGregor, however cordial his address. He was a thin, dark, stiff man, fastidious of manner, soberly dressed amongst all the colourful Scots nobles and notables. Rob and he were apt to find, during that morning, their eyes fixed one upon another.

All forenoon further guests were arriving, mainly from the North-East, including the Earl Marischal and the Master of Sinclair. There were notably few from Edinburgh, Lothian and the South.

Gregor had brought his best tartans, wrapped in a bundle on the back of his pack-pony. In them he made an eye-catching figure, quite outshining the Lowland lords and achieving a notable success with the Maule ladies. In the matter of enthusiasm he more than atoned for his uncle.

* * *

'His Majesty is five years older – and, if I may make so bold as to say so, my lords, more than that wiser.' Hooke's voice was harsh, unmelodious, and with little trace of any Irish intonation. And though his steel-grey eyes swept the company as he spoke, they always seemed to come back to rest on those of Rob Roy MacGregor. 'He is determined, this time, to put his fortunes to the test, and under God's will, believes that what is his by right shall be his indeed.'

The statement was loyally acclaimed, Gregor being by no means backward in his plaudits. Rob Roy said nothing.

'His Majesty has been serving in King Louis' army, the better to fit himself for the stern tasks ahead. He acquitted himself nobly at Malplaquet, as I myself can witness. He now more fully understands the military requirements of a successful rising, gentlemen.'

There was some significant nodding, at that.

'Moreover, the time undoubtedly is growing ripe,' Hooke went on. 'As you all will agree, yearly, monthly, almost daily, the Union grows less popular in Scotland. This new Malt Tax is aimed deliberately at killing the Scots trade in malted liquors – just as the Salt Tax was to destroy your salted-herring exports, and the duty on linen to kill that industry. England covets your foreign trade, and will use her Parliamentary majority to see that she gets it. All trade with the Americas is to be carried only in English ships. . . .'

'Aye, we know all that, Colonel – only too well!' Pan-mure interrupted. 'But there is nothing new, there. 'Tis only a matter of degree.'

'Your Lordship will admit that degree, in timing, is vitally important, and that the trading interests in Scotland are ripe for revolt? The people always hated the Union, but the merchants were in favour. And now, with the lairds and landowners hit by the Malt Tax . . .'

'You were not after coming all the way from Lorraine to be telling us this, Colonel?' Rob mentioned, pleasantly enough.

'No, sir. But it is wise that we should have the background clear in our minds. There is more than that. One of His Majesty's agents in London is close to Queen Anne's court. He tells us that the Queen is sickening, of a disease which cannot but prove fatal!'

'A-a-a-ah!' Everywhere men sat up and forward at this intelligence.

'I need not inform you, gentlemen, of what this could mean. Anne's death would transform the political situation. Besides his gracious Majesty, there can be no other claimants to the throne than the aged Electress Sophia, and her bumbling son George of Hanover – a man who cannot even speak English! Moreover, Anne, it is known, cordially dislikes both of them, especially George, who refused her as a bride years ago. She has intimated that she will do all in her power to prevent him from ultimately succeeding her. In her dark days, it seems, she is turning more and more towards her gracious brother whom she has so grievously wronged, in remorse. And even a dying monarch can do much to influence the appointment of a successor.'

'How desperate is the woman's illness?' Lord Kilsyth asked forcefully. 'How soon can we expect the throne to be vacant?'

There were a few murmurs at this bluntness – but all awaited the answer eagerly.

'Only the all-knowing God can tell that,' the Puritan Hooke declared piously. 'But it is thought by her physicians that she cannot live more than perhaps a year.' He paused. 'In which case it behoves us, my lords, to have our plans laid and ready, the fire truly set and the tinder only awaiting the spark. That is why I am here.'

There was no doubting that Hooke had the company

with him, now. There was a clamour of excited talk.

The Irishman looked at Rob.

That man stroked his red beard. 'Is Queen Anne to put His Majesty on his throne – or are we?' he wondered, his voice stilling the chatter.

'Both, I hope,' the other answered. 'The Queen, His Majesty trusts, will name him as her successor. But there will be strong opposition from his enemies, from the Whigs and Hanoverians, and from, H'mm . . .' He coughed slightly. '. . . from those who cry Popery!' The religious problem was always a stumbling-block – especially so to the Puritan envoy of a Catholic Pretender. 'It will be necessary to have a large and well-equipped army ready to strike, here in Scotland – to take advantage of the situation as it develops.'

No one contested that – although it was noticeable that more glances than Hooke's flickered towards the Mac-Gregors.

Hurriedly the envoy went on. 'It may not be necessary to fight. But the presence of a powerful force, poised ready to strike in Scotland, would be of enormous encouragement and help to His Majesty's supporters in England. As you will know, the Tories are gaining favour and influence daily. Oxford and Bolingbroke have high hopes that Anne may turn to them to take over the government – and, with a demonstration of fervour from Scotland, they believe that they may be able to swing the whole Tory camp in His Majesty's support.'

The veteran Sir Hugh Patterson grunted. 'Aye, aye, man,' he declared in his broad Doric. 'Fine, that. But the Whig-maleeries still *are* the Government, wi' an army in Scotland to do their bidding. We canna openly raise a force here, and hold it standing awaiting Queen Anne's pleesure to dee! No' withoot a clash.'

'Yes, sir – that is true. As far as the Lowlands are concerned.' Hooke coughed again. 'But the Highlands are a different story, are they not? We all know that no southern army can really penetrate to any depth into the roadless Highlands. Behind the barrier of the mountains a Highland army could assemble and prepare without fear of interference. Word would leak out that it was there, no doubt – but it could not be brought to battle until it was ready to move out. The threat of such an army, my lords and gentlemen, in a few months time, might well be all that is needed to set King James upon his throne!'

A pregnant silence greeted this conclusion. All eyes were now frankly bent on Rob Roy – with varying expressions that ranged from anticipation and encouragement, through question and doubt, to suspicion and even alarm. The Highlands and the Lowlands ever made uneasy partners in Scotland. While most of the lords and lairds present undoubtedly would be well pleased if the Highland clans were to bear the brunt of the business and run the early risks, others would see the danger of the Highland influence growing too strong, and the rewards of success going in the wrong directions.

A born actor, Rob Roy took his time to speak. 'A Highland army is not a thing to be growing like leaves upon a tree,' he pointed out mildly. 'Indeed, there is no such thing, at all. Many little small armies there are, one to each clan – and och, they are not great at loving each other! It is a hard thing to bring them all to the assembly. And when you have them brought, to make them agree.'

' 'Pon my oath – that's the truth!' Keith, the Earl Marischal, said grimly.

Rob nodded. 'That being so, *ipso facto*, you cannot be having a Highland *standing* army. It just will not stand, whatever. The only way to be holding it together is to keep it moving and keep it fighting. Otherwise the clans will be at each other's throats, see you. I do not see any army raised and waiting for Queen Anne to die, behind the Highland Line.'

'I understand that,' Hooke said. 'I am not wholly ignorant of your Highland ways, you will recollect. I do not suggest that this army shall actually stand assembled. Only that each chief shall promise the King a certain number of men, and give his word that they will be at a certain place of assembly within so many days of a given signal. That is all.'

'You would trust to the chiefs' words so completely?' Viscount Fentoun, no lover of the Highlands, demanded.

'I would, my lord,' Hooke replied – and again looked at the MacGregor.

It was neatly done. Rob could not but uphold the honour of his fellow Gaels. He could not suggest that such a scheme would not work through any failure on the part of the chiefs. Nor could he claim that the clansmen might not follow their leaders. He was out-manoeuvred – and smiled slightly in somewhat rueful acknowledgment of the fact.

Gregor, however, did more than smile. He was not one to leave anything in doubt where Highland honour was concerned. 'Are you after suggesting, sir,' he cried, half-rising from his chair and staring at the viscount, 'that the word of a chief or any Highland gentleman is *not* to be trusted completely?'

'Lord – nothing of the sort, Glengyle, I assure you!' Panmure intervened hastily. 'Fentoun meant no such thing, I'll warrant. I take it that all he meant was could Colonel Hooke be satisfied with such word-of-mouth communications to assemble an army. That was your point, Fentoun, was it not?'

The peer from East Lothian mumbled something approximately affirmative.

'I think that you need have no fear,' Hooke went on smoothly. 'The chiefs all will be approached as soon as possible for their agreement and promises, and thereafter will be given as long warning as may be as to the date and place of assembly. I foresee no serious difficulties . . . if Mr MacGregor will consent to act as His Majesty's representative and ambassador to the clans, as he has done before?'

'And who would that man be, at all?' Rob asked gently, of the heraldic plaster ceiling apparently. 'This *Mister* MacGregor?'

'H'rr'mmm.' The Irishman blinked rapidly. 'Inversnaid, I mean, of course. I apologise, sir. A slip of the tongue. I have been away from the North for years. My regrets, Inversnaid.'

'Accepted, Colonel,' the MacGregor replied graciously. 'In this company, Rob will serve very well. But a gentleman of the MacGregors is Mister in no company, whatever, you will remember? *Dia* – he is not!'

The niceties of Highland and Gregorach dignity thus suitably established, Rob sat back. 'So it is myself that you will have to be doing all the toil and the striving?' he went on. 'Me it is that has to be seeing the chiefs and convincing the clans?'

'None could do it better. Or so well. The chiefs all trust you – even the Campbells! Which is a thing I doubt if any other man in Scotland could say!' And Hooke smiled his wintry smile.

'The Campbells may trust me – but that is not to say that I am trusting the Campbells!' Rob Roy observed dryly. 'But I'm thinking that more than trust is needed. The clans have rallied twice to King James's banner, already – and both times he has failed them. They will not be so eager now, I'm thinking.'

'All the more reason why it should be you who approaches them, Rob,' Harry Maule intervened quietly, fingering the long curls of his great wig. 'They will accept your assurances when you explain the situation in London. And that His Majesty has learned a great deal in these five years. And when you tell them that the prospects for the cause were never fairer.'

'For the cause, perhaps, friend – but what of the prospects for the *clans*? It would seem that they will bear the weight of any bloodshed that there may be. Not for the first time. I have to be thinking of them also, see you.'

Fentoun's chair scraped back. 'You put your chiefs before your king, MacGregor!' he cried.

Other voices rose in his support.

'I put the benefit of the people before that of any one man, my lord – even of James Stewart!'

'S'death! Is this His Majesty's envoy to the clans?' the viscount demanded hotly. 'God help King James if this is the voice of the Highlands!'

'No, no. Peace. Fentoun – in Heaven's name!' Panmure said. 'You mistake him. . . .'

'Would the gentleman prefer to play the envoy his own self?' Rob wondered. 'To go round the clans in person? I shall be happy . . .'

'Gentlemen – my lords,' Hooke broke in. 'This is folly. Let us not excite ourselves over nothing. Inversnaid . . . er, Rob . . . is perfectly right to concern himself for the people, *his* people. The interests of the country as a whole must be considered. His Majesty is equally concerned for the people, for his loyal clansmen – more so, if I may dare suggest it, as their divinely appointed ruler and protector. But fortunately, in this instance, the King's and the clans' interests coincide.' The Irishman tipped thin lips with his tongue. 'The usurping Government in London hates the clans. Witness our friend Rob's own personal predicament. The victim of animosity and greed, he is convicted in his absence on a trumped-up charge, declared bankrupt, and outlawed by the Government. He suffers more than any of us from the King's enemies. Therefore he has the right to be cautious, lest he suffers more.'

The MacGregor stirred in his chair. The man was wickedly subtle, seeing two or three moves ahead all the time. Never had Rob been manoeuvred so skilfully into a corner. To use his outlawry to commit him was clever; but to hint at over-caution, linked with the name and reputation of Rob Roy MacGregor, was masterly.

Gregor took the bait like an eager salmon. 'You are not suggesting, sir, that it is caution that concerns my uncle?' he demanded. 'God's death – you little know us if that is your opinion of the Gregorach!'

'Quiet, Greg lad,' Rob interposed. 'Colonel Hooke understands the MacGregors very well, I think – too well, perhaps!'

'I know that I have never yet called upon you in vain – whatever has been my experience elsewhere,' the Irishman said handsomely. 'I am sure that I will not this time either, my friend?'

'I fear that perhaps you will,' the other answered, shrugging. 'I have other things to do, see you.'

Gregor glanced at his uncle sharply.

'But . . . nothing so important that it can prevent you from doing this great service for your King, surely? And country likewise, of course,' Hooke added hurriedly.

'I think that it could, yes.'

'I need not mention, need I, that His Majesty will reward gratefully and suitably such services done to him?'

'As Royal's my Race – I do not serve my country for reward!'

'No. No – er, that is understood, of course . . .'

'But what is there that you must be doing, Rob, that is so important?' Lord Panmure asked. 'You are outlawed, more or less a fugitive in the heather, if all that we hear is true. How can you be so tied with affairs . . . ?'

'Sink me – I'd have wagered that you would welcome the chance, man, to get away from dodging the red-coats and living as a hunted man!' Lord Southesk declared. 'I vow *I* should!'

'Your lordship's preferences are your own. Put it that I have a debt to settle,' Rob mentioned. 'A notable debt.'

Hooke eyed the MacGregor shrewdly. 'I take it that you

mean with his Grace of Montrose?'

'With Montrose, yes. And with another.'

'That is understandable. And a debt of honour is not to be denied,' the other agreed sympathetically. 'But I put it to you that the best way to pay your debt to Montrose is to bring down the Government of which he is a member, to ensure his political downfall and the end of his position of privilege. Put King James on his throne, Rob, and Montrose is at your mercy! And others with him.'

'Aye, aye.'

'Truly spoken.'

There was sense in that, Rob could not deny. But a MacGregor's vengeance was not of the sort that could be put quietly by till times were more propitious. 'That may be true,' he said stubbornly. 'But I do not intend to wait so long, at all.'

'But . . . mercy on us – the need for this service is urgent!' Hooke cried, for once nettled into irritation. 'The King's cause cannot wait!'

Into the silence, it was Gregor MacGregor's voice that spoke. 'If my uncle cannot find the time for this service, then *I* will go to the clans,' he said. 'I am not so notable a man as he, nor yet a famed warrior. Not yet. But I am chieftain of Clan Dougal Ciar of the Gregorach, and that is enough for any clan's chief under heaven, whatever! The King shall be served!'

There was a momentary pause as men looked from nephew to uncle and back again. Then the applause broke out and continued.

Rob stared straight ahead of him. Then his first quick frown was displaced by a smile. 'You are a brave fellow, Greg,' he said. 'A very paladin! But we will discuss this later, see you.'

Hooke judiciously decided that the moment was ripe to change the subject. 'Now, my lords,' he said. 'I think that we can turn to the consideration of how much each of you can promise to contribute in money, horses and materials. And men also, of course. You, my lord of Panmure, have already promised an excellent provision. As has Mr Harry. Now, perhaps my Lord Glamis . . . ?'

* * *

That evening, in the privacy of their own room, the two MacGregors faced each other, so dissimilar in appearance yet so basically alike.

'I tell you I am no longer your pupil! Your tutoring days are over!' the younger man declared warmly. 'Wanting a high chief of MacGregor, no man is my master. I choose my own road . . .'

'Aye, boy – but in matters of war I'd remind you that *I* am Captain of Clan Alpine still. And this is warfare.'

'Not yet, it is not. This is a matter between myself and my king! When the clan is to be led, you will lead it, and I will serve under you. But until that day, Glengyle is his own master!'

'*Dia* – you crow like any cockerel on a midden! How think you the chiefs – veteran fighters like Maclean of Duart, and Locheil, and old Coll of Keppoch – will heed the words of a stripling like yourself! How will *you* contest the evasions of that fox MacDonald of Sleat? Is the proud Clanranald likely to give his promises through young Gregor of Glengyle?'

His nephew swallowed, and his eager face sank a little at the mention of these famous and resounding names. 'I . . . I do not know,' he admitted, his voice suddenly subdued. 'I can but try them – do my best with them. Somebody must go to them, if you cannot. . . .'

'They will scorn you, boy – or cozen you. They will talk you round and about, and shout you down, and twist you round their fingers. They are devils for pride and double-talking. I know them – I know the way of them, and the way round them. They have to be played off, one against another, played like salmon, handled like the slippery eels they are! Or the King will never see his army. . . .' Rob paused, tugging at his beard.

Looking at his uncle, Gregor opened his mouth to speak, and then shut it again – for once wisely holding his peace.

The older man took to pacing the floor of that little bedroom up within the steep roof of the castle. 'Difficult it is,' he muttered. 'If I thought . . . If James was to be failing the clans again, I would never have myself forgiven. Yet, if Anne dies, the word of a force in arms here in Scotland might turn the tide. . . .'

'Is it for policy's sake that you will not go to the chiefs, Rob – or because of John Graham of Killearn?' Gregor asked, then.

His uncle paused in his pacing. 'Both, lad,' he said. 'Both. Though it may be that Hooke has the right of it, this time. I swore that I would never again lead good Highlandmen out to risk their blood for a spineless fool, king or none! But, if Anne dies, and only a fat German is to succeed her . . .'

'It is not policy that holds you back, then, so much. It is Killearn, just?'

'Aye – I suppose that it is, lad.'

'But, Rob – Killearn will keep. I said that before, and it is truth. If the king wins, then Killearn's master falls, and Killearn with him. You can hunt him where you will – the Lowlands will be open to you. They will hide him no longer. You must see that?'

'Would you so wait, Greg, if it had been Glengyle House burned, and *your* Mary and bairns driven out into the night?'

'I do not know. I do not know, at all,' the other admitted soberly. 'Probably not, then. But you are a wiser man than I am, Rob. And, see you – there is this to it. How are you to get at Killearn, anyway? He keeps himself well hidden down there in the Lennox. If you make to go in there, you *may* kill Killearn – but you will never win back to Inversnaid. You, a man well known to all by sight, and with a great price on your head. And the clan is like to need its Captain. But if you wait – wait until February. The Quarter-day – Candlemas. Killearn always has to come north to collect Montrose's rents. *Then* you can reach him, in our own country. That is the time. A bare two months. As factor, he must come for the rents. Then you can pay him yours, my God!'

Slowly Rob Roy nodded. 'Aye,' he said, at last. 'The Candlemas Quarter-day. I believe that you are right, Greg – I do so! I had not thought of that. Yes, I will have him then. Even if he has a regiment of red-coats to guard him, I will have him! Aye.'

'Then . . . you have two months. You will go to the chiefs?'

His uncle smiled. 'I will go, fire-eater.'

'Fine! Fine! Then I will go with you. . . .'

'You will not. No, Greg. I go alone. With red-coats at Inversnaid, your place is with your Mary and the children at Glengyle. The clan needs you there, too. I go alone. But . . . I will be back . . . for Candlemas!'

Gregor sighed. 'Aye,' he said.

CHAPTER TEN

DESPITE all his legendary speed of travel, and the urgency that gnawed within him, Rob was only just able to fulfil his declared intention of being back in his own countryside by Candlemas Quarter-day. Traversing the remote and savage Highlands of the north and west at dead of winter, with snow-choked passes, every stream a foaming torrent, sea-lochs lashed with winds, and the islands often storm-bound for days on end, was a trying and unpredictable business, a succession of challenges, that made a mockery of haste. Nor were the calls that he had had to make such as could be rushed, or disposed of to any timetable. The chiefs, small kings in their own territories, and prouder than any en-throned monarchs, could not be forced into any definite undertakings to supply armed men for James Stewart in the course of, say, an evening's chat. The thing had to be approached suitably, discreetly, in accordance with dignity, and discussed with much diplomacy – frequently, the smaller the chief the greater the diplomacy required. Men had to be coaxed and wheedled, flattered and tempted, and played off one against another. If MacDonald of Barrasdale could be screwed up to promising fifty men, then the chances were that MacDonald of Arnisdale would feel bound to offer at least seventy-five – but again, MacDonald of Glenelg would not join in at all if he heard that the other two were involved, and *he* could produce at least a hundred. Then the great chiefs – Maclean of Duart, Clanranald, Glengarry, Sleat, Macleod, Seaforth and the rest – had to be angled for with probable advantages and honours and promises, as well as having their mutual jealousies and antagonisms played upon. Only the most expert, knowledgeable and trusted of emissaries, could hope to achieve any success in this task; even Rob Roy MacGregor could not rush matters as he would have liked.

So it was the last day of January, after leaving Mac-Dougall of Lorne's castle of Dunollie, before Rob made his way, somewhat wearily for that man, up the fair Glen Orchy that had once been the MacGregors', and round below Beinn Dorain's cloud-hung peak, to Auch and his family. There, any hopes that he might have cherished as to the healing effects of his two months' absence on his wife's spiritual wounds were speedily dissipated. Mary treated him exactly as she had done previously. Her health appeared to be good, she ate adequately, cherished her children as a mother should, worked about the house and at spinning and weaving and dyeing, and in all other respects behaved as normally — save perhaps that her great eyes still held a strange light at times, and she showed less interest in her appearance than formerly; but where Rob was concerned — indeed, where any and all men were concerned — she was as blank as a wall lacking doors or windows. Her husband's stories of his mission to the chiefs, and what he intended for John Graham of Killearn when he came up to collect his master's rents in a day or two's time, equally failed to arouse any discernible reaction in her. The following morning, Rob flung out of the house under Beinn Dorain set-faced, thankful that his errand left him no time for delay.

That night he was at the cave on Cruach Tuirc, where he found only MacAlastair, living a hermit's life in apparent content. Donald, it seemed, had been gone for nearly a month, back to the haunts of men — and likewise women. It appeared that a couple of weeks after Rob's departure, a fleet of boats had come up Loch Lomond from the south, and had taken all the soldiers away. They had gone by night, as they had come, leaving no word, no explanations, no threats even — only much litter, equal quantities of scorn and hatred, and the foundations of the new fort up on Tom na Bairlinn. Presumably they would come back in due course. Meantime the MacGregors, without waiting for Rob Roy's instructions in the matter, had demolished such masonry as had been erected on the foundations, and carted the hewn stones over to the site of Rob's burnt-out house at the other side of the burn, for eventual rebuilding. Life in Inversnaid and the glens, therefore, had returned more or less to normal. MacAlastair forbore either to cheer or to prophesy.

Rob was well enough content with what all this might indicate — but at the moment he was more interested in the doings of Graham of Killearn than those of the military. The Duke of Montrose, from his base of Buchanan Castle in the low country at the foot of Loch Lomond, had inherited and acquired vast estates right up to the edge of the Highland Line — and in one or two instances, even over it. Much of this bordered on the MacGregor territories of Craigroyston and Aberfoyle, and was therefore, from the Lowlander's point of view, on the wrong side of the elementary safety line. It was the custom in Scotland to collect rents quarterly, at the term-days of Candlemas, Whitsun, Lammas and Martinmas — and since the tenants by no means would, or could, travel long distances to pay, it behoved the lairds to send their factors to recognised assembly points to receive their tribute in cash or kind. Thus, every three months, Graham of Killearn had to come north to visit various known venues on his master's behalf. The venues could not be changed without ample notification to all concerned — or no rents would be collected. Rob Roy could hardly go wrong.

At noon, for instance, next day, the second of February, John Graham was due to be at the ale-house of Duchray, only a few miles from Aberfoyle. Very well so.

The three men were in position early, amongst the heather and scattered pines above the clachan of Duchray. The small grey Graham castle stood on its knoll below them to the left, and to the right, beyond three or four cot-houses, lay the inn, scheduled scene of today's collection. It was a brilliant sparkling morning of hoar frost, and the snow-covered mountains gleamed and glittered in the dazzling sunlight, a trial to the eyes.

One or two tenants had arrived before Rob, and all morning they came in, singly and in little groups, driving a cow or a couple of sheep, or a pannier-pony laden with sacks of grain or crates of poultry – for by no means all paid their dues in cash. Hidden, the watchers high above, waited – and wished that they could help to keep the cold out with some of Colin the Inn's cheer, as did the over-punctual tenants.

Just before noon the still frosty air rang to a different sort of sound to the scuffle and clop of the hooves of cows and garrons – the ring of iron-shod hooves on the ice-bound track. Many hooves. Round a bend in the drove-road from the east trotted a purposeful cavalcade.

'*Dia* – he does not ride unprotected, does John Graham!' Donald MacGregor exclaimed. 'It is an army, whatever!'

'Half a troop, say,' Rob amended. 'And what did you expect? If I was John Graham, I would have brought more than that.' He paused for a moment. 'No, my God,' he added grimly ' – I would not have come, at all!'

The company consisted of about thirty red-coated dragoons, with three men in civilian clothing. They clattered past the inn, with scarcely a glance at the waiting countrymen, and on to the castle.

'He wants his dinner, from Duchray, before he attends to the tenantry scum!' Donald commented. 'Always Kill-earn loved his belly.'

The civilians and one of the soldiers – the officer, no doubt – dismounted and entered the castle doorway, while the dragoons disposed themselves as best they could. There was a sizeable crowd now, about the ale-house, and much livestock, some of it vociferous. All waited with what patience was in them.

Rob waited, too – waited for over an hour till the factor's party emerged from Duchray Castle and moved over to the inn, escorted by the soldiery; waited for longer than that, waited all afternoon in fact, despite the cold and Donald's increasing restiveness – while tenants came and went and the herd of beasts grew, and the soldiers scattered about and relaxed in their boredom. Donald was for action, unspecified but dramatic, all the time, but Rob would not be rushed. The longer that they could delay, the better, he pointed out; there would be the more beasts in the pens behind the inn, the dragoons were growing less and less watchful and drinking more and more of Colin's ale, and the more substantial tenants would be arriving late when, according to established custom, the factor would provide refreshments for these favoured folk at the end of the day. Moreover, dusk and the oncoming night, would aid them in anything that they attempted. The waiting game could be the winning game.

Lights indeed had been lit within the little inn before at length Rob decided that the time was ripe. Stiff and cramped with cold, the three men rose up out of the heather amongst the shadows of the dark pines, with the sun down behind Beinn Lomond and no certainty about anything in sight save the twinkling lights below.

'You have it clear, what you have to be at?' Rob charged his lieutenants. 'Work you down, unseen, to behind the house. Get a barrier down in the pens, there. Och, you will manage that, easy. Then out with the beasts – get them running downhill into the haughs of the Duchray Water. No torches this time, MacAlastair – you will have to be shouting, just. Noise is the thing, see you – once you are ready for them. Get the beasts running, and you amongst them – och, and the soldiers will be running after you. It is soft down in the haughs – boggy; they will not do much with their fine horses there. Splash you across the burn and up into the thick woods beyond. They will not find you in there, in the dark, those ones – but keep you on with the shouting, so that they follow you. You have it?'

'The cattle – the beasts, Rob?' Donald demanded. 'We'll never can manage the cattle through the thick wood. . . .'

'Let the beasts go where they will, man. Leave them. They will scatter – and take a deal of gathering again. In the dark, the soldiers will be hearing them crashing about and thinking it is yourselves. Och, it will be child's-play, just. All I am wanting is fifteen minutes to myself with John Graham – no more. Keep you the soldiers busy for that, and Killearn is mine. I will meet you, later, at the garrons back up here. You have your pistols primed, to be firing a shot or two. . . . ?'

Rob watched them slip away down hill like shadows. Very soon the dusk had swallowed them into its obscurity. He waited, once more.

His friends seemed to take an unconscionable time about their business. Not that this mattered greatly, for the darker the evening the better for their purposes – unless they delayed long enough for Killearn to finish his work at the inn and retire to the castle for the night, in which case all was lost. But that was unlikely, unless he was going to dispense with the usual refreshments. . . .

Then, abruptly, pandemonium broke out below. A shot, sharp in the crisp air, sparked it off, then a volley of yells, followed by much bellowing of alarmed cattle and the thunder of trampling stamping hooves. Cries and shouts rose from all around now, and two more shots rang out. In the din, Rob could distinguish the barked commands of authority. He nodded to himself, satisfied.

He gave them a minute or two, by which time the principal sources of noise were already obviously moving away down towards the water meadows, before looking to the priming of his own pistol and himself slipping away downhill.

Probably Rob followed approximately the same route as his colleagues. The pines and birches gave him cover right down to the level of the drove-road. He darted across it, and circled round towards the back of the inn. The hullabuloo was still proceeding, but it was now some distance off, down about the waterside.

Rob made for the inn's back door. There seemed to be nobody around the rear of the house – only one or two restive tethered garrons, a few agitated sheep, and the broken-down barricading of the cattle pens. So far, so good.

The back door was shut, but not bolted. However carefully he pushed it open, it creaked a little – but there was a chatter of voices upraised within that would cover the noise. He edged inside, closed the door behind him, and quietly slid home the bolt.

He was in a narrow passage, at either end of which were open doors through which light streamed. He was acquainted with the place, and knew that the apartment to the right was the large public room of the inn, that to the left being the proprietor's private kitchen. A ladder midway led up to rough sleeping-quarters in the loft.

Rob moved along the passage to the right, his rawhide brogans making no sound on the earthen floor. Keeping well back in the shadow, he approached the doorway.

There seemed to be about a dozen men within, all talking and gesticulating at the same time, some peering out through the open front door, some crowding around a window that faced down towards the waterside. All but three were dressed in the rough hodden grey and blue bonnet of the low country farmer. Colin the Inn was standing at the table with a steaming dish of collops. Of the two others, one was in Montrose livery, a thin stooping man who looked like a clerk — and an unhappy one. The last man, well dressed in broadcloth and wearing a cocked hat somewhat askew, stood well back from the outer door, turned away from Rob. In his hand was a drawn pistol — though he did not seem to be gripping it with any degree of confidence.

All this the MacGregor, with no eyes in his direction, took in during a swift survey of the room, by the wavering smoky light of the tallow dips. Bottles and tankards stood about everywhere; benches lay overturned as though upset when men rose hastily to their feet; the table, apart from its victuals, was heaped with ledgers and paper, with stacks of coins, and with bulging money-bags.

Rob's own pistol was now thrust forward, his thumb on the lock. He smiled, but not pleasantly, and took a pace into the room.

'Graham!' he said simply, not loudly but vibrantly enough for the word to penetrate the chatter.

The other man turned round — and as he did so, a dirk, hurled with savage force and accuracy, struck the wrist of his pistol hand. It was the haft that struck, not the point, but even so both weapons clattered to the floor, and the man uttered a yelp of pain.

Rob Roy uttered an exclamation too, part surprise and part curse. The pistol barrel that he had raised to point at the other's chest wavered for a moment.

'Gorthie!' he got out. '*Diabhol* — you! A plague on it — where is Killearn?'

'MacGregor!' the injured man gasped, his features contorted. 'I . . . you . . . God's curse on you, you devil!'

It was the wrong man — Mungo Graham of Gorthie, Montrose's chamberlain, not his factor.

*   *   *

Rob's upset and hesitation was short-lived — as was the wavering of that pistol. The weapon swept menacingly all around the room, for now every head was turned and every eye upon him.

'Your pardon, gentlemen all,' he called. 'I shall not be disturbing you for long, at all. Och, no. Colin – close me that door, man. Bolt it. Quickly. I thank you.' He turned back to Graham. 'This is strange work for you, Gorthie, is it not? I had expected to see Killearn . . . with whom I have my own small account to settle. Regrettable it is that he is not with us.'

The chamberlain answered nothing. No man spoke.

The MacGregor went on. 'My apologies if I have hurt your hand, Gorthie. I trust that it will not incommode you for the signing of receipts and the like? Colin – pick me up Gorthie's pistol; it will be safe with me.' He drew a long breath. 'Now, to business, gentlemen. I have not got long with you, more's the pity. All have paid their rents by this, I hope? Och, yes.' He scanned the many alarmed and anxious faces. 'Good. All have obtained their due and legal receipts from his Grace's chamberlain?' And, more sharply, as all gaped but none answered, '*Have* you, gentlemen? For your own sakes it is important that you hold receipts.'

'Och, I'm no' needin' ony receipt,' one man declared.

'Nor me, neither. . . .'

'That is foolish. Is it not, Gorthie? Gorthie will give you one, now.'

Rob jerked his pistol at the thin stooping clerkly man. 'You, fellow – write these gentlemen their receipts. Gorthie will sign them. Quickly, man. His Grace would have all done in proper fashion, surely?'

'What . . . what do you intend, MacGregor?' Graham asked, biting his lip – whether with pain or agitation was a moot point. He was a very different man from the dour bull-like Killearn, older and more sensitive in manner, though of similar build.

'Nothing that is not just and suitable,' Rob assured him

easily. 'Never fear, man Mungo – all will be done in order. *Exitus acta probat!*'

'You will suffer for it, I promise you. . . .'

'It may be that I have done my suffering already, my friend!' And to the clerk. 'Haste you with your scribbling, fellow.'

For a few moments there was no sound in that room save the scraping of the quill and some very deep breathing. From outside a lively shouting still prevailed, but it seemed to come from a long way off.

As the clerk laid down the pen, Rob took it up and handed it to Gorthie. 'Sign, you,' he directed. 'With your left hand, if need be.' And as the other hesitated, 'Go on, man – it is no more than your plain duty. These tenants have paid you – they are entitled to your receipt.'

With ill grace Graham took the quill with his left hand, and scratched some sort of signature.

'Good. Now, a piece of paper for my own self.' Rob transferred the pistol to his left hand, and took up the pen himself. 'Mark you all,' he mentioned pleasantly, 'that I can shoot equally exactly with either hand!' Leaning against the table, he dipped pen in ink and began to write, raising his eyes between each word. He enunciated the words as he wrote.

'Received from James Graham, Duke of Montrose, the sum of . . .' He paused. 'Does this excellent ledger tell how much coin has been received, fellow?' he asked of the clerk. 'As distinct from cattle and the like?'

'Eh? Aye – och, yes. But I've no' added it yet. . . .'

'Then do so now, man – and quickly. All must be done in order. Tell me at the end of this, and I will write the sum in. Just what you have collected in coin, see you. The beasts would be an inconvenience.' He started again, with the pen.

'. . . the sum of . . . being rents received in coin from all tenants due to pay at Duchray on this day Candlemas the year of grace seventeen hundred and fourteen, the said tenants all having received Gorthie's due receipts. I acknowledge that the said moneys have been duly accepted by me from Graham of Gorthie, as agent for his Grace, in part payment of the debt owing me by the said Duke James. As witness to which my signature is hereby appended.' And he signed the paper with a flourish, 'Robert MacGregor of Inversnaid and Craigroyston.'

'God damn you, MacGregor – you canna do this!' Gorthie burst out. 'It is plain and shameless robbery! Before all these witnesses, I charge you . . .'

'Wheesht, man – wheesht! Clerk – the sum total, if you please?'

'Och, sir – I canna just get it right. I'll tot it up again . . .'

'*Dia* – never trouble! I do not want it to the nearest groat. Give it to me in pounds Scots, man.'

'Pounds Scots . . . it'll be eight hunnerd an' saxty-five, aboot. I made it so the first time. . . .'

'That will serve well enough. Leave it now. Put you all the coin in the one bag – the large one. Quickly, now. In with it. Every groat of it, yes. Quiet, Gorthie, while I write in the figures. You would not have me make an error in an important receipt such as this, would you? Eight hundred and sixty-five, was it not? Pounds Scots. Good. That is it, then. Let the ink dry on that, and all is done in proper style. . . .'

'You are a villain, MacGregor – a barefaced thief and a murderous cateran!'

'Tut, man – not so. Not at all,' Rob denied, transferring the pistol and taking up the heavy bag of coin in his left hand. He seemed to weigh it, judicially, as he did so. 'Nothing has been done here but what is fair and seemly. Your master, Montrose, has unlawfully and maliciously deprived me of my ability to earn my living, whatever. Moreover he has had my house burned on me, my chattels destroyed, and much of my livestock purloined. It follows that he must keep me and my family, out of his bounty, until such time as I am permitted to do the same for myself again. . . .'

Rob stopped short. There was a rattle at the front door, and then a banging thereon. He grimaced. 'We seem to be disturbed, gentlemen. But och, I think our business is satisfactorily done. You have your receipts from Gorthie for your rents. You cannot suffer. Gorthie has his receipt from myself, for this payment on account. What could be fairer . . . ?'

The banging resumed, more urgently.

Rob shook his head. 'Impatient, they are. A pity. I'll bid you good-day, then, gentlemen . . . until the Whitsun term! God preserve all honest men!' And cocked pistol in one hand and money-bag in the other, he backed out of that room and into the passage. From the rear door he shouted, 'Colin, man open up and do not keep the gentlemen waiting!'

Then he was out into the night. Nobody seemed to be at the back of the house. Fleet as any deer he ran for the cover of the first trees.

As he had promised his friends, it had all been child's-play. But practically wasted effort, unfortunately. Killearn still went unpunished.

CHAPTER ELEVEN

ROB did not have long to fret over his disappointment. He had agreed to make a report on his mission to the chiefs to Nathaniel Hooke, and now there was nothing that more urgently demanded his attention. Taking Gregor along with him once more, with MacAlastair in attendance, and leaving Donald to keep in touch with the household at Auch, two days later he was on his way east to Kelly Castle again.

But Hooke was no longer based at Harry Maule's grey house by the grey sea. He had travelled north, it seemed, on receipt of an important message from London, making for Mar Castle on the upper Dee. Rob whistled when he heard this news – for John, Earl of Mar, was Secretary of State for Scotland in Anne's Government and no known Jacobite.

A day later the three MacGregors were on their way northwards likewise.

They went discreetly, as ever, avoiding Forfar and Kirriemuir and deliberately making for the snow-bound hills where, whatever the discomforts, they could travel openly and without skulking. They followed Glen Clova right up to its head amongst the great hump-backed Grampian mountains and then struck northwards over the high snow-choked passes that led down into Glen Muick and so to the wide strath of Dee near the Pass of Ballater. This was not the route that Hooke would have taken, undoubtedly, but it spared them many distractions other than the purely physical ones that anyway came to these three as second nature. Moreover, it gave Rob ample opportunity to ponder the problem of the Earl of Mar.

That Hooke apparently should be making a rendezvous

with London's Secretary of State for Scotland was on the face of it alarming. But the Colonel was no fool, and presumably his information satisfied him. Besides, it was significant perhaps that this journey was being made, not to Alloa House, Mar's Lowland home near Stirling, but to the remote and semi-ruinous Deeside castle from which the earl took his ancient title. This, surely, could only have been at Mar's own request. The man, known as Bobbing John on account of his facility for changing political parties, presumably must be considering changing dynastic sides – which could be a good augury indeed. His mother, of course had been Lady Mary Maule, a sister of Panmure, and his wife, recently dead, had been a sister of the Jacobite Earl of Kinnoull, while his own sister had married Sir Hugh Patterson of Bannockburn – so that, whatever his politics, he was closely connected with many of King James's most prominent supporters. Rob was doubtful, nevertheless, of the wisdom of having dealings with a man of his reputation who was in a position to do their cause infinite harm if he so wished; the uncomplicatedly honest and straightforward Gregor of Glengyle was not doubtful at all – he was deadset against it.

Up the Dee, in darkness, they came inconspicuously to Mar Castle on its rock, to find it not only ruinous but deserted. Discreet investigations revealed that its lord was lodging at the house of Farquharson of Invercauld a few miles down the strath – a very doubtful Jacobite indeed. Not too happily the MacGregors repaired thereto.

They used MacAlastair to make enquiries. Colonel Hooke was found to be at Invercauld also. He came out to welcome Rob eagerly for so stiff a man, and took the MacGregors down to the inn by the riverside where they could talk freely. There he expressed himself as delighted with the report of Rob's mission in the North-west, and more than satisfied with the promises of men and support elicited from the chiefs. He further declared that this information had come at a most auspicious moment – for he could pass it on to Mar, to whose conversion it might well prove decisive.

At Rob's strongly phrased objection to any such betrayal of the chiefs' confidence, Hooke explained. Mar was a Jacobite at heart. Though a member of the Whiggish Government, he had been growing more and more convinced that the future lay with the Tories. With the prospect of Queen Anne's death, he was prepared not only to go over to the Opposition but to throw in his lot with the supporters of King James if he could be assured that they were in the temper and position to take fullest advantage of the dynastic vacuum. Mar himself had sought this meeting, and had gone to no little trouble to effect it. His declared concern, throughout the negotiations with the Colonel, had been doubts as to the numbers of troops that the Jacobites could put into the field quickly enough to keep the Government forces from dominating all strong-points in Scotland in the event of a sudden crisis. Rob's news and figures from the western seaboard would go a long way towards reassuring him.

The MacGregors' doubts about disclosing this information to the Government's chief minion in Scotland, incriminating the clans, were swept aside by Hooke, who pointed out that these chiefs of the North-west were known by all to be King James's men as it was, and the only question was how many broadswords they were likely to put on the field. The numbers that Rob had gained promises for, amounting in all to seven thousand, were highly satisfactory. There could be no harm in informing Mar – for even if he was minded to do the cause hurt, he could by no means reach these chiefs behind their endless ramparts of mountain.

But there was more to it than that. Mar was ready to be convinced, and the greater the weight of support that could be demonstrated for King James, the faster the earl would come over. And he was prepared, it seemed, to continue on in his present important position of Secretary of State, not to make any open break meantime with his Whig colleagues – and so could prove to be of the very greatest assistance to the Jacobite cause as an informer sitting at the very council table of the enemy. Moreover, a sympathetic Secretary of State could greatly ease Jacobite preparations in Scotland, and wink at much that might otherwise be banned. The stakes were high, as they must see.

Rob saw – though he did not fail to see, also, that an informer could work in two directions, and a double-dealer could play more sides false than one. Gregor, for his part, was entirely shocked, and said so.

But Hooke's mind obviously was made up. He was going to tell Mar, and all the MacGregors' doubts would not stop him. He left them at the inn, promising to see them again on the morrow. Being the Gregorach they were, once the Colonel was gone, they prudently left the hostelry and found less vulnerable quarters for themselves in a charcoal-burner's hut in the pine forest. It behoved those who entered the devil's kitchen, said Rob, to see that they left the door open behind them.

It was afternoon next day before Hooke contacted the MacGregors again. Then he came smirking his satisfaction. Mar was convinced. He would throw in his lot with the Jacobites – though not publicly of course – and act positively for them behind the scenes at Whitehall. A dukedom in due course, promised in the name of King James, had nicely clinched the matter.

Gregor made some remarks in the Gaelic which it was probably as well that Hooke did not understand.

It was decided that there was no point in the Mac-Gregors seeing Mar. Hooke suggested that it might be an embarrassment for the Secretary of State to meet socially a wanted outlaw with a price on his head – though Rob gave it as his opinion that a minister who would swallow the salmon of betraying his own Government would not puke at a minnow such as that. However, as it happened, he had no desire himself to talk to the man – and Gregor would have refused to do so anyway.

Hooke, moreover, had other urgent plans for the Mac-Gregors. He himself was about to travel further north still, to fully implicate and enlist the Marquis of Huntly and all his Gordons. These were English-speaking; but the clans further inland, in Badenoch and the great Spey valley, were not – the Shaws, Macphersons, Cattanachs, Mackintoshes, Cummings and Grants. To these he desired Rob and Gregor to go, on the same errand as heretofore – especially to seek to use the influence of Rob's old friend MacAlpine Grant of Rothiemurchus to sway others of that large clan against the Whig tendencies of their chief, the Laird of Grant. Rob had performed an exactly similar service in 1707, with a certain amount of success. It would be a lengthy and difficult employment, but Hooke, who appeared now to be in possession of considerable funds, no doubt raised from the low-country lords, promised that it would be a well-paid one. Gregor MacGregor tut-tutted at the introduction of such sordid considerations into the loyal service of His Majesty, but his uncle was differently minded and believed that the labourer was worthy of his hire – particularly when the said hire came out of the deep pockets of purse-proud Lowland magnates. Amongst other attributes, Rob Roy was not least a notable business-man. In agreeing to undertake this second embassy he drove a fairly shrewd bargain. Mary and the boys, back at Auch, would not starve yet awhile.

So the following day, as Mar rode south and Hooke north, the MacGregors headed westwards through the vast and daunting mountains of the Monadh Ruadh, by the passes of Glen Geldie and Glen Feshie, for Badenoch and the uplands of Spey. Rob was not altogether sorry, perhaps to have his mind and time so fully occupied with the King's business.

CHAPTER TWELVE

POLITICS and such high affairs did not so wholly fill his mind, however, that Rob forgot his promised engagement with Montrose's good tenants for the next rent day, the Whitsun term. His work on Speyside still unfinished – it had not only prolonged itself as the result of the evasiveness and obstinacy of men and the effects of melting snows on river-dominated terrain, but had extended itself into the heights of Moray and the Great Glen areas – he allowed himself a temporary respite and relaxation, and set off for the south at the beginning of May, in good time he trusted to do what had to be done. Gregor he had already sent home a good month previously – partly for his young wife's sake, partly to keep an eye on the Gregorach, and partly because his distinctly straightforward and all too honest nephew did not make the best of negotiators.

Rob and MacAlastair made their way out of Badenoch by the Pass of Drumochter, down long Loch Ericht-side and across the waterlogged wastes of Rannoch Moor to Orchy and Auch. This time Rob did not look for any notable welcome from his Mary – and so was not disappointed. But he had had ample time for thought and cogitation during his months in the north, and he arrived home with certain decisions firm upon him. Consequently, when he came to intimate something of his Whitsun Quarter-day programme, he added as an after-thought, but crisply, that he was going to take his wife with him on this occasion.

Mary's statuesque armour of reserve, almost impenetrable as it was, wilted just a little at this announcement. She actually blinked. 'What . . . I . . . such jesting is ill-judged,' she said.

'It is no jesting,' he assured.

'Then it is folly,' she gave back, as briefly.

'That is a matter of opinion,' he shrugged. 'But you come, nevertheless, *a graidh.*'

'Indeed I do not.'

'Yes, you do. You are my wife yet, see you – little as you may act the part these days. You will do as I say, woman.'

'Have you . . . have you taken leave of your wits?' she cried.

'It may be so – in which case there will be the two of us in that state! Still, I think not. But you will ride with me tomorrow, whatever.'

Helplessly the woman stared at him. 'But, why? Where would you take me? How can I be leaving here? The children – I cannot leave my children. It is unthinkable. . . .'

'The children will do finely with Marsala. It will not be for long, at all. A holiday it will be for them, just.' Rob changed his tone. 'Och, you rode with me on many of my ploys in the old days, Mary – and liked it well. We had good times together. You have been too long penned in a house. We used to work finely in harness. . . .'

'Those days are gone.' She shook her lovely head. 'Dead.'

'Perhaps not, *a graidh.* But sleeping, it may be.'

'Dead,' she repeated, flatly. 'You killed them.'

'I . . . ?' He raised wide shoulders. 'Have it as you will. But you ride with me tomorrow!'

'No! I will not! Are you crazy-mad? You cannot do this.'

'Some things I cannot do, woman, I grant you. But this I can! And will! As Royal's my Race – you ride tomorrow. Be you ready, early.' And turning about, the man stamped out of that house.

So, with the mists still low on Beinn Dorain next morning, a stiff-faced and stiffly-held woman was hoisted up in front of Rob Roy on his garron – for when he said that she was to ride with him, he meant just that, and did not allow her even a horse for herself. Her parting from the wondering children and startled Marsala had been strained, but there had been no scene – for Mary MacGregor was not a woman who indulged in scenes. They rode off, the impassive MacAlastair a discreet distance in the rear, with only Rob's hand waving farewell and his cheerful voice upraised.

There is little scope for distance-keeping and any effective display of sustained hostility and disapproval between two people on the back of a single trotting jolting pony. Rob found it expedient to hold his passenger fairly tightly within his arms throughout, a pressure which the passenger was in no position to resist. The jouncing motion of the horse flung body against body so consistently that any maintenance of attempts to avoid such would have been as absurd as it was fruitless. Markedly uneven ground and frequent steep climbing, both up and down, forced the woman to clutch the man's arm constantly for elementary balance's sake, and a sportive breeze continually blew her long dark hair in the rider's face with an undeniable sense of intimacy. Nevertheless, throughout a long day's riding, Mary MacGregor managed to preserve a detachment and cold aloofness that was little short of miraculous, giving the impression that she found her companion to be no more than some impersonal if deplorable force of nature that must be put up with. She did not actually refuse to answer all remarks addressed to her, but such responses as she made were so brief and non-commital as to serve only to emphasise her dissent and protest. Rob fairly soon gave up attempts at conversation.

It was not until they were plodding over the long braes that rise out of Glen Falloch and give access to the head of Balquhidder, after a full day's riding, that Mary, no doubt having struggled against it for hours, fell asleep. Thereafter she lay comfortably and naturally relaxed within the man's arms, her head nestled against his broad chest. Rob smiled then and frequently in the ensuing couple of hours that brought them down into Glen Gyle, holding her still closer. And more than once he surreptitiously brushed his lips over the heavy raven tresses so close to his chin, and grieved at the white strands so recently invading the black. Those were the happiest two hours that he had spent in half a year.

He did not take his wife to the cave on Cruach Tuirc, of course, but to the large and comfortable House of Glengyle – though still he held to his self-imposed ordinance of not entering under Gregor's, or any other clansman's, roof. Delivering Mary over to the welcoming arms of the younger Mary, and sternly refusing to be drawn into any explanations save that he would call for her again next morning, he drew Gregor aside and went walking with him through the May dusk, eating as they went.

The two men had much to tell each other, but Rob's questions prevailed, and were particular rather than general. Much anent Montrose's Quarter-day arrangements for this area he queried, and was answered just as he anticipated. Killearn was less likely than ever to venture north of the Highland Line, or anywhere near to it, after what had happened at Candlemas. But arrangements had been made for the grain collections to be held at different centres than was usual, and a day earlier than was normal – no doubt in an effort to circumvent any gestures by Rob Roy.

The Whitsun quarter was distinguished from the other three by the emphasis laid on the payment of rent by grain and meal, rather than either cash or cattle. This was understandable – at least from the landlords' point of view. The long winter was over, but the new season's pasture, up in these northern latitudes, was not yet available; consequently feed for the cattle, the basis of the Highland economy, was always in desperately short supply by May. Oats were all but worth their weight in gold. Shrewd landlords, therefore, made a point of insisting that at least some proportion of this quarter's rents should be paid in grain and fodder, albeit at a time when their tenants could least afford it – in the interest of their own hungry herds. Girnels, or collecting stores, were appointed in each area – and well guarded.

Rob learned more than all this from Gregor. He heard that the military were back – Major Selby and a full Company, at Inverarklet on Loch Lomond, plus a large number of masons and builders. They were working hard at the new fort on Tom na Bairlinn again. The soldiers were not otherwise proving themselves to be very objectionable to the clan, however, being there apparently, at this stage, purely to guard the builders and their work. The MacGregors, in accordance with Rob's unpopular instructions, were leaving them severely alone. For the rest, it had been a bad winter for the beasts, and Rob's great swollen herds were in bad shape, stock dying off every day for lack of fodder.

None of this was unexpected. Rob nodded grimly, and asked only for the brief loan of half a dozen Glengyle gillies, for service unspecified and anonymous.

*   *   *

Sometime during the next day, the majority of the Montrose tenants in the Aberfoyle, Gartmore and Menteith areas – all the more substantial ones, at any rate – were visited by a messenger bearing a short but authoritative letter, impressively stamped and sealed with the Montrose seal. This informed them that his Grace, having had warning of the rascal Robert MacGregor's baleful intentions, had decided to put the grain collection forward for still another day, and had changed the venue once again, in order to checkmate any knavish MacGregor tricks. The tenant was ordered to appear, therefore, with his oats conveniently bagged, on the thirteenth day of the month – that was, the day following – between the hours of noon and three o'clock, at the mill at Port of Menteith, on pain of his Grace's stern displeasure. God Save Queen Anne. If any of the said tenants noted that the messengers were not dressed in the usual Montrose livery but in assorted and ill-fitting Lowland garb and yet managed to sound extremely like Highlandmen – who were they, individually, to question the ways of their betters? And there was no arguing with that magnificent heraldic seal. Rob had retained possession of this trinket as a memento of a former business partnership, in which he frequently had had occasion to act on behalf of James Graham in the buying and selling of livestock. None of the tenants were likely to notice that the coronet depicted thereon was still that of an earl and not of a duke.

The following early morning, therefore, refusing any further assistance from Gregor – who of course had some of his own rent-collecting to attend to – Rob took Mary once more up before him on his garron, and again with only MacAlastair and Donald as lieutenants, rode off eastwards. Mary remained true to her former attitude – no relenting, no co-operation, but no scenes.

By a carefully thought-out route, avoiding the dwellings of men, even of MacGregors, travelling by the south side of Loch Katrine, the flanks of Beinn Venue, and the long ridge of high ground that stretches eastwards from there, they came down eventually to the wide green levels of the Forth Valley, to Port of Menteith on the north shore of its great lake, a good two hours before noon. Rob had selected this place with care. It was ideally situated for his purpose, the mill standing at the foot of a leafy lane beside a confluence of stream and loch, with only this one access road. Moreover, the miller was a Graham and a surly oaf, and so fair game.

They approached the mill quite openly, and while Rob installed Mary in such comfort as the main barn could offer, MacAlastair and Donald went in and locked up the miller and his wife and daughter in one of their own upper rooms, with fierce looks and blood-curdling threats. Thereafter they brought out a kitchen-table and chairs and set them up just inside the door of the barn. Then, after reconnoitring the neighbouring woodlands thoroughly, the two henchmen went to take up their positions to regulate the flow of traffic, Donald at the head of the lane, MacAlastair at the mill itself.

Rob sat Mary beside him at the table, facing the doorway, and with pens and ink and paper spread before him, filled in the time with the writing of receipts. He suggested, mildly, after a while that Mary might care to do likewise? She answered with a cold negative, whereupon he pointed out reasonably that what was being attempted was solely to the detriment of her hated enemies the Grahams and not for his own private benefit – so that she need feel no qualms about aiding him if that was her trouble. This specious argument received the response it deserved – but, after perhaps another twenty minutes of waiting, the woman suddenly reached out and took up a pen, and inking it, commenced to copy out one of Rob's blank receipt forms. The man at her side said nothing, but within him his heart lifted a little.

The two pens scratched thereafter busily, in unison.

The first tenant arrived well before noon, a substantial farmer, one Drummond in Ballabog, leading three pack-ponies laden with sacks of oats. MacAlastair directed him into the barn, where Rob greeted him pleasantly.

'Aha, Ballabog – you are more than punctual.' he cried. 'I trust that I see you well, whatever? An ill winter it has been. The Lady Inversnaid, maybe, you do not know?'

That the farmer was astonished goes without saying; flabbergasted might better describe his state. Mouthing like a stranded fish, he stared. No words came.

'A welcome on behalf of his Grace of Montrose,' Rob went on, genially. 'He cannot have the satisfaction of greeting all his tenants in person – so I am acting for him in the matter. But I have all the due receipts ready and in order, see you. Let me see, now – how much is your payment, at all?'

'Eh . . . ah . . . I . . . och, mercy on us,' the other stammered. 'Goad save us a'.'

'Tut, man – that will not be necessary, on this occasion! How much?'

'Och, T't'twal'bolls o' oats, an' forty pun Scots, jist. But . . .'

'But too much, I agree, Ballabog. Too much, after a bad winter. Don't you agree, my dear?' That to his wife.

Mary looked away biting her lip. But she nodded.

'Aye, then. Too much. What would you say, Ballabog, was a fair quarter's rent, in the circumstances?'

'Eh . . . ? Och, Goad kens, sir – I dinna!' the farmer faltered.

'Come, man – you must have some idea. If you have not, who has? It has been a hard time for the beasts, and prices are bad. What do you say – *eight* bags and *twenty* pounds?'

'Guidsakes!'

'That would satisfy you, eh? Very well, so. Eight bags and twenty pounds Scots, it is. His Grace perhaps lacks understanding in these matters – dukes often do. So I will make out your receipt for the full amount – the twelve bags and the forty pounds, you see – which will satisfy both his Grace and you – but I will take from you only the eight bags and twenty pounds, which will satisfy me whatever! Och, I am a reasonable man, as anyone will tell you!' Rob scratched busily with his pen.

'But, man – you canna dae that!' the perplexed farmer exclaimed. 'It's . . . it's no' lawfu'.'

'What is unlawful about it my friend? I am accepting payment on behalf of his Grace. Not for the first time. You will have heard that we were in partnership together – a partnership that has never been legally dissolved, see you? I am giving you a receipt, in his name, for the full amount of the rent. If I choose to take only part of it, the responsibility is mine. Is it not?'

'Well. . . .'

'Good, then. There is the one thing, just. I will be needing your garrons to be carrying the grain, see you. I see that you have three fine beasts out there. I will take two of them and leave you the one to be carrying back your four bags of oats – that will be a bit help for your own cattle-feed, I've no doubt? You will have my personal receipt for them, and the word of Rob Roy MacGregor that you will receive them back in good order within two days. You understand?'

'Och, aye – I mean, no! I'm hearing you – but . . .'

'*Dia* – you are no doubting my word are you, Ballabog!'

'No, no! Lordie – no! Save us a' – never think it! It's jist . . .'

'You *want* to be spared half your silver, and your four bags of oats, I take it?'

'Ooh, aye – surely. Surely. . . .'

'Very well, then. Here are your two receipts. Your garrons will be delivered back to Ballabog in due course. Mac-Alastair there, will show you to your ale and bannocks – refreshment that you may accept as a token of his Grace's goodwill! And a very good day to you, Ballabog. The Lady Inversnaid sends her greetings to your gudewife, likewise – do you not, my dear? Exactly. MacAlastair – show Ballabog his refreshment. Ah – you have another tenant waiting then? I fear that I do not just mind the name, for the moment . . . ? Och yes, then – Erskine, Gartfarren. Of course. Come away in, Gartfarren. You are welcome. My wife, the Lady Inversnaid . . .'

That was the pattern of the business. There were varying details with each tenant, but the basic strategy was the same. More effort and eloquence had to be expended on some than on others. Some were more difficult, others actually co-operated. None, when it came to the crux, refused to pay. Which was scarcely to be wondered at. Rob Roy was not a man to argue with, especially for small farmers – and he could be expected to have hordes of his fierce clansmen in hiding just around the corner, to enforce his wishes; by dealing with the tenants one by one, and then seeing that MacAlastair and Donald got them fairly quickly out of the way, he faced each with an individual choice and prevented any mutual encouragement to resist, any united front. Also, of course, none of them could be quite sure just how much of it all was trickery and how much fair dealing. Few of the payers had any love for their absentee ducal landlord, and most of their sympathies would lie with Rob rather than with Montrose – so long as it did not cost them dear. And Rob had baited his trap cunningly, remitting them a substantial part of their payments yet giving them a receipt for it all; he knew the minds of peasant-farmers. No doubt there was, too, that the presence of Mary Mac-Gregor sitting there, helped greatly to engender a suitably respectable atmosphere from the start, and to prevent acrimonious dispute; in a matter of this sort, first impressions were important.

Before mid-afternoon, then, an impressive concourse of garrons and pannier-ponies, with their burdens of grain and fodder, were tethered in rows behind the mill – necessitating the hiring of sundry small boys who had materialised as small boys will, to watch and ward them – and a sizeable heap of silver merks had accumulated in the barn. Rob was beginning to get just a little bit concerned, as time went on – for of course it could be taken as granted that the mulcted tenants would talk once they were away from the mill area, and the possibility of such excited talk rushing round the district and reaching ears hostile to the MacGregors could not be ruled out. Reactions might follow – though it was improbable that any large force could be summoned against them locally at short notice, or that the military escort for the factor's party would arrive in the district until the morrow.

At length, even with three or four tenants still to come, Rob called a halt. There was no point in risking all for the sake of a small fraction – for there remained much to be done yet. A band of sturdy Gregorach gillies would have solved his problems – but that was not to be. He pinned a writing on the barn-door instructing the late coming tenants to deliver their rents to such of the poor and needy as they might select, and left signed and sealed receipts for the full amount thereof skewered near by on a dirk; whether or not they actually followed these instructions was not the vital issue – which was to deny the rents to Montrose if possible. Then, piling all the coin into a bag, and recalling Mac-Alastair and Donald, he made ready to move.

There proved to be no fewer than sixty-three ponies assembled behind the barn, bearing on an average three hundredweights of oats apiece – a total of nearly ten tons of grain. They would make a long pack-train for three riders to control, most obviously. Rob turned to his wife.

'Mary, *a graidh*,' he said. 'You will notice that we are something lacking in hands. One extra rider, even, could be a help whatever. Will you do it?'

'Yes,' she said simply, quietly.

The man's blue eyes lit up, but he forbore to comment, containing himself with finding a suitable beast for her to ride, and sharing out its load elsewhere. He sent Mac-Alastair to release the miller's family.

Pairing up the horses, and linking each couple with grass rope from the mill, they set out in a long procession. Donald led, on this occasion, and Rob brought up the rear – for he reckoned that it was from there that any trouble might be looked for – with MacAlastair and Mary in the centre. They made an irritatingly deliberate cavalcade, necessarily reduced to the pace of the slowest laden garron.

They headed back by approximately the same route that

they had come – but of course there was no possibility of doing so secretly; sixty-odd horses in a string take a deal of hiding on bare hillsides. Rob imagined that once they were beyond the Pass of Aberfoyle, and so into MacGregor territory, no persons short of the military would dare to interfere with them. But they had five or six exposed miles to cover before that.

They were crossing the long rolling heather flanks of Creag Dubh, the southern buttress of the shapeless Menteith Hills, and still a couple of miles short of Aberfoyle, when MacAlastair, mounting a knoll ahead and looking backwards, gestured urgently, pointing. From the rear of the long column, Rob turned to stare. Following them, and just emerging into sight from out of the birch-clad braes below, was a scattered but extensive concourse of people. Concourse was almost the only name that could be put to it, so far, since it seemed to have no shape nor form nor any coherence; but it was composed of a lot of men, quite clearly, a lot of horses, and the afternoon sun glinted on a notable amount of steel of one sort or another.

Rob hurried forward to the knoll at a canter, where Mary had already joined MacAlastair; Donald was away at the front with the leading pair of garrons.

'Many men,' the gillie greeted him grimly. 'You will not talk *these* round one at a time, I'm thinking!'

'No – more there are than I bargained for!' his master admitted, shading his eyes with his hand. 'There seem to be some good horses in the front – Graham lairdies, no doubt. They must have gathered together more of their folk than I thought possible at short notice.' He frowned, eyes busy. 'There could be a hundred in it – though, och, a lot will be come out to stare rather than to fight, at all.'

'With the half of them starers even, we still have scarcely the advantage!' the other observed dryly. 'Three of us – and all these beasts to be managing . . .'

'Four!' Rob corrected sharply. 'Do not be forgetting

Mary.' And he glanced sidelong at his wife. 'A quarter of our strength – and her making the better men of us!'

'We fight them then?'

'If we must.'

'What can you do . . . against so many?' Mary asked, a little breathlessly. 'Save flee?'

'We cannot flee with all these laden garrons – and I will not flee without them,' Rob declared.

'What, then . . . ?'

'See you – they are not just rushing upon their fate, these heroes,' her husband pointed out. 'Circumspect they are, for so many.' That seemed to be true. The concourse, now fully revealed in its ragged and far-flung extent, appeared to be anything but impetuous in its advance, following them with a caution that seemed excessive for so large a company in pursuit of three men and a woman. Rob gestured. 'That could be meaning one of two things, maybe. Either that they do not wish to be fighting us at all, but only to be scaring us away from the garrons and the grain – in which case they do not know Rob Roy at all! Or else they think, maybe, that they know Rob Roy too well, and do not believe that he is ever attended by less than a regiment of the fierce Gregorach! It could be that they think that there must be many more of us – but in hiding.'

MacAlastair nodded thoughtfully.

'If that is so, since we must disappoint them in the first notion, it would be a great pity to do so in the second, would it not?'

Mary shook her head in mystification, but the gillie began to look about him keenly.

Rob did the same, making one of his swift surveys of the lie of the land. He pointed here and there and there again, swinging his arm round. At each gesture MacAlastair nodded briefly.

'You down below, by the burn-channel there. In those hollows,' Rob went on. 'Donald up above – making noise

156

enough for many. Och, it is worth the trying.'

'Aye, then. And the garrons . . . ?'

'I will lead them,' Mary interposed. 'I think that I see what you would be at. I will look after the garrons – keep them moving.'

'Nothing could be more convenient,' Rob agreed, smiling. 'Off you get then, forward – the pair of you. Myself, I will just be taking a bit of a rest, see you!'

* * *

For a while it almost looked as though Rob Roy meant what he said about taking a rest. While the other two hurried forward, and Mary relieved Donald at the head of the cavalcade, Rob dawdled on at the rear. In fact, he fell further and further behind. Occasionally he glanced behind him at the pursuit – which, however restrained their ardour for the attack, could not help overtaking this dilatory quarry.

If Rob's outstanding person and identity must by then have been entirely clear to the enemy, the same, to some extent, could be said of the chase. At five hundred yards or so they were still too far away readily to pick out individuals from the mass – though the great fat man on the enormous horse well to the front could be none other than Graham of Rednock, cousin to Gorthie. What was evident was the motley nature of the force, comprising young and old, aged ploughmen and stripling herd-boys, bonnet-lairds and men who might be grooms or house-servants. All were mounted on as extraordinary a selection of horseflesh as ever assembled in one company, and appeared to be equipped with an armoury of which scythes and hayforks were the chief components. The MacGregor snorted strongly at the notion of such a crew daring to sally out against Rob Roy – though he reminded himself that there almost certainly would be many good muskets and pistols, and numerous stout hearts, amongst them quite sufficient to deal effectively with even three MacGregors and a woman.

The sudden yittering call of a curlew, high, clear and prolonged, from well above him on the hillside, answered almost immediately by a similar call from below, produced an extraordinary effect on Rob. His lounging was replaced by action. Raising two fingers to his mouth, he produced a series of shrill and penetrating whistles that shattered the balmy atmosphere of the afternoon. Again and again he whistled, and there was no doubt that all within a good mile's radius must hear him. Then, striking a posture on his garron, he began to point. And to shout.

His shouts were not wild or disonnected. Indeed, they were noticeably clear and were very distinctly amplified by his gestures. Obvious for all to see, he was directing various unseen persons to move from where they were hidden to somewhere else – and, by the sweeping and dramatic motions of his arms, to move fast in large numbers. Jabbing, pointing and signalling, he continued to bellow his commands. Any fool could see, even from a distance, that they meant close in and attack the pursuit from above and below.

Much yelling from hidden points up and down hill thereupon ensued. It seemed quite extraordinary that it could all be made by two men, one of them so preternaturally silent as MacAlastair. Savagely threatening those cries were, with 'Gregalach! Gregalach!' in various keys and intonations prominent amongst them. That terrible war-cry was worth a score of broadswords in itself.

Behind them, on the lower ground, the hunt came to an abrupt and most obvious halt. Despite its lack of form and cohesion, this step at least had every appearance of unanimity. A council-of-war, many councils-of-war, developed spontaneously.

Rob moved up on to an eminence from which he could, as it were, direct the battle. He was growing a little hoarse from all his shouting. His two henchmen must be still more so – and breathless too, for clearly they were darting about, out of sight, seeking to give the impression that their cries came from many men scattered over quite an area of the broken hillside.

A shot rang out. Startled, Rob glanced to his right – for the report had come, not from the ranks of Menteith nor yet from either of his busy lieutenants above or below, but from the westwards, in front of the now distant column of ponies. Anxiety flickered across the man's mind. Could it be an ambush of some sort – with Mary alone up there? Had he sent her into danger . . . ?

Another report echoed over the braes. It sounded like a pistol rather than a musket. Not the volleys of fire that might be expected in an ambush. More like a signal. . . . No cries or shouting sounded from there – if only his two collaborators would cease their wretched braying for a moment, to let him listen properly! It could not be Mary herself? She had no pistol. But she might just have borrowed one from Donald – Donald who was always armed to the teeth like any desperado? If it was herself . . . ?

Whatever it was, the shots had by no means put new heart into the halted and thoughtful pursuit. Increased agitation became plainly discernible. The noise of gunfire always sounds daunting to unprofessional warriors – more so than mere shoutings and slogans. The councils-of-war appeared to be breaking up.

Then a new noise smote Rob's anxious ears – also coming from the west – the drum-beat of hooves, many hooves, that rose swiftly to a rumble, to a thunder. There could be no question as to what that meant. Horses, garrons, in panic flight.

Biting his lip, Rob started forward. He could see, now, the confusion in front. Some part of the long string of ponies was still plodding ahead, but the leading beasts of the cavalcade had turned and were coming plunging back in scrabbling swaying alarm. Their train was no longer a column but a frantic stampede of various pairs and groups linked together and straining this way and that, their burdens jouncing about crazily. And above this tide of frightened horseflesh, like a raft riding a torrent, Mary MacGregor came, her arms waving wildly.

Cursing, Rob urged his mount onwards. And then, something about his wife's seat on her garron's back, the fact that she seemed to be shouting, gave him pause. He realised that she was actually whacking laden ponies on either side of her as she passed them. The man perceived that she was far from flotsam whirled helplessly on the spate of events, but indeed was directing the flood, probably was the creator of it. His held breath escaped from him in an exclamation, part oath, part chuckle, wholly appreciative. That was his Mary, to be sure.

If the effect of the woman's activities on her husband had been dramatic, the effect on the opposition was still more so. Possibly from their distance off they would not perceive that it was a woman, or just one person, at all; probably all that they saw, in the main, was a mass of horseflesh galloping over the hill towards them. Whether any large proportion of them realised that these were the same packhorses that had plodded patiently away from them, was not to be known. What certainly counted with most was that these horses were coming back, towards them – and in a hurry. That, added to the cumulative effect of the shouts and the shots, the gesticulations and the war-cries, completed the weight of evidence necessary to convince the vast majority there that the entire expedition was ill-advised, frought with danger, and likely to be unprofitable. Incoherent and unconcerted to the last, the company began to break up piecemeal, first in ones and twos, then in groups and parties. Soon all were streaming away whence they had come – only a lot faster – save for the little group of lairds at the front, whose dignity at least demanded that they give the others a start. No excessively lengthy start seemed to be called for, however, and with the dreaded slogan of 'Gregalach! Gregalach!' coming down to them with redoubled vigour and clarity, these too turned for home. There are occasions undoubtedly when even the instincts of bumpkins and ploughboys are to be trusted.

As Rob rode forward to halt Mary's headlong career – and that of such of the runaway garrons as he could influence – he was laughing hugely. But Mary did not laugh as she came up. Breathless she was, and flushed, her eyes brighter than the man had seen them for many a day; but she did not laugh back at him. She did not even smile.

'They are gone, I see,' she said. And if she had difficulty in controlling the enunciation of her words, she appeared to have none in keeping their tone cool and impersonal. 'For good?'

'Aye, they are gone, lass – thanks to yourself at the latter end. And I'll wager they won't turn again. *A graidh*, you were magnificent! You sent them running like a flock of sheep. Och, that was the woman I married, whatever!'

'It was not,' she answered, shortly. 'That woman is dead. I did little – only what it was obvious should be done. And what I did, I did that it might hurt the Grahams. That only.'

The man, his laughter gone, shook his red head. 'I don't understand you, Mary,' he said unhappily.

'No – you do not,' she agreed. 'Do you not think that it is time that you went and gathered together these foolish scattered beasts?'

Tugging at his beard Rob went, muttering.

With the help of MacAlastair and Donald they managed to get the dispersed and demoralised ponies back into some sort of order and on their way once more. A little of the grain was spilt, but it was only a small fraction of the whole. Donald was uproariously gleeful, but MacAlastair permitted himself no hint of elation – it was to be doubted indeed whether that man knew what elation was. So that, despite their bloodless victory and the notable haul of excellent cattle-feed acquired, it was a less jubilant party than might have been anticipated that found it's way back, without further interference, into the MacGregor mountains – for Rob had become markedly silent and preoccupied, and Mary had reverted to her former reserve.

In the anonymity of that night, many very willing hands took and distributed the treasured feeding-stuff to secret stores over a wide area, from which conveniently and judiciously it could be crushed and bruised and dolled out to the hungry MacGregor cattle. All acknowledged it as a Godsend. Since it could be anticipated that Montrose, in his wrath, would bring to bear every weapon at his wide disposal against his former partner, including Major Selby's redcoats at Inverarklet, Rob slipped away northwards again at first light next morning, duty done and his given word implemented. The last thing that he wanted was, by lingering in the neighbourhood, to bring down trouble on his clan's people.

On the journey back to Auch, Mary rode her own garron – and tended to ride it as far out of talking distance of her husband as she might. Yesterday's excitements might never have been. Rob did not enjoy defeat on any front, and it is to be feared that on this occasion he did not entirely succeed in hiding the fact.

It was perhaps as well that his political mission in Badenoch and Speyside was still far from completed.

CHAPTER THIRTEEN

ROB ROY put in another couple of months of fruitful activity on behalf of King James, amongst the clans of Badenoch, Inverness and Lochaber, in the doing of which, to some extent, he was able to put his personal problems behind him. Then, one thundery evening in mid-July, Gregor of Glengyle ferreted him out in a glen deep in the Chisholm country of Strathglass; his nephew had been on his trail for days, tracing him across the breadth of Highland Scotland. He came chock-full of news, local and national, that could not but affect his uncle's activities.

First of all, Queen Anne was very ill and sinking fast. A new Government had evolved in London, so-called Tory but in fact neither one thing nor another, a Government of time-servers and fence-sitters, more or less waiting to see which side in the dynastic struggle was likely to be the most advantageous to support. This was less than had been hoped, but at least it meant that no very vigorous anti-Jacobite measures were likely meantime; indeed, that the more public support for King James was evidenced, the more impressed and helpful this apology for a Government was likely to be. Mar, that expert jockey, had managed to change horses skilfully and timeously, and was still Secretary of State for Scotland; Montrose also retained the Privy Seal – but he was less happily placed, his background being too notoriously anti-Jacobite. Moreover, General the Duke of Argyll, Red John of the Battles, had been brought back from Spain and appointed Commander-in-Chief in Scotland – and though he was a firm Whig, he was also a personal enemy of Montrose. The Campbells and the Grahams were ever at loggerheads.

Already this situation, Gregor revealed, had had its repercussions, in Scotland in general, and in the MacGregor country in particular. No longer were the military forces, now under Argyll's command, at the beck and call of the Lord Privy Seal and available to advance his private enterprises. The garrison at Inverarklet, guarding the fort-builders, had been cut down by two-thirds and Major Selby transferred elsewhere. Work on the fort itself still went on, and was indeed nearing completion, but the military escort's attitude towards the MacGregors had changed noticeably. No longer was there oppression or any parade of authority. In consequence, the Gregorach were reverting contentedly to their normal activities, and Rob's orders about not being aggressive or provocative had become out of date and pointless. Again, rumours of an imminent Jacobite rising were filling the country, and since the MacGregors knew that they would be in the thick of anything of the sort, a martial and defiant spirit was becoming predominant. Without hinting that his own chieftainly authority was insufficient to control his people, Gregor indicated that it was perhaps time that Rob Roy came home.

Moreover there was another aspect of the impingement of the murky politics of the day upon the Gregorach. Since Archibald MacGregor of Kilmanan's presumed death in Ireland in 1708, there had been no High Chief of Clan Alpine, the chiefly line of Glenstrae dying with him. Rob was Captain of the clan, yes – but that was a different thing. Now, this curious Government in London was seeking to buy the allegiance of the Highlands by offering pensions to the clan chiefs, at the rate of over four thousand pounds Scots per annum – £360 sterling. Alastair MacGregor of Balhaldies, who was one of the claimants to be senior cadet of Clan Alpine, thought it a pity that such splendid largesse should pass good men by when it could be had, as it were, for the picking up. Admittedly its acceptance was meant to insure that the recipient did not join in any rising against the Government – but that was not a matter that need weigh heavily with sensible men. Accordingly Balhaldies proposed that he should be elected High Chief of Clan Alpine, in the room or the late Kilmanan, and he in turn would agree to apportion out the pension amongst the other senior cadets who might otherwise be his rivals. For this laudable purpose there must be a council, a meeting of the chief men of the clan – and Rob of course must be there. In fact, it was to be left to Rob to convene and preside at the meeting, as Captain.

Rob smiled grimly at this information – for he did not trust Alastair of Balhaldies much further than he could see him. But it was true that the clan needed its High Chief, for various reasons – more especially with its Captain outlawed. And Balhaldies was a cunning fellow, highly intelligent, educated, and married to an influential wife, a daughter of Lochiel, no less. And her brother, Alan Cameron, was powerful in court circles – which in such times might have its advantages. They might do a lot worse for their figure-head – so long as Rob himself remained Captain and in effective control of the clan. He might come south, as Gregor suggested, and amongst other things convene this meeting.

Rob had every intention of returning south fairly soon anyhow, of course – for the pursuance of his quarter-day vendetta with the Grahams. It would soon be Lammas term, the first day of August, three months on from Whit-sun, and it would be a pity to disappoint anyone. He had naturally been turning over in his mind sundry possibilities in this connection – though undoubtedly Montrose and his minions on this occasion would be taking every precaution. It all seemed to mean that he must travel south just a little earlier than he had intended. . . .

So, since Rob's commitments and negotiations with the

northern chiefs did not permit of any hasty and unceremonious breakings-off, Gregor was dispatched forthwith to the south again, with various instructions, his uncle promising to follow in a few days' time. It occurred to Rob that Mary's peculiar state of mind, which was probably the result of too much solitary meditation, might well benefit from some enforced company of her own kind. He told Gregor, therefore, to summon, not a clan council, but a meeting of the principal MacGregor cadets, chieftains of septs such as Glengyle's own Clan Dougal Ciar, for Auch itself, to consider the matter of Balhaldies. And since the Lammas Quarter-day fell on the first of August, and Rob was liable to be busy about then, let the meeting be called for, say, five days previously; that is, for the twenty-seventh day of July. That would give Gregor twelve days in which to make the arrangements – time enough, surely. As an afterthought, Rob mentioned that he had better warn his aunt in passing, that she would be having visitors.

*   *   *

Rob Roy as it happened, delayed after a riotous night with young MacIan of Glencoe, was the last of the select band of Gregorach notables to arrive at the little house of Auch under Beinn Dorain's frowning brow – with something of a frowning brow himself, as a consequence of a splitting head; young MacIan, with bloody memories to drown, was a hard man to outdrink.

The company awaiting him was colourful and resounding. It included Gregor MacGregor of Roro – who probably had a better title to the High Chiefship than Balhaldies, but who lacked the necessary ambition – and his son; Duncan of Dunan, and his son; Donald of Coiletter; Malcolm of Marchfield; Gregor of Bracklie and his sons – another possible contender; Gregor in Ardmacmoine; and of course young Gregor of Glengyle himself. Curiously enough Alastair of Balhaldies was not present – though he sent numerous apologies, assurances and affirmations; Rob Roy was neither astonished nor seriously disappointed at this. Balhaldies was a shrewd man if hot-tempered, and probably reckoned that in that proud and touchy company his case would go better lacking his presence.

Mary seemed to be coping with the invasion with a cool competence that failed nothing in the demands of hospitality, yet conceded nothing in warmth and approval. No man there failed to be aware of the fact. Her long-absent husband she greeted as one more guest to whom, unfortunately, courtesies must be extended. Rob should not have been disappointed in this either, by now – but he was.

He hid it, of course – better perhaps than he managed to hide the effects of MacIan's brand of hospitality. He turned to greet the galaxy of red MacGregor tartans and eagles' feathers, gallantly.

'Gentlemen, you do my heart and spirit a power of good – as Royal's our Race you do!' he cried. 'A nobler array of our Highland spirit and valour never assembled together, I declare. Welcome to this poor hovel – all that his Grace of Montrose has left to a humble but honest cattle-dealer.'

There was considerable outcry at this sally, and the visitors obviously began to feel more at ease. Since the little house patently was quite incapable of accommodating the twelve of them, not to mention their attendants – for each had felt it necessary to support his style and dignity by bringing at least two running gillies – Rob proposed that they hold their deliberations on the greensward outside, the weather being fine. This was another relief, for the somewhat daunting presence of their lovely but difficult hostess was less potent out of doors, undoubtedly. Moreover, Rob had taken the precaution of bringing along with him a pony's load of liquid refreshment, the distilled perfection of various glens on his route – including that of Glen Coe – and this quickly served to thaw out any residual stiffness. Eloquence very soon began to mark the day, and continued to wax and flourish increasingly, like an exotic bloom in the smile of the sun – for the Gregorach were ever as notable in talk as in action. Only Roro, who inclined to the pompous, perhaps failed to measure up to the full flowering of MacGregor oratory. Rob, who himself barely sipped at the regalement, made a point of plying Roro's horn lavishly until such time as pomposity faded into incoherence.

When he judged the atmosphere to be approximately right and suitable, Rob turned to business. 'You all will be aware that Balhaldies has gained the notion that he might adorn the office of High Chief of Clan Alpine,' he mentioned. 'Likewise that the government is after looking for chiefs to give fine pensions to, out of the depths of its wisdom. Now, I am not the man to be saying that I agree entirely with Balhaldies – nor even to be sure in my mind that the pensions will be paid for very long. But it seems to me that, as practical men, we might do well to support Balhaldies in this matter. I do not necessarily believe that he will make any heaven born chief, see you – any more than I recognise his claim as being established. Roro here, or Bracklie, or young Glengyle, all have as good a claim, no doubt, as chieftains of septs as senior as Balhaldies. But . . .'

'My God, yes!'

'Damnation – that is the truth!'

'Yes. But there is more to it than just that, my friends,' Rob went on. 'Such a chief would be of great value to the clan – more than many hundreds of pounds of pensions. A chief who can speak for the clan in high places – as I cannot do, being outlawed, and a humble man moreover. A chief who moves in circles close to Edinburgh and London, who hears of moves and intrigues long before I can do so. How many can do that?'

There was no answer.

'And another way of it. This rising that is projected – if it is a success, that will be fine. Och, just fine. The clan will come well out of it. But it was to be failing, now – and risings *can* be failing, mind you – that would be a pity. The Gregorach would be in trouble, then. It would pay the clan, in such case, to be having a High Chief that the Government could be making an example of . . . if you understand me? Instead of the clan itself. Och, they like a man, those ones, that they can punish, instead of a whole clan. Easier it is. Don't I know it! One man then might save many.'

'*Dia* – you do not mean a, a sort of a *sacrifice*!' his nephew exclaimed, shocked once more. 'Not that, Rob?'

'To be a sacrifice can be no light honour, Greg. Does your Bible not tell you so?' the older man answered.

'But deliberately to use a man so . . . ?'

'Tush, lad – if a man would bear the honour and title of High Chief of Clan Alpine, then surely he must be prepared to give all for the clan. The style has no meaning, otherwise. Just as I, being Captain, must take the forefront of the battle, and risk death first, so much the High Chief, in his sphere, be bearing a similar risk. Glory never lacks its dangers. I but remind all here of the fact.'

Gregor was silent, though others proclaimed hearty agreement.

'The clan is what counts whatever – in this as in all else,' Rob declared vigorously. 'I charge you not to forget it.'

'Rob has the right of it,' Bracklie substantiated loudly. 'It is the clan first, for sure. Up, the Gregorach!'

'Aye.'

'Then, I take it you will not challenge Balhaldies appointment, Bracklie?' Rob asked, mild of a sudden.

'Me? Och, no – not me, Rob.'

'Nor you, Roro?'

Roro was in no position to do more than blink owlishly, but his son shook an urgent head for him.

'And what say you, Dunan?' That was merely a gesture,

though a calculated one, for Dunan was far out of line for the chiefship.

'I say let Balhaldies have it, Rob. So long as you are Captain, it matters not.'

Coiletter and Marchfield, both far-out cousins of Rob's own, and therefore junior to Gregor of Glengyle, looked at their young chieftain – as did his uncle. That man of honour shook his blond head.

'I do not seek the High Chiefship on this occasion,' he said slowly. 'But not because I would see Balhaldies made scapegoat for the clan. If our enterprise for the King should fail – which God forbid – then we all must pay the price equally.'

'Bravo! Spoken like a hero!' Rob declared, but dryly. And swiftly, 'Then we are all agreed. The thing is unanimous. Balhaldies it is. We will draw up a paper to the effect that Alastair of Balhaldies is hereby elected and appointed rightful, lawful and undoubted Head, Chief and Chieftain of our clan of MacGregor, commonly called Clan Alpine, *et hoc genus omne* and we will all sign it, as is proper. Drink up, gentlemen – for this business is thirsty work. I will get me quill and ink. . . .'

In the house as Rob sought the writing materials, Gregor came to him.

'That was ill done, I think,' he said quietly.

'Do you, then? I am sorry for that. And how would you have done it, lad?'

'Honestly, I hope. Without ill-will to the man who will be our chief. Without appeal to, to the baser instincts of these others.'

'So! And you think that by such lofty means you would ever have prevailed upon these prideful men to abate one jot of their own pretensions? Think you that they could ever be got to agree to forgo their own claims and dignity, save by playing upon what you priggishly name their baser instincts? *Dia* – for all I taught you, you know not men yet!'

'I know that men can be easily corrupted, yes. You taught me that, too. But not that *we* should be the corrupters!'

'Save us, boy – enough of this! Mind your tongue. Can you not see it – we play for high stakes, for survival as a clan. A clan that is hated in high places, proscribed, all but landless – doomed unless her leaders are farseeing, cunning, single-minded . . .'

'Single-minded, say you? Or double-tongued?'

'Aye, single-minded. Where the clan is concerned – always.'

'For the clan, then you would forget honour?'

'Honour! Lord – always you prate of honour! What is honour? Answer you me that. No two men will answer that alike. Aye, for the clan, Greg, I will do all things – all things that my conscience permits.'

'Your conscience, now! *You* speak of conscience!'

'Aye, I do so,' his uncle said, sombrely. 'But *my* conscience – not yours, boy! A man's conscience, not a stripling's. Now – leave me to cherish it, if I may, for sweet mercy's sake!'

As he turned his head, in an imperious gesture towards the door, his eyes met those of Mary as she stood there behind them. It was Rob's that fell.

Muttering into his red beard, he stamped outside behind his nephew. He was scarcely at his best or sweetest, that day – MacIan of Glencoe's fault, perhaps.

*　　*　　*

His manner changed noticeably, after he had dashed off for signature an affirmation much briefer and less florid than was usually considered suitable. Rob set about collecting from the assembled company the numbers of men whom they might provide for the MacGregor contingent of the Jacobite army. In this case he adopted a technique, Gregor noted, markedly different from that he had used amongst the clan chiefs of the north and west, not merely refraining from using mutual jealousy and pride to work up the numbers promised, but actually damping down undue ardour. Numbers were not everything, he pointed out. A good well-disciplined, well-trained, compact force for special duties, was a much more valuable contribution to King James's cause than any mere swollen rabble. Let them be selective. A total of three hundred would perhaps meet the case – a handy, manageable number.

Keeping the numbers down to three hundred, as it happened proved to be quite a task – for Gregor himself had proposed to bring out fully two hundred. But Rob was adamant – and autocratic – and as Captain of the Clan claimed that decision lay with him. At length he lost patience with the business, declared that he would inform them all, in due course, exactly what numbers he would require of each, and announced that meantime he required to rest himself. He was tired. Food for their journey home his wife would provide. But if any of them would see some sport, he added, as an afterthought – let them meet with him in the Pass of Aberfoyle two days hence at sundown. He thought that on that occasion he could promise them better entertainment than he had done here.

Gregor, for one, wondered. He could not remember his uncle ever complaining of feeling tired before.

*   *   *

Rob Roy usually was as good as his word. Two evenings later, he did not fail such of his fellows as had accepted his invitation to entertainment. Most of them had come, intrigued – all, indeed, except old Roro from Glen Lyon.

The promised sport was not confined to the wooded defile of the Pass of Aberfoyle; it proved to be neither more nor less than the greatest raid that had ever taken place upon the much-harried fair land of Menteith, the ancient

Graham earldom that was now Montrose's. Rob had worked hard and fast at the organisation of the affair – reassured by the knowledge that it was changed days for the Lord Privy Seal, and that his own old friend and patron, Argyll the Commander-in-Chief, probably would not for his part frown too heavily on any high-spirited cantrips by the Mac-Gregors, so long as they were merely directed against his personal foe and rival Montrose and were innocently un-seditious in character. From what Rob had learned, his own people of Inversnaid, Craigroyston and Glen Arklet were in need of his firm directing hand, also. This night's enter-tainment, therefore, had a dual objective.

In consequence, for the first time since Rob's outlawry, large numbers of MacGregors were involved – though dis-creetly, of course, and not so that they would be evident or readily identifiable. They were not even evident in the Pass of Aberfoyle for the visitors to see, being scattered by then far and wide, in little groups, over a great area of that green level country that surrounded the vast waterlogged wilder-ness of the Flanders Moss and the Lake of Menteith. Some few men there were in the Pass – no more than a dozen – whose efforts would be engaged near at hand, and who therefore must await the cover of darkness.

Rob entertained his guests first at the little ale-house on the MacGregor side of the Pass, until the shades of night were well advanced. Then, mounted on garrons, he led them quietly – or as quietly as he could enforce – through the shadows, slipping to the south of the Clachan of Aber-foyle and heading eastwards into the low country of Gart-more and Shannochill – Graham territory. But they were not provocative, avoiding all habitations. Presently the ground beneath their garrons' hooves became wetter and wetter, and the great empty flats of Flanders Moss spread dark and mysterious before them. Rob ordered his party to ride exactly in file behind him, treading only where he trod. None were so foolish as to disobey, for the name and nature of this place were only too well known and respected.

Flanders Moss was a land unto itself – a land that consisted largely of water. Covering an area of some fifty square miles, where the stripling Forth, new won out of its confining womb of mountains, poured out extravagantly into a huge level plain so low-lying as to be in places only a foot or two above the level of the distant sea, it became a vast trap for the drainage of hill ranges to north, west and south. A wilderness of endlessly twisting, coiling rivers and streams and burnlets, of lochs and ponds and pools, of meres and bogs and slimy morasses, it remained useless, shunned of men, feared even, empty save for the wildfowl and the flitting roe-deer – unknown and unknowable. Save to Rob Roy MacGregor, that is – and therefore to MacAlastair his shadow, and to a lesser extent to Gregor. Rob all his life had revelled in the place's strange atmosphere and loneliness – and some knowledge of its secrets was part of the learning that, as Tutor of Glengyle, he had imparted to his pupil. For it held secrets worth knowing to bold men. There were routes, tortuous and intricate, through that quaking emerald treachery, islands of firm ground amongst the endless reed-beds, fords in the still network of waterways, even causeways sunken beneath the dark surface – for in times beyond ken it had served as a last place of refuge from the invader. Here even the Roman legions had come to a final halt, baffled at last.

On this occasion, of course, Rob had no intention of penetrating really deep into the benighted fastnesses. He was only concerned meantime with one comparatively small north-western corner of it, known as the Gartrenich Moss. Into this he now led his careful following, twisting this way and that, frequently doubling almost back on his path, pausing every few yards to align his crazy course by unseen landmarks. He did not speak, so keen was his concentration – and none sought to disturb him. Only the squatter and quack of disturbed wildfowl, the creak and whistle of pinnions and the lonely calling of the night birds broke the hush.

After something over a mile of this plowtering, by which time all concerned were wet and mud-spattered to their waists, mounted as they were, Rob called a halt. They found that they were actually based on solid ground, and though in the darkness it was difficult to perceive their position, it became evident that they were on a fairly extensive island in the marshes. Trees of a sort grew here, willow and alder scrub, instead of the man-high sedges and bulrushes.

Refreshments had been brought along, and Rob urged his guests to make themselves comfortable. Meanwhile, he and Gregor, with MacAlastair, had a night's work to do.

That was no exaggeration. The three of them had few idle moments for the rest of that night. Separately they each made their way back through the moss to previously appointed positions, not on the outer edge of it, but, as it were, on an inner secret ring. To these points, north, west and south, presently began to arrive mud-stained weary cattle, in the care of MacGregor gillies, from small parcels of four or half-a-dozen to fair-sized herds – beef-cattle, stirks, breeding-stock and heifers. And as soon as a sufficient number was made up, a gillie was left to meet new arrivals, and the guide, be he Rob, Gregor or MacAlastair, set off with the rest, deeper into the quagmire, to lead the beasts by devious watery routes to the chosen island in the centre – a tiring, trying task that demanded an infinity of patience, though indeed the cattle seemed to have a better instinct than had men for where to tread. At their destination they were turned loose; there was lush pasture in plenty amongst the surrounding water-meadows – and no danger of beasts straying far.

All the night the cattle continued to arrive, so that soon Rob's guests were enrolled to do duty as guides for limited stretches. None complained, for nothing appealed more to

MacGregor fancies, high and low, than the handling of other men's cattle – as Rob well knew.

By the first rosy flush of dawn on the thirtieth day of July, the MacGregors were all slipping away quietly out of the Flanders Moss, through the white early-morning mists, to their several homes, duty done. They left behind them under the supervision of a mere two or three watchful gillies, fully a couple of thousand head of prime cattle, the cream of Menteith's livestock. No tenant of any substance had been spared. It had been done quietly, advisedly, solicitously; no heads had been broken, no roofs lit, no woman harried – and where foolish opposition had unfortunately been offered, the shouting of varied clan slogans other than MacGregor, and yells of Balquhidder! Balquhidder! had served to make rash and sleep-bemused farmers think again, and think moreover along suitably mistaken lines. None would be able to swear that it was Gregorach work, any more than any would be able to assert just whence their beasts had disappeared – even though some might have a shrewd idea; that Moss would hold its secret from more potent folk than these, for an entire army could remain hidden in those endless reed-beds, and if the lowing of a querulous beast or two sounded faintly across the miles of sedge, that provided no uncomfortable proof for peaceful husbandmen who valued their own skins.

So it was that, two days later, on Lammas Term-day, the first of August, the Duke of Montrose's representatives – excluding John Graham of Killearn once more – escorted this time by bands of specially hired bullies in lieu of the military, were met by a solid phalanx of vociferously protesting tenants, none of whom had the wherewithal to pay their rents – all, indeed demanding protection from their landlord whose duty it was to guard and insure them from such disgraceful spoliation and pillage. This was the quarter before the cattle-sales, when rents were necessarily paid in livestock – so that the factors could nowise obtain cash instead of kind, bluster as they would. Sadly frustrated, at each assembly-point they were forced to turn away empty-handed. No MacGregor showed his face in all Menteith.

But Rob was not finished yet. He had no particular quarrel with Montrose's tenantry, as such, and the cattle taken from them far outvalued their quarter's rents. Accordingly on the next two or three nights after term-day, there was considerable if unadvertised movement of livestock northwards by devious ways from the vicinity of Flanders Moss through the mountain passes into Breadalbane. And thereafter, the word spread around Menteith, started who knows how, but sustained and factual, that the missing cattle would all be put up for sale at Killin in a few days time; it might well be seemly and profitable for former owners to be present.

Killin, of course, up at the head of Loch Tay, was well inside the Highland Line, indeed the capital of the Camp-bell kingdom of Breadalbane, under the very walls of the Earl's castle of Finlarig, and so safely out of reach of Mont-rose. And there, a few days later, at a special sale, the dis-puted livestock changed hands once again. It was a very special sale indeed. Rob Roy, though unseen, very much dominated the proceedings. And though large numbers of spectators had turned up, bidding was low, almost non-existent. In fact, it became known at an early stage in the proceedings that any offers for these beasts, from others than their former owners, not only would be frowned upon but simply would not be accepted. In consequence of which the Menteith tenants, or their representatives, were able to buy back their missing stock at mere token figures, with none other than themselves bidding – a quite extraordinary proceeding. Cattle that day made the lowest prices ever recorded in Scots agrarian history, before or since – such token moneys being merely to cover the cost of transportation, as one whisper put it, while other sugges-ted that the small proceeds were to form a contribution to

King James's war-chest. It was a mysterious affair altogether, and many must have wondered at the whys and wherefores of it – as they were meant to do. But the results were plain for all to recognise, and to draw their own conclusions. The Menteith tenants were soon all driving their errant beasts home through the passes of Glen Ogle and Strathyre – with the aid of a quite surprising number of suddenly available Highland volunteer drovers – at a cost to each which worked out at almost exactly the amount of their quarter's rent, a rent which they had nowise been able to pay to their ducal landlord. Nor would Montrose be able to claim any sort of back-payment, for each tenant could justifiably assert that he had had to buy back his own stock, at whatever price he chose fit to state, for no receipts or figures were produced on this occasion. All the land seethed with the story, its refinements and elaborations and mirthful implications. Never had a great landlord and national figure been made to look more foolish, inept, and utterly helpless than his Grace James of Montrose.

Rob would have admitted the affair's over-elaboration; but then it was all planned with the multiple purpose of humiliating Montrose to the utmost degree, rather than merely depriving him of his rents; of involving John Campbell Earl of Breadalbane to some extent, if possible; of making a combined operation for his MacGregors, to demonstrate to them that the Rob Roy hand was once more firmly on the helm, and undisciplined private enterprise no longer to be tolerated; and of offering the Gregorach chieftains not only the promised entertainment but an intimation that though Alastair of Balhaldies might be elected High Chief, Rob Roy MacGregor remained undisputedly the master of the clan.

There is no doubt that little of this ambitious demonstration missed its mark. Certainly it would be talked about and magnified and chuckled over when many others of its perpetrators' more valuable exploits were gone and forgotten. There was only the one man on whom it all fell rather flat – and that was Rob himself. Though he carried on with his scheme, as planned, to the end, his preoccupation was apt to be elsewhere. Partly up at Auchinchisallan, where his manhood suffered continual defeat, but more urgently even further away; for that Lammas Term-day of 1714 was conspicuous for another event altogether. On August the first Queen Anne died in London, and word to that effect from Nathaniel Hooke reached Rob Roy in the midst of his stirring activities.

CHAPTER FOURTEEN

WELL might Rob be preoccupied. So much was to hinge on
the Queen's death – poor, weak, unlamented Anne. All the
Jacobite plans were geared to this event – the sudden
vacancy of the throne. All Rob's missions had been to prepare for action now. This was the moment of fate.

And yet nothing seemed to happen. Everything went on
exactly as before. No orders came for Rob from Hooke or
anyone else. On his own authority he sent orders round the
MacGregor chieftains, requiring them to have given numbers of men armed and ready to join him at a moment's
notice. No doubt other chiefs who had given their word to
him were doing the same. But as for orders, directions and
declarations from the centre, nothing happened.

A peculiar inertia, indeed, seemed to have stricken both
sides in the dynastic tug-of-war. Perhaps the heat of high
August had something to do with it. The feeble semi-Tory
Government in London sat still in office and did nothing,
apparently only awaiting a new monarch to appoint a successor to it. Its days were numbered, anyway, for Anne, unpredictable and unreliable to the end, had on her death-bed
handed the Treasurer's white staff of office to the Whig
Duke of Shrewsbury. Constitutionally, therefore, the Whig
and Hanoverian party may have had authority to take over
in the interim. But there were doubts and hesitations there
also, as well as bitter jealousies. The old Electress Sophia,
grand-daughter of James Sixth and First, had died only a
few weeks before Anne, and it was said that her son George
of Hanover was extremely reluctant to leave his Germanic

fleshpots for a disunited country that had a bad habit of dethroning and even executing its kings. He temporised. In the meantime a Regency Council of eighteen noblemen of England, with seven Lord Justices, sat over the affairs of state and twiddled their thumbs likewise. Though they did issue a proclamation ordering the payment of one hundred thousand pounds sterling to anyone who should seize and secure the Pretender should he land in Great Britain or Ireland. This was practically the only official notice taken of James, Prince of Wales, that some called King James the Eighth and Third.

All this was unedifying, but less fraught with consequence than was the inactivity of the Jacobite side – for, after all, these people represented the *status quo*, and as ever possession amounted to the major part of the law. It was up to James's supporters to take advantage of the situation. But this, despite all the plans, no one in authority seemed ready to do. James himself, instead of sailing forthwith, issued an erudite and historically accurate Declaration to the world, setting forth his undoubted right to the three thrones of his fathers, and then went from Lorraine to the French court – but to obtain formal recognition of his new status rather than to raise any French expeditionary force apparently. The Duke of Berwick, an illegitimate half-brother of himself and of Anne, and a professional soldier, whom it was expected would be appointed Jacobite commander-in-chief, was not sent – it was said because the ageing King Louis refused to release him, as a French Marshal and subject. In London, Bolingbroke was still nominally Prime Minister, but he had quarrelled with Oxford and did not seem to be prepared to act on James's behalf alone. No others of that curious administration were of sufficient statue, vigour or Jacobite leanings – save perhaps Mar. And Mar was Mar.

Bobbing John was the biggest question-mark of all. Despite all his intrigues and time-serving, he chose this moment to embrace conjugal bliss for the second time. A few days before the Queen's eventual expiry, he married the Lady Frances Pierrepont, a Whig, and daughter of the powerful Duke of Kingston. Thereafter, though he was still Secretary of State for Scotland, he deserted high politics apparently for choicer delights, and no more was heard of him meantime.

In Scotland, no one was appointed leader. Nathaniel Hooke was an emissary, not a commander, and of the many Jacobite lords and chiefs, none was given any authority over another. King George was proclaimed in Edinburgh by the Lord Advocate.

Restless in their mountains, the MacGregors fretted and fumed, waiting while the ship of state swung this way and that, rudderless. It was all ominously like what had happened in 1707 and 1708.

Rob sent urgent messages to Hooke, in Angus. He went and saw old Sir Hugh Patterson of Bannockburn. He himself proclaimed King James at the Cross of Crieff – and though not all cheered him, none shouted him down.

So passed an unsatisfactory and uneasy August.

Then, in mid-September, word swept the country that George of Hanover at least had made up his mind. He had declared himself to be King, dismissed Bolingbroke as Prime Minister at long range from Germany, and had actually set sail for England. Now there could be no more holding back, surely? The issue must be put to the test before it was too late.

But no. Word came that James had dispatched £4,000 in specie, to aid his brave supporters in Scotland – but nothing more militant transpired. George arrived, unopposed if not riotously welcomed, at Greenwich, with his extraordinary entourage of fat German mistresses, and sat down stodgily on the throne. A man of no enthusiasms himself, he appeared not to notice the lack of the commodity in his reception. The fact that he knew no English, nor had intention of learning any, undoubtedly helped. Gott save the Koenig!

Then occurred an incident that might have changed the course of history – an incident variously interpreted. John, twenty-seventh Earl of Mar, premier earl of Scotland, Hereditary Keeper of Stirling Castle, and his Majesty's Secretary of State for his ancient Kingdom of Scotland, emerged from domestic felicity and presented himself before the occupant of the throne. And Majesty did not see him, would not look upon him, turned its dumpy back upon him – and a day or two later had him relieved of his seals of office. George's manners were bad, admittedly – but this almost seemed to indicate that he had had better information services over in Hanover than had been realised. Mar, seasoned trimmer as he might be, could not smile away such studied and public insult from the source of power and patronage. Within the week word was reaching the north that he was now body and soul for King James and would in due course put himself at the head of his Majesty's loyal subjects in Scotland. The Jacobite cause had at last, it appeared, found its reluctant and belated champion.

Rob Roy, when he heard this intelligence, stormed out and sought solace in the empty hills.

Rob had been living, since Lammas, in a new cave, less remote and more convenient than his old one on Cruach Tuirc – indeed, less than a mile over the hill from his burned-out house of Inversnaid, on the wooded side of Loch Lomond. Here he was entirely free, yet could face a winter with some degree of comfort; he could keep an eye on his own folk, and at the same time on the small and now very unambitious garrison at Inverarklet guarding the fort-builders. The fort itself was practically completed, most of the masons having gone, and only the carpenters remaining on interior work. On this too, needless to say, Rob kept an eye.

Such was the position at the onset of winter of 1714, one eventful year after Rob's outlawry and the shattering of his home.

Donald MacGregor was waiting with the news when Rob returned to his cave after a visit to Glen Gyle, one early evening of November.

'A man has come,' he said excitedly. 'The chief contractor man it is no less, they say. All the way from Edinburgh. For the fort. They do be saying that the fort is finished now. This man – Nasmyth or suchlike the name is – has now to be inspecting it, and to give it to the soldiers, some way.'

'Nasmyth? Yes, that was the contractor's name,' Rob nodded. 'He is here, then? Now? Where? And how did he get here, at all?'

'At the damned fort he is, now. He came with six redcoats. They were after meeting him at Aberfoyle. Some of our people followed them, and brought me word. The soldiers were from Inverarklet, and they went to meet him. They were saying to Callum the Inn, at Aberfoyle – while they were waiting for the man, see you – that they would not be shivering in their tents many nights more, but would be snug in the fort.'

'So-o-o!' Rob tapped his knee, in thought. It had come to a decision for him too, now. He had been wondering about that fort. And hesitating – which was not like Rob Roy. He had been hoping, rather feebly perhaps, that with the coming of hard weather again, the military might return whence they had come, with the workmen, until the winter was over. If he himself did not provoke them. They had been little trouble to each other, that summer. Argyll clearly was for *avoiding* trouble, offering no provocation to his old protégé. But this news changed the situation.

'If Nasmyth has come it can only be to hand over the completed fort to the soldiers,' he agreed, as much to himself at to Donald and MacAlastair. 'It is still the contractor's property – och, he will not be able to get his money for it until he has the local commander's acceptance of it in good order.'

The others nodded.

'If the soldiers are for moving into it, out of their tents, then that means that they are going to garrison it all the time – that they are not going to be leaving us for the winter. And, *Dia* – they will be a nuisance in there, whatever!'

He was not contradicted about that, either. 'I have wondered, my own self, why you have not swept that fort away again before this,' Donald admitted. 'The thing is an insult, just, to our clan.'

'Aye,' Rob said heavily. 'I will tell you why. I like it less than you do – but it has been the lesser of two evils. *Mac Cailean Mhòr* – Argyll – has been using me gently, see you. As is only right and just. To strike at Montrose is good and well – that is a *private* matter, and Argyll need not be concerned. But to strike at this fort is different – even though Montrose it was who ordered it to be built. It is for the Government, the fort – for the military. If I should strike at it, Argyll likely cannot be looking the other way, even if he would. We do not want an army of red-coats here at Inversnaid again. Not when we ourselves may be off to the wars any day.'

There was silence in the cave, now.

Rob was tapping at that hairy knee again, a sure sign of deep cogitation. 'And yet, and yet . . .' he said. 'The fort is an ill thing, there – and could be dangerous for the King James's cause, garrisoned against him. I am wondering – wondering whether Argyll would take it less hard, maybe, if the fort was to suffer some damage *before* the military took it over, at all – while it was still by way of being the contractor's property? Och, he might just prefer it that way, see you!'

'But . . . but . . . the man is here,' Donald pointed out. 'It is too late, Rob.'

'Maybe not too late yet. The man Nasmyth will need tomorrow for his inspection. He will not hand over the place until tomorrow, I'm thinking. We have tonight.'

'Tonight!' the younger man cried. 'But can we do it? We cannot get the clan roused, in the time . . .'

'There will be no rousing of the clan,' Rob declared sternly. 'This is against the Government, you will remember not just Montrose. I will not have the clan involved – not until there is a general rising. Myself, I dealt with the fort before – I must needs do so again.'

'But, how? The fort is strong, now. Barred and locked at night. It is not just foundations any more. . . .'

'Wheesht, you! Hush your chatter man, and let me think. That one – the man Nasmyth from Edinburgh – will not have much love for tents of a November night, I'm thinking . . . ?'

*   *   *

There were lights shining from the small barred windows of the fort on the top of Tom na Bairlinn that night, a thing that had not been seen before – for the builders throughout had been taken down at nightfall to the safety of the army camp at Inverarklet and the place locked up, with two sentries posted. Those two sentries still patrolled faithfully, patiently, after almost a year's fruitless vigil.

Their fall, that night, was not exactly simultaneous, nor was it entirely soundless – though fortunately it was the second victim who emitted a small squawk and so did not alarm the first. This lack of fullest synchronisation was occasioned wholly by Rob's insistence that on no account must either of the sentries be killed. Half-hearted methods always tended to be the more clumsy.

A little later – but not so late that the lights in the fort were out and all bedded down – two red-coated figures came up to the great iron-studded and barred door, thumping thereon with their musket-butts and calling to be admitted. It was Rob's voice that did the calling, however, in his best Cockney.

The visitors had been prepared for a certain amount of questioning, and Rob was ready with his answers. But such were not required. A lamp was brought to the iron-grating, its light was shone out, less than efficiently, on the two uniformed men. Then, its bearer apparently satisfied, the bolts were drawn and the small wicket door opened.

What followed happened more swiftly than it may be described. The two red-coated figures stepped within, one at either side, and Rob Roy leapt in between them, pistol in one hand and broadsword in the other. The door slammed shut behind him. A musket-butt shattered the lamp upheld by the door-opener – who proved to be the foreman mason – and left only the firelight's flicker to illuminate the scene within.

In the main room of the fort three men stood staring, over by the fire on its wide hearth – and none were in uniform. If there were other men elsewhere in the building, the noise had not brought them out. These three clearly had just jumped up, startled, from a table by the fire, whereon lay papers and tankards.

Rob strode into the room, eyes busy. 'Your pardon, gentlemen, for this intrusion,' he jerked. 'Sometimes I must be more precipitate than I would wish. Do not be alarmed – no hurt is intended towards you. Tell me only – is there anyone else in this building, at all?'

None of the three moved lips to speak, but one managed to shake his head.

Rob came forward, and laid his weapons on the table, as though no longer required. 'My name is MacGregor of Inversnaid,' he mentioned modestly. 'You may not have heard of me – but, och, it is my land on which you stand.' He bowed towards the better dressed of the trio, a heavy red-faced man with spectacles. 'You, sir, I take to be Mr Nasmyth, of Edinburgh?'

The other still did not answer. He was looking now past Rob to the two red-coated imposters, obviously bewildered.

'Ah – I see. These are friends of mine,' the Highlandman explained. 'I am fortunate in my friends. But sit down, gentlemen. It may be sometime yet before I need request you to vacate this building.'

Mr Nasmyth drew a sharp breath at this. 'What . . . what do you mean, sir?' he got out unsteadily.

'Just that it will be necessary for me, unfortunately, to demolish these excellent premises that you have so efficiently erected, sir. You see, contrary to all law and civility, my permission was not sought when it was decided rashly to build this place on my land. As proprietor here, I find it an inconvenience and an obstruction to the view. Therefore I must take steps to clear it away. It grieves me to lay violent hands on such excellent craftsmanship.' Here Rob bowed to the foreman mason, the foreman carpenter and the little clerk of works, who had elected to spend the night with their employer going over the plans and estimates. 'But perhaps you were remiss in not ascertaining that the land had been properly conveyed by me to . . . to your clients. Och, a small thing – but important, whatever!'

'But . . . my God – you cannot do this!' Nasmyth cried. 'You cannot . . .'

'On the contrary, sir, I can – and shall! My only regret is that I have insufficient gunpowder available to do it with fitting thoroughness. But we have enough to serve, see you – and these excellent plans of yours will be helping me to be placing my charges to the best advantage!'

'I protest . . . !'

'Yes, sir – that is to be expected. I suggest that you make your protest – and a strong one, whatever – to his Grace of Montrose. I hear that his Grace is newly appointed Secretary of State for Scotland, in room of my Lord of Mar. Since his Grace it was who made the original mistake here, it is most appropriate that now he should right it. I should demand heavy compensation, Mr Nasmyth – you deserve it. And then I further suggest that you take your workmen and build your fort elsewhere – preferably in his Grace's property of Buchanan! It would look nicely there.' Rob bowed again. 'Now, gentlemen your pardon – but we have labours to perform.' And he took up the plans from the table – also his weapons.

So while the unhappy builders sat there, under the fleering eye and cocked pistol of Donald MacGregor, Rob and MacAlastair went to work. They went outside to the hidden ponies and brought in the kegs that represented the residue of the Gregorach stock of gunpowder. These they disposed in strategic positions, amongst the foundations, under arches and lintels, in corners – the plans proving valuable in showing constructional key-points. Then systematically and with vigour and ruthlessness that must have wrung the hearts of the watching craftsmen, they wrenched off, broke down, shattered and smashed up all the woodwork in the establishment, using tools amply to hand on the premises. It was all pitch-pine, and would blaze like a torch.

Rob had lengths of fuse this time, procured by nimble fingers mainly from the stone-masons' own quarrying equipment. When these were fixed and all was ready, the prisoners were conducted outside into the night.

'Think you that she will go up bravely, or not?' Rob asked of Nasmyth, interestedly. 'We have less powder than I would have liked. You will be knowledgeable about such matters, I have no doubt?'

He obtained no reply from the unfortunate contractor.

Rob lit the various and adequate fuses himself, and on this occasion there was no unseemly scramble for safety necessary. There was time even for the panting Rob to stand back with the others, and watch.

It made a peculiar explosion. There was scarcely any effect of blast or detonation to be observed. A couple of unexceptional flashes, and Tom na Bairlinn seemed to shrug itself beneath the watchers. Then one end of the fort appeared to lift slowly upward, while the opposite end sank and shrank in on itself. But neither of them violently, eruptively. There was a hiccupping sort of rumble, more flashes, and a further heaving and twisting of the building. Finally a sort of sigh on the night air. That was all. Compared with the blowing up of the dam that other time, it was all most undramatic and disappointing.

But, after a due wait – in case of any delayed fuses – close inspection supplied a different impression. The entire building, though superficially it retained its outward shape, leaned and sagged drunkenly. The gables were riven, no wall was sound, cracks and seams forked everywhere, and craters yawned amongst the foundations. What had been left of the woodwork was already blazing furiously. That fort would require to be rebuilt from the bottom up. A year's work had been destroyed in a few seconds.

Rob forebore to look at Nasmyth and his men just then.

They lit the bonfire of the carpenter's handiwork, using the working plans and estimates as tinder, and in a few moments the resinous wood was sending great crimson tongues of flame leaping skywards. There would be no need to stoke that fire.

Rob turned at length to the contractor. 'Mr Nasmyth – you have my sympathies,' he said, courteously. 'But no doubt you will console and recoup yourself with other Government contracts. But I advise that you act smartly about it – as about your claim for compensation. For there may be a new Government very soon, which may not smile kindly on contractors who built forts to harry loyal Highlandmen. A difficult position for men of business? Now – no doubt your companions will conduct you safely down to the tents at Inverarklet for the night? Och, yes. If you will wait for one minute, just, my two friends will restore to a couple of soldiers their borrowed clothing. Och, we would not wish to misuse any Government equipment, see you. Then you can all go down together, and at a good pace – for the soldiers may be cold a little. A good night to you gentlemen.

Oh – there is a small matter that you might be mentioning to the officer down there. It is that this operation was performed by the proprietor of the lands personally, as a private transaction whatever. Not by the Clan of MacGregor – who indeed know nothing of the business. You will not forget. . . . ?'

And so the two little parties went their different ways – and the ruins of the fort on the Hill of Warning stared gauntly across the Snaid Burn at the ruins of Inversnaid House, by the red light of the flaming pile.

CHAPTER FIFTEEN

IT took Rob Roy some little time to learn the reaction of
Red John of the Battles, Duke of Argyll, to that night's per-
formance – Argyll having much on his mind just then. His
was a difficult position, commander-in-chief in a country
– and his own country – for an unsteady Government
and a new and unpopular monarch, with neither of whom
the majority of his countrymen had any sympathy. A Highlander himself, he knew the pull of loyalties and interests
only too well – for his own clan was split, the Campbells of
Argyll following their chief as good Whigs, and the Campbells of Breadalbane being Jacobites. He was none too sure
of the loyalty of his Scottish troops, at a pinch, and had
to place his reliance on English soldiers and foreign mercenaries. Moreover, despite his battles and victories, he
was a humane and reasonable man, and like most good
soldiers, abhorred above all else the idea of civil war. And,
of course, Rob was an old friend, and indeed a very far-
away relation.

Then there was Montrose to complicate matters, his
fellow-duke and traditional enemy, who had once more, on
the political see-saw, manoeuvred himself into a strong position with King George, and was now Mar's successor as
Secretary of State for Scotland – the man with whom
Argyll must deal most closely, in fact. Montrose, enraged
by Rob Roy's campaign against him, was demanding the
use of troops against the MacGregors – especially with the
Martinmas Quarter-day nearly upon them – claiming that
the entire Highlands were in danger of blazing up in sedi-

tious rebellion, and that a strong hand must be shown. Argyll temporised, claimed that he must concentrate his available forces to hold the strong-points of Edinburgh, Stirling, Dumbarton and the like, in case of a rising, not scatter them over the face of the land. But the pressure was strong, and the effeminate but steely Montrose had all the civil power in his pocket.

The demolition of Inversnaid Fort was a bad blow, that could nowise be overlooked. And then, only a few days later, the countryside rang with the story of a new provocation. Despite the utmost secrecy, intricate last-minute changes of venue, the eventual appointment of remote Chapellaroch as meeting-place, and the darkness of evening as cover, individual tenants being met and escorted by sheriff-officers and hired bravoes – despite all this, Rob Roy was there first, concealed himself in the inn loft above the place of payment, and, towards the end of the business got his minions to set the place afire by the age-old method of firing burning arrows from a distance into the thatch. In the subsequent panic and confusion, he leapt down through the smoke and showering sparks, grabbed up most of the bagged rent-money, and bolted for the nearby Flanders Moss – in the first quagmires of which, presently, he bogged his rash pursuers.

Montrose now was like a man possessed. There was no containing his rage and spleen. But he was shrewd, still. He claimed it all as a Jacobite outrage – robbing law-abiding citizens to fill the Pretender's coffers. He demanded energetic measures by the State – and was in a fair position to insist upon them. Edinburgh rang with alarmist and inflammable speeches.

Argyll had to go some way to meet him. Though he refused to parcel out his all too few reliable troops in small numbers and put them at the disposal of sheriffs and other civil authorities, he did accede to Montrose's demand that loyal and faithful tenants of areas flanking the deplorable

Highland Line – by which he meant Montrose tenants – should be supplied with arms and ammunition to preserve King George's peace and their loyal lives . . . if the military were unable to do it for them. The Commander-in-Chief would have to have been very sure of his position indeed to refuse such request to the Secretary of State.

And so the royal arsenals were thrown open to the Grahams. Into lairds' houses and farms, villages and mills, cottages and change-houses, the stream of weapons flowed.

Meanwhile, on the wider scene, action hung fire. Bolingbroke fled to Lorraine, where James appointed him his Secretary of State. The Duke of Ormonde and other prominent English Jacobites followed him – so that it seemed obvious that there was going to be no uprising in England. Scotland must act first, and probably alone, if the cause was not to go by default.

And in Scotland, though talk there was in plenty, gestures were made, and even some enthusiasts locked up, action did not follow. The winter of course, was no time for any sort of military campaign in the Highlands – and it was to the Highlands that Scotland looked. But the Highlands, as Rob Roy had so often pointed out, though warlike and ready for the fray, were split into numerous mutually antagonistic clans. The men were there, but they would not unite save under someone high above their own prideful jealousies and feuds. None such had been appointed. If James had come over in person, the clans would have flocked to him in their scores of thousands – his half-brother Berwick, likewise. Any royal appointee, provided that he was sufficiently warlike and distinguished for proud chiefs to serve under, would have done. But none emerged. There were some who suggested that Rob Roy himself should take the lead in this impasse, at least for a start – Gregor of Glengyle prominent amongst them. But Rob shook his red head. He was no general, he said; a guerilla commander, yes – but no field officer. Besides, the great chiefs, though they might accept him on occasion as an equal, would never consent to actually serve under such as himself. Moreover, daring and incautious as he could be personally, Rob was not the man to plunge his clan into armed revolt prematurely, where others might not follow; too much was at stake for the MacGregors.

Strangely enough, the only prominent man who seemed to be deeply agitated by the continuing delay was John, Earl of Mar. Whatever else he might be, of course, Mar was a manoeuvrer, with a keen eye for the main chance, a shrewdness for the moment of advantage. He bombarded with urgent letters both James in Lorraine and the Jacobite notables in Scotland, succeeding in offending both by his importunity to action, and the implication that he himself was authoritatively involved. He did not urge his own name as commander in the field – for he was a politician and no soldier – but others with a more military background suspected and resented his eagerness nevertheless.

Thus the months went by, and while some supporters of James grew the more frustratedly impatient, others' ardours cooled noticeably. The Duke of Atholl, who had long flirted with the Jacobites, went south to make his peace with King George. Others did likewise. Breadalbane, claiming to be too old and sick to attend at Court, sent fervent protestations of loyalty – though privately the old scoundrel assured his good cousin Rob Roy that five hundred Campbell broadswords under Glendaruel would be available for King James at three days' notice. In the north and west the clans were deep in winter hibernation and local homicide.

Rob maintained his feud with Montrose, in quarterly instalments – but automatically, now, as a duty, with most of the fire and verve gone out of the business. Killearn might have emigrated to the furthest Indies for all that was heard of him, and stealing rents from this unseen ducal adversary began to pall on Rob. The current disease of inertia and frustration seemed almost as though it might have infected even Rob Roy MacGregor. Curiously enough, it was Mary MacGregor who saved him from that.

Rob still visited Auch at irregular intervals, making duty calls as father rather than husband. During one such visit in the early spring, after snowstorms had kept Rob in the small house amongst her feet for three days on end, Mary abruptly if temporarily abandoned her rigidly maintained attitude of chill aloofness for one of sheer and very human exasperation.

'Mercy upon us!' she cried out. 'Can you be a man, at all, Robert MacGregor – sitting there day after day with nothing in the world to concern you, your hand as idle as it will be in the grave! Is it dead you are, before your time, or what?'

Startled, the man jumped up. 'Lord – what's this?' he said. '*Me* dead! Save us – I think you have it head to tail, woman!'

'Naturally mine is the fault!' she flung back at him. 'Not the great Rob Roy!' The sudden surge of animation did wonders for her, bringing a flush to her almost too perfect features, sparkling her lovely eyes, flaring her chiselled nostrils. The man, despite all, was not unaware of it.

He shook his head. 'Why do you hate me so, Mary?' he asked.

Only for a moment did she hesitate. 'I said naught of hating you,' she answered. 'I cried out upon your idleness.'

'But, what is there to be doing in this snow? The beasts are safe and well. There is wood and peats in plenty, for the fire. What would you . . . ?'

'And is your life, your world, these small four walls? Is not a king in danger of losing his crown, and do not the Grahams ride ever higher – while you sit and watch my peats burn?'

'*Dia* – think you that *I* can win James Stewart his throne for him? I have done my best – I have done more than most. More than he has done himself, whatever! I am ready for his orders. I cannot *make* his orders for him. And have I not done as I said, and made Montrose keep me? Have I not made him a laughing-stock? Snapped my fingers under his woman's nose? Killearn is beyond my reach . . . as yet, God's curse on him! But him I will have too, in time. Till then I make a fool of him also. He is his master's factor, responsible for Montrose's rents. Those rents I take each quarter-day. . . .'

'Rents! Money!' Mary broke in. 'Think you that is all that matters — money, beasts, fodder? Is that all that you would take from the Grahams? Montrose has money in plenty. And cattle. He rules Scotland now. You will never make a pauper of James Graham. Will a few pounds, a few cattle-beasts, redeem your honour — since mine will never be redeemed?'

'But . . . what can I do more? How else can I come at them? You know how I am limited.'

'I know that you have the means of hurting James Graham, and aiding your king, both. If you would.'

'Eh? How could that be? What mean you. . . . ?'

'I have heard that Montrose arms all his tenants with weapons from Argyll. That is true, is it not? Those weapons lie now in each Graham house — for the taking, one by one. They could arm men for King James.'

Rob stared at her, lips moving for a moment wordlessly. 'Merciful Mother of God!' he got out, at length. 'Why thought I not of that? Heaven's angels could not have conceived a choicer design, whatever! Mary,' he declared, looking at her admiringly. 'I think sometimes that you should have been born a man!'

'Would to God I had!' she said, wearily, suddenly deflated again, and turned away.

Rob was now the excited one. 'If this thing, this notable conception, could be done — and I believe that it could — would you aid me in it, lass? Come with me?'

She shook her head.

'But it is your notion, your concern. You would see it successful?'

'I want no part in it – nor any of your man's concerns,' she answered dully.

'Not even against the Grahams?'

'That is *your* duty, not mine.'

'But, woman – you have just said . . . you have told me . . .'

'I have told you your duty. It is for you to do it, not me.'

'But, Mary . . . see you – if I do this thing, if I succeed in this plan of yours – will you then perhaps smile upon me a little more kindly, in return?' That, from Rob Roy Mac-Gregor came as near to complete surrender as was in the man.

She turned to look at him, slowly, deliberately, strangely, her expression at once wondering, scornful, perhaps even a little pitying. 'No,' she said briefly, finally, and left the kitchen.

Rob, of course, was not the man to let personal disappointment interfere with the course of duty – and such pleasant duty. Very shortly thereafter, despite the weather, and the failings and inertia of others, began a prolonged campaign that was to keep himself, MacAlastair and Donald MacGregor fairly fully engaged throughout the spring of 1715 and well into the summer. It was not a concentrated revolution; by its very nature it had to be a sporadic business, comprising innumerable small incidents, wide-scattered and sometimes with quite lengthy intervals between. And other activities, local and national, were not entirely neglected. But it was a recognisable campaign nevertheless, and no one failed so to recognise it – more especially the House of Graham.

All along the borders of the Highland Line no Graham house was safe, no tenant of Montrose, or of any of his cadets, slept at peace in his bed – until relieved of the

198

controversial weapons issued from Government arsenals. Raids were unpredictable, varying in character, and almost impossible to counter. Many were modest in scope and simple to a degree, but others were ambitious and elaborately planned; most were perpetrated in darkness, but others in broad daylight. Physical violence was eschewed wherever possible – but immunity was by no means guaranteed to stubborn men. No hiding-places were inviolable – as ravaged marital beds that had concealed muskets, and the harried crypts of Graham churches, bore witness. Indeed, hiding was worse than useless, for the MacGregors appeared to have veritable noses for powder and shot, and smelt it out no matter how closely hidden, leaving a trail of ruin, burned thatches and the like behind them. Defence against attack proved equally unavailing, even for the larger lairds, for none could afford to maintain an armed guard permanently on duty, day and night, waiting for a blow that might never fall – and where the enemy seemed to have a most excellent intelligence system warning him of the presence of opposition; anyway, the name and fame of Rob Roy paralysed most local resistance at source, most wise men preferring to be rid of arms that they had never particularly wanted rather than clash with the dreaded freebooter – especially as they all duly received a receipt for the weapons, signed by Rob Roy, taking them over in the name of and for the use of King James the Eighth, God save him.

In the circumstances, perhaps, it was not surprising, as time went on, that many of the as yet unraided tenants had second thoughts about the whole business, and ended up by insisting on having the arms returned whence they had come, for safety's sake. News of this move spread, and presently it became something of a race between Rob and the prudent ones as to the ultimate destination of the guns and muskets.

The MacGregor arsenals grew apace. Instead of being a

disarmed clan, as the law described them, they were well on the way to becoming the best armed in all the land.

Rob almost forgot wider disappointments.

CHAPTER SIXTEEN

WHAT drove Mar to take the final drastic step is not to be known. Some said that he feared for his life in the south – though why that should be it might be hard to explain, even admitting that Oxford was impeached on 16th July and committed to the Tower of London; others suggested that the move was to forestall somebody else – who, was not specified. The more probable explanation was that the man just suddenly got sick and tired of waiting. Certainly his letters both to France and Scotland had been growing increasingly urgent and importunate. Whatever the reason, he abruptly changed the entire course of his life. Secretly, on 2nd August, he left London, stealing away on a coal boat of all things, and sailed from the Thames for Fife.

And now there was no more delay. Once in Scotland, Mar announced himself to be King James's Lieutenant in Scotland – omitting to mention that he held no commission to that effect – and summoned all loyal supporters of His Majesty to assemble for a *tinchal*, or hunting-match, on the Braes of Mar – the traditional and accepted step to raising the standard of revolt – in one week's time.

Bobbing John had bobbed up again to some effect.

It is eloquent of the climate of impatience and frustration prevailing in Scotland that so many men of name and fame did flock to Aberdeenshire in answer to that summons – for Mar, despite his anicent lineage and premier earldom, was held in scant esteem throughout the land, and known as a turncoat. Yet they rallied to his hunting-match in their scores and hundreds – eight hundred it was said attended the *tinchal*, of which three hundred ranked as nobility and major gentry – not to mention the still more exclusive company of twenty-six Highland chiefs and captains of clans.

Rob was there, of course, as was Gregor – and Balhaldies, or the Laird of MacGregor as he now preferred to be called also, the first occasion on which both the new High Chief and the Captain of Clan Alpine had appeared together officially. Happily there was no embarrassment or clash of interests; Rob did not even wear the three eagle's feathers to which, in war, his captaincy entitled him, contenting himself with the single plume of a modest cadet; whilst Balhaldies, who was a discreet and diplomatic individual, however ambitious, dressed on this occasion in Lowland garb, deferred to Rob on all matters military, and indeed appeared almost to have more interest in the position of his wife's clan, the Camerons, than the MacGregors; Gregor it was who provided the splendour for the trio, a yellow-maned giant clad in fullest panoply of Highland magnificence, his two feathers the tallest and proudest ever grown by eagle.

As *tinchals* went, the one on the Braes of Mar was a success. The need for action and an end to delay was so evident to all concerned that it was possible to reduce the preliminaries to a minimum. Inevitably there was a certain amount of argument over precedence, but this was on a minor key, and social rather than military. Men held their hands, and to some extent their tongues, meantime.

Hunting was not altogether neglected, and numerous deer died in Glens Cluny and Quoich.

Some of the island chiefs and the Lowland lords from the Borders, with long distances to travel, could not but arrive late. But there was one other who came late who had not that excuse. He was Alexander, Marquis of Huntly, heir to the old Duke of Gordon, celebrated Cock o' the North. Others of the Gordons had been present from the first – the young Earl of Aboyne, General Alexander Gordon, Glenbucket. But Huntly, the acknowledged leader of the great half-Lowland half-Highland house that could put men into the field in their thousands, Huntly came late and came sulking. Probably he did not come purposely to make trouble – but trouble followed nevertheless. He was proud, headstrong, and he despised Mar. He could call out a hundred broadswords for other men's ten. He was heir to a duke – and it was for dukes to lead armies. And he was Cock o' the North. To most people it should have been obvious who should lead the King's forces. He did not actually say this in as many words, of course. But a few misunderstood him, and not a few tended to agree with him. He could not be any less of a soldier than Mar, at any rate.

But Mar was cautious. He did not say that he himself wished to be Commander-in-Chief. He seemed to go on the assumption that James himself, or at least the Duke of Berwick, would be over from France in a week or so to take command, and that his task therefore was merely to organise and set the campaign moving. In fact, a loyal address to his Majesty urging him to do that very thing was one of the first matters attended to. In the circumstances it was difficult to accuse Mar of seeking to impose himself upon them.

Fortunately or otherwise, there were so many practical details to discuss and arrange that the inevitable battle of personalities that bedevils any and every Scottish corporate venture was much restricted. Thanks to Mar's undoubted flair for organisation and his keen eye for priorities, decisions were reached at a remarkable speed, all things considered. It was agreed that the actual standard of revolt should be raised, and by Mar himself, in one week's time, and as nearly simultaneously as possible King James should be proclaimed in as many towns and cities as the Jacobites could control. Sundry small and local expeditions should be made, where victory was assured, for the sake of prestige and to encourage waverers. Meanwhile, the components of the army should be assembling – the main striking force and backbone therefore, naturally, in the clan territories to north and west. The strategic south Highland passes should be closed, and held for King James. It was now the 28th of August. Two weeks should suffice to assemble the clans, or most of them. They should then march south, to place themselves somewhere near the edge of the Highland Line, and in convenient communication with Perth, by the end of September. At Perth, dominated by the staunchly Jacobite house of Drummond, the Lowland forces would assemble. By then, it was hoped, His Majesty would be present to take over the command, and a two-pronged advance on Stirling and Edinburgh would commence.

Rob had considerable part in all these decisions, and it was noticeable that Mar placed much reliance on his views and advice. Rob himself would have liked, of course, to return to the MacGregor country, raise his own clan, and see to the blocking of the passes of Balmaha and Aberfoyle. But Mar, no doubt wisely, had more vital work for him; his assistance in co-ordinating and bringing the main clans to the assembly in the north-west would be invaluable – others could bring out the MacGregors. This latter duty and privilege, therefore, fell to Gregor of Glengyle, for Balhaldies had volunteered to go and use his influence with his brother-in-law Locheil and the Camerons, who were hanging back. Gregor was nothing loth.

The *tinchal* broke up on an unfortunate note. Huntly, disappointed and offended, went off home to Strathbogie before the end, refusing any assurance of active support. Others followed his lead, notably the Lord Erroll, Traquair and Stormont. But that was only to be expected. By and large the meeting had succeeded.

The rising was launched. The majority were committed. Mar remained in effective control.

*　　*　　*

The weeks that followed were thrilling or alarming ones for Scotland – and for England too, to a lesser extent – depending upon one's point of view. Inverness fell like a ripe plum to the veteran MacKintosh of Borlum. Aberdeen opted for James, and the King was proclaimed there by the Earl Marischal. In Dundee, Viscount Dundee, though a Graham, performed a like service, and was cheered to the echo. In Dunkeld, Montrose, Brechin, Forfar, indeed all the North-East, it was the same. In Fife the rival factions came to blows, but steadily the Jacobites gained the upper hand. Almost all over the Highlands the clans were mustering, and only the small Government garrison at Fort William remained, practically beleaguered. The Mac-Gregors held the Highland Line – and not passively, either – the best-armed Jacobites of all, thanks to Montrose, and panic spread far further south than Stirling. Argyll, arriving in Edinburgh from the west, complained bitterly that he had a striking force of no more than 1400 men – four regiments of foot and four of cavalry. How was he to defend Scotland with that?

No battles had been fought, but more than half the land was King James's already.

It was in these conditions that, at the end of September, with Mar's headquarters already set up in Perth, Rob Roy led a glittering and colourful array southwards through Lochaber, Glen Coe and Glen Orchy. Perhaps even Rob, hardened campaigner as he was, felt a surge of pride to be marching at its head – for this was the main Highland Division of King James's army, the largest massing of clansman seen for centuries – and largely the fruit of Rob's own work. It might even be suggested that it was the said pride that brought the great company by that route at all – for this was by no means the only road south; but it was the route that passed the little house of Auchinchisallan, under Beinn Dorain.

So Rob rode up to Mary's doorstep in the most resplendent and resounding company that any Highlandman could imagine. Clanranald was there, and Glengarry, and two brothers of Sir Donald of Sleat, with all Clan Donald at their backs. MacDougall of Lorne and the Laird of Mac-Kinnon; Grant of Invermoriston and MacIan of Glencoe; Maclean of Duart and Chisholm of Strathglass; and Mackenzie of Applecross, forerunner of Seaforth's great clan, still assembling. And behind them followed the endless serried ranks of their clansmen, in their gallant thousands.

Some might possibly have sensed a degree of pathos in the way that Rob Roy presented this offering before his wife, in the eager, almost anxious fashion in which he watched her reception of it. More perhaps might have found it in their hearts to pity him for the utter blankness of those glorious eyes as they turned away from him and what he brought.

The chiefs rode on, and Rob with them, to camp in Strathfillan – where the Robertsons of Struan, the Stewarts of Appin and the Breadalbane Campbells were to join them. It took their followers two hours to pass the door of Auch, and the flourish of their bagpipes filled the glens. The young MacGregors cheered until their throats would croak no more. Their mother watched expressionless – but her strong slender fingers tore and tore at the edge of her red and black plaid.

Major-General Gordon of Auchintoul was appointed to take field command of the Highland Division, and Rob returned to his MacGregors, who were manning the passes of the Highland Line.

King James did not appear.

CHAPTER SEVENTEEN

JOHN, Earl of Mar, now styled Captain-General of King James's army – some said that his commission to that effect was not only a forgery but was in his own handwriting – faced his officers and commanders with that expression of mild distaste which was habitual with him, even when, as now, he seemed slightly on the defensive, and which did nothing to endear him to his associates.

'I think that we dare wait no longer, my lords and gentlemen,' he said. 'His Majesty undoubtedly is coming – but he is delayed. As you know, King Louis of France has died, and on the representations of Stair, Ambassador from London, Orleans the Regent has refused to allow King James's flotilla to sail. There are twelve good ships lying in Havre de Grace, loaded with 2000 men, 12,000 muskets, 18,000 swords, 4000 barrels of powder, and a dozen brass field pieces. But Orleans has ordered them to be unloaded. I have urged that his Majesty sail without them, secretly if need be – but others advise differently. We cannot be sure that he will leave France within the month.' He did not add that he had in his pocket a letter from the same Majesty declaring that he wished that his supporters in Scotland, however loyal, would not move in advance of his royal authorisation.

There was some muttering amongst his hearers. The less knowledgeable and more ingenuous amongst them had been daily expecting the King's arrival.

Mar went on, a little wearily. 'Argyll, as you are aware, is at Stirling. His skirmishers are as far out as Bridge of

Allan – not much more than a score of miles from this city of Perth. He has no more than two thousand regular troops – but I have reliable tidings that he is daily expecting reinforcements. Six thousand Dutch mercenaries are on the sea, to aid him, and the first have actually landed. Every day that we wait for His Majesty, Argyll grows stronger.'

'We have waited over long already, by the good Lord God!' the fiery Clanranald cried.

'Aye, we have!' Campbell of Glendaruel, Breadalbane's lieutenant, exclaimed bitterly. 'There is scarce a bag of meal, a living cow, a stick of firewood, or an unravished woman left in all Breadalbane – thanks to the MacDonald horde!' And he glared angrily at the tight group of Clan Donald chiefs. 'Let us be on – and see if some can fight as well as they pillage!' The Highland Division of 10,000 clansmen, enforcedly idle, had been a little hard on Breadalbane of the Campbells, admittedly. It had been too good an opportunity to be missed.

Clanranald's hand slapped down resoundingly on the silver basket-hilt of his great broadsword. 'Did a toad croak?' he demanded of the room at large. 'Did a sheep bleat?'

As from a pack of dogs the growls arose.

'Gentlemen! Gentlemen!' Mar cried, his rather thin voice cracking. 'Peace, I beseech you. Let us mind what we are at.' But the altercation, so typical, so normal, had given his nimble mind another aspect of their situation to stress. 'An army inevitably bears hardly on any local population. The burghers of Perth are not backwards in their complaints either, I can assure you! And idleness in irregular troops is helpful to none. Even the bravest.' And he glanced placatingly at the MacDonalds. 'It is time, I think, that we put our case to the test.'

No man could in honesty say differently. It was 9th November, and since 22nd September Mar had lingered at Perth, ostensibly awaiting the King's presence. He had been reinforced by the reluctant Marquis of Huntly with 2500 more Gordons, the Earl of Seaforth with nearly a thousand MacKenzies, the Earl Marischal with 700, the Mackintosh with his clan, and many others, so that Perth groaned under the crushing weight of its deliverers. At the behest of the impatient and to relieve the pressure, as well as to attempt to keep spirited men from each other's throats, Mar had sent off sundry minor expeditions, probing attacks, and feints. Practically all his cavalry, eating its head off on the Inches of Perth, had been dispatched to Fife, under Lord Drummond and the Master of Sinclair, and now that semi-island county was strongly held for King James and threatening the Lothian coast across the Firth of Forth. Brigadier Mackintosh of Borlum, possibly the best soldier in the Jacobite ranks, had crossed from Fife to Leith in a daring seaborne escapade, capturing that seaport and its citadel, and menacing the Capital itself. The pugnacious MacGregors had been detailed to make a comprehensive sweep of Loch Lomond to capture every boat on its lengthy surface – for it was feared that Argyll, denied the use of the Forth estuary, would bring in his Continental mercenary reinforcements at the Clyde, and use the loch and its boats as a means of outflanking the insurgent line to the west. Rob Roy had been recalled personally from this congenial occupation – in which he had been able to deliver a few shrewd blows at the southern Graham lands of Buchanan and Endrick – to take part in still another diversionary expedition, which pleased him less. This was a raid on Inveraray, Argyll's own capital town on Loch Fyne, made in the hope of distracting the Government Commander-in-Chief into making a rescue bid and dispersing his forces, and at the same time giving the restive Highland Division still camped at Strathfillan something to do. It had not been as successful a business as it might have been – for Inveraray was in a strong water-guarded position and did not lack Campbell manpower to defend it – and it may be that Rob Roy was not too unhappy about that, for he had some sympathy and kindly feeling towards the harassed Argyll. It was from this employment that Mar had abruptly recalled the Highland Division leaders, Rob especially named amongst them, for this special council in Perth.

None would deny, then, that the insurgent army had waited long enough for its royal commander, or that it was not time to put the cause to the test. Already Simon Fraser of Lovat had whistled home 300 of his clan, and others from the glens were drifting away from lack of employment.

'You have a plan of action, my lord?' It was Huntly who spoke, stressing the word action, and not troubling to disguise the scorn in his voice. He made no secret of his continuing hostility to Mar and his conviction that he was militarily incompetent.

'I have taken good advice, my lord,' the other answered mildly. 'I believe it to be sound.' And he glanced over towards Major-General Gordon, a veteran of Czar Peter's wars.

Huntly could not publicly question the advice given by so notable a member of his own clan. He shrugged, and with but ill grace held his peace.

'Here is what I – what *we* – propose,' Mar went on. 'Argyll holds Stirling Bridge, and watches it like a hawk. There is no bridge lower across the Forth, nor any higher save up at Aberfoyle, twenty miles away. Only boats – ferries. Argyll knows that we cannot bring an army over those, in his teeth. To our cost it has been a wet autumn, and the rivers are running high. So Argyll concentrates his force at Stirling, watches Aberfoyle – and has us held.'

His hearers knew that, every one, all too well. They waited.

Mar, examining his nails went on. 'Our good friend Mac-Gregor of Inversnaid tells me that there are certain fords across the Forth, known to few. Indeed, I understand, known to practically none save himself and one or two of his people. He has, it seems, sometimes found them useful, in the past.'

There were smiles, there – and it was not often that Bobbing John raised a smile.

'These fords, which I believe are set in the midst of a great bog or moss, will be in no good state after these rains. Indeed, to speak in a general way, they will be impassable. They are always impassable, save under skilled guidance. Ordinary troops could not use them, certainly. But Rob Roy believes that he could get special troops across – lightly armed men, used to fording torrents, linked together, using ropes. He believes, gentlemen, that he could get most of of the Highland Division across, given time.'

There was no doubt that he had the interest of all now. An eager hum of talk broke out. A dozen men turned to question Rob.

Mar made his thin voice heard only after banging on his table. 'Once across these fords, the Highland Division could outflank Argyll's left, move in behind him, and cut his communications with Edinburgh and the south. And with the west likewise, so that his reinforcements from the Clyde could not reach him. He would be in a hose-net, gentlemen, surrounded. Lost.'

'If he did not learn about the crossing of the fords, and strike before the fording was finished,' the Earl Marischal objected.

'Precisely, my lord. I said, you will recollect, that Rob could get the Highland Division across, given *time*. That time, my lord, *we* would have to give him.' Mar paused. 'We should have to move forward from Perth here, directly down as though for an attack on Stirling Bridge itself. Our main horsed army. Openly. Very openly. At the same time, our forces in Fife would also move westwards, towards Stirling. Even the Highland Division would break camp and march eastwards, by Strathyre, Callander and Doune, as though making likewise for Stirling Bridge – and only at the last moment, at night, would turn back to make for these fords. Argyll has all too many spies. He would not fail to hear that we are moving on Stirling and the bridge. There is nowhere else that we could be moving against, there. He lacks men. He would concentrate all to hold the bridge. He could do no other.'

There was silence as men digested this, and many nods of approval and agreement. There were head-shakes too, of course. The plan was far from foolproof.

'The venture seems to me sound,' Panmure declared.

'I do not care for it,' Huntly mentioned, shrugging.

Choosing his time Mar brought Rob Roy into it. 'Rob,' he said, 'have you anything to add?'

'Only that I must have time *first*, to be visiting all the fords. I must see the state that they are in, with all this rain. And send you word, before you move, whatever.'

'That is understood.'

'Why are these fords passable only to Highlanders?' that same Viscount Fentoun who had been so anti-Highland at Kelly Castle two years before, demanded. 'Why the Highland Division? If men can cross, horses can cross. Let the cavalry do it. Once across, we can overrun the land faster and to better purpose, cut off Argyll more swiftly. This is work for horse, not foot.'

There was considerable sympathy with this point of view, the Lowland cavaliers much objecting to having to make in effect a mere feint in order to offer the Highlanders a chance for glory.

Nothing more was needed to swing the clan chiefs solidly in favour of the project. Loudly, hands on their claymores, they swore that they would ford that river or nobody would. Neither flood nor man nor devil would stop them – certainly not any trousered Lowlanders.

Mar, who had been prepared to temporise and compromise, as ever, hurriedly changed his mind. All would have their fill of fighting and glory, he assured – though it is doubtful if many heard him in the uproar – for Argyll was not the man to surrender tamely. And promptly, probably wisely, he closed the council.

Rob Roy was given two days to make his inspection and report on the state of the fords of Forth. Meanwhile the entire army in its three divisions would make ready to move.

CHAPTER EIGHTEEN

WEARY, mud-spattered and soaking wet, Rob, stripped to only his kilt, stood back as two MacGregors with great mallets drove a stake firmly into the sloping river-bank and tied the stout grass-rope securely thereto. But though wet, and the night chill and indeed frosty, Rob was far from cold; all night he had laboured as hard as any of his men, much of the time in the icy waters of the swollen Forth, probing, directing, even swimming. The fords, all four of them in the Frew area, had been marked, tested and roped, and reasonably sound tracks through the quaking moss to each of them surveyed and roughly but clearly signposted. Gregorach guides were placed at every difficult point along the routes that the clans would use, scores of men being required for this task; indeed, the entire MacGregor contingent was engaged on this special duty. The river was running high and the fords were not pleasant to use; but with care, and the use of handropes, bold men should be able to retain their footing, and cross.

This Frew area that Rob had chosen was not in the deepest and most daunting part of the Flanders Moss; even he could never have got an army through that. But it was sufficiently desolate and remote for secrecy, the actual fords lying some three miles out into the wilderness south of the village of Thornhill and half that distance north of Kippen on the enemy side, roughly midway up the winding Forth between Stirling and Aberfoyle. There was a fair track down as far as the Mill of Goodie, a mile north of the fords – the miller of which found his lonely premises requisitioned as the night's headquarters. It was near the mill that Rob stood now – for this Goodie Burn had to be crossed also before the clans could reach the main fords, and though a comparatively small stream, it was running faster than the great river, and required to be roped likewise.

It was nearly four o'clock on the morning of 13th November, and Rob was growing just a little anxious. He had been looking for advance parties of the Highland army for over an hour now. Around midnight a courier had brought him the information that the clan army, after marching east and south all day, according to plan, had duly turned back westwards at Doune, under cover of darkness, heading for here. Doune was a bare seven miles away, and he had expected the vanguard ere this. It would be daylight in three hours, and it was vital that at least the majority of the army should be across the fords and fanning out beyond by that time. It would be a slow process, inevitably.

The drumming hooves of a fast-ridden horse sounded on the frosty night. Rob heard it draw up at the mill, and then hurrying footsteps as a gillie brought the messenger to him. This would be General Gordon's forerunner, announcing that the army was approaching.

But as he loomed out of the dark, Rob perceived that the courier was no Highlander but an officer dressed in Lowland fashion.

'Are you MacGregor? MacGregor of Inversnaid . . . Rob Roy?' he demanded, peering doubtfully at the half-naked and mud-stained apparition.

'None other, sir.'

'I have had the devil's own trouble finding you,' the other complained. 'I have orders for you, from the Captain-General. You are to leave here at once, and proceed with your MacGregor contingent with all speed to Ardoch on the River Allan, there to rejoin the Highland Division.'

Rob Roy stared. 'Good God, man – are you crazy?' he

cried. 'Ardoch, you said? Near to Dunblane? Rejoin the Highland Division . . . ?'

'Yes, As quick as you may. Those are my lord of Mar's orders.'

'But . . . *diabhol* – the Highland Division is here, whatever! Or nearly. What folly is this?'

'The Highland Division is turned back, sir. Has been these four hours. Marching for Ardoch. It is joining the main army there. It should be there before daylight. All plans are changed.'

'But . . .' Rob swallowed, his great fists clenching. 'Why?' Why, man – in the name of Heaven?'

'Because Argyll has outwitted us. Stolen his march on us. He did not wait for us behind Stirling Bridge. Hearing that we were on the move, damn him, he has moved himself, north to meet us – it is believed in order to drive a wedge between our main force and the Highland Division. He lies on the south slopes of Sheriff Muir now, and we lie on the north.'

'*Dia* – he does? Red John of the Battles is a man for you!' Rob exclaimed in involuntary admiration. 'With less than half our numbers, he does not sit and wait for us. He attacks! But . . . what is Mar at, man? Why has he changed the plan?'

'I should have thought that would be obvious, sir. Argyll seeks to drive up the Allan Water between our divisions, and so split us. The Captain-General, by quickly altering his plans will bring in the Highland Division to join him at Ardoch and so spoil the enemy's manoeuvre. By acting thus swiftly he will present Argyll with a united army. There was just time for it to be done . . .'

'By acting thus, Mother of God, he is throwing away his greatest advantage!' Rob interrupted. 'Can you not see it? We still have to cross the Forth. The Highland Division *behind* Argyll's back, would be worth three times what it is facing him. Red John's move forwards make our move twice as good as it was, whatever. Clearly he knows naught of our plan – of this crossing of the fords – or he would never have dared to leave Stirling. It is all the more important that we cross here, as arranged. We can sweep round behind him, take Stirling and its bridge like ripe plums – and he is trapped between the Forth and Mar. Can you not see it, man?'

The officer shrugged. 'Whether I see this or that is no matter, sir. Your orders are to retire to Ardoch forthwith.'

'But this is folly. Your orders are folly. What fool gave Mar such advice?'

'It is the Captain-General's own decision, sir.'

'Then the Captain-General is a fool!' Rob roared. 'Curse him for a fool, as well as a craven and a turncoat! Men's lives hang on this – many lives of better men than Bobbing John. Not to mention a throne, whatever!'

The courier had stepped back a pace or two in the face of Rob's towering wrath – as many another had done before him. But he held his ground in other respects. 'Sir, I think that you forget yourself,' he said, if with little confidence. 'It is not for you, nor myself, to question the orders of the Captain-General. . . .'

'Orders can be changed,' Rob rapped. 'Especially the orders of a fool! They *must* be changed. It may not yet be too late. The Highland Division must be turned again – back to cross these fords. You must turn them. . . .'

'I will do no such thing, 'fore God!' the other declared strongly.

'Then *I* will! I will ride, at once, I will see Gordon. If he will not heed me, then Clanranald will. And Glengarry. And Duart, and the rest. I . . .'

'You are too late, MacGregor. However fast you ride, they will be at Ardoch before you. Hours before. Even now they will be nearing the camp. You are too late. Battle may be joined before you could get there.'

Panting with his anger and frustration, Rob glared at the

man – and knew that what he said was true. It was too late. The die was cast. The sinews of neither man nor beast could bring him to the clan army before it joined Mar. Nor bring him to Ardoch before daylight. Even if foolish men would listen to him when he got there. Something like a groan escaped him.

The courier heard – and wisely reckoned that the time was ripe to take his departure. 'You . . . you will bring your MacGregors as quickly as may be?' he reminded falteringly – and without awaiting any answer, turned and strode back towards the mill and his horse.

For long Rob Roy stared into the empty darkness, biting his lip, tugging his beard, a prey to his most savage emotions. Then, at length, he sighed, and turned to the matter on hand. It would take time, considerable time, to reassemble his men. They were scattered widely, individually and in parties, at strategic points over a large area of the morass and its approaches. And Gregor, with an advance party, was already across the fords of Frew, keeping watch on the enemy side. Wearily, Rob sent for his running gillies.

*　　*　　*

The MacGregors, reinforced by a detachment of Badenoch MacPhersons from Cluny's contingent, sent by General Gordon to aid them at the fords, were delayed in rejoining the main army for a number of reasons. The first was obvious; there were almost a score of rough miles between Frew and Ardoch, and the Gregorach had been arduously employed for thirty-six hours without a break already. Then, about 10 o'clock on a sparkling cold morning, another courier found them, up on the long Braes of Doune, from General Gordon. He informed them that the two armies were already in contact, manoeuvring for position about the long ridge of the Sheriff Muir, and that the MacGregors were now to change direction and make to cross the Allan Water at Kinbuck, and so to connect up with the right wing of the Highland Division, which was of course on the right of Mar's line. Rob Roy accordingly turned his tired company south by east.

Long before they reached the neighbourhood of Kinbuck and its ford, the sound of gunfire was rumbling across the wide strath to them. That could only be Argyll's cannon, for the Jacobite artillery unfortunately was still in France. Everywhere men's lips tightened and weary bodies tensed.

Then, as they hurried down the green haughlands of the Lodge Burn, still a couple of miles from Kinbuck, one of Rob's scouts came back to report that the way ahead was blocked. A party of cavalry was halted in the grassy valley around a bend in front, apparently eating mid-day lunch – and though they were not red-coated dragoons there were red-coats amongst them. Cursing, Rob and Gregor crept forward to investigate.

Sure enough by accident or design, their road was barred. What looked like a full squadron of light horse filled the haughland. By their motley dress they might have been Jacobite insurgents – were it not for the few red-coated regulars vivid amongst them. Almost certainly they were a mounted detachment of the Glasgow Whig Fencibles that Argyll had recruited, stiffened by Light Dragoon officers. Whether they were here as providing defence in depth for the ford at Kinbuck – the first point at which the Allan Water could be crossed above Dunblane – or whether they had merely halted for a meal on their way elsewhere, could not be known. But there they were.

A council of war followed. To attack, or to move back discreetly and cross this Lodge Burn higher up, to seek to come at Kinbuck by another approach? Discussion of the matter was little more than a formality, of course – for these were Gregorach and not noted for discreet withdrawals; moreover, fatigue not withstanding, they were spoiling for a fight, what with one thing and another. And with their 300, against little more than half that number – even of cavalry – self-respect was at stake.

'Three parties of a hundred each,' Rob directed. 'Glengyle on the right, Coiletter on the left. Myself, I am getting old and will take the centre, for peace and quiet! The enemy are all on this side of the burn. Coiletter will make a wide circuit and come up at them from below. Glengyle will cross the burn up here, out of sight, and come down on them openly on the far side. They will have to cross to get at him – and while they are at it and their backs turned, myself I will descend upon them safely! Och, it will be simplicity itself, just.'

The best military manoeuvres are always the simplest. After Coiletter's hundred had been given some fifteen minutes to get into position further down, Gregor and his men, stripped to only their kilts, plunged across the stream. It was running high but came only up to their breasts – nothing to men who had spent the night coping with the swirling Forth. Once across, they proceeded down the far side – and the moment that they came within sight of the enemy, still some three hundred yards off, they fired a random volley of shots, drew their broadswords, and with a wild shouting of 'Gregalach! Gregalach!' charged downstream.

The effect on the Fencibles was remarkable. It was as though an ants' nest had been disturbed. The shouting there was almost as loud as was the MacGregors'. But bellowed commands gradually prevailed, reinforced by blaring bugle calls, and in some fashion the squadron proceeded to mount and raggedly to cross the burn to meet its insolent attackers.

Gregor and his men, in consequence of this delayed reaction, were almost at the waterside to meet them as the first troopers came splashing and clambering out. Broadswords clashed with sabres, pistols banged, men bawled, and horses whinnied and screamed. In effect, Gregor's clansmen were lining the far bank, waiting for the cavalrymen as they came straggling over.

The dragoon officers soon saw the folly of this, and the bugles blew again and again to bring order and cohesion to the excited volunteers. It was then that a wild slogan-shouting from downstream turned all eyes thitherwards. Coiletter's party was coming storming up, on both sides of the burn, distant yet but vociferous. Orders and bugle notes grew the more urgent, if no less confused.

Grimly laughing, Rob waited behind the summit of the steep bank above, holding back his impatient men. One troop of the enemy, seeming to be somewhat better disciplined than the others, was beginning to splash across the stream, half-right, towards a point where they could clamber out unimpeded and so keep the two Gregorach parties from joining up. Gregor, perceiving the danger, promptly detached a proportion of his men to head them off – thereby weakening his retaining force. Orders for a concerted charge towards him were shouted.

Rob glanced over at Coiletter's racing warriors, nodded, and raised his arm, broadswords drawn. With a roar, in which the MacPherson slogan mingled with that of MacGregor and dreaded name of Rob Roy, the third party hurled itself directly down the steep slope.

It was too much for amateur soldiers, however gallant. Not knowing which way to turn, which officer to obey, nor where the next blow might fall, and obviously outnumbered, the Fencibles lost their heads completely. Better trained men than these have done the same at less provocation, frequently – without Rob Roy's terrible name being thrown into the scales.

There was comparatively little blood-letting, in the end, most of the actual killing being done by Gregor's men on first reaching the bank; mounted men at least have this advantage that they can usually extract themselves with greater success from the clutches of the unhorsed. Thus, as with one accord if in varying directions, the Fencibles proceeded to do without further delay. Their regular officers appeared to see no point in lingering far behind. Whooping with triumph, the Highlanders speeded their departure from the scene as best they might, and stared resentfully at those who had insisted on surrendering.

There was more plunder, undoubtedly, than would have been the case with a regular unit. And the midday meal had happily been left almost untouched.

It was some little time before Rob was able to resume his march for Kinbuck. The Artillery fire had died away, he noted.

*   *   *

Climbing out of the valley of the Lodge Burn, in order to cut off a corner, the MacGregors reached the crest of the little ridge that separated it from the wide gently sloping strath of Allan. And there they halted abruptly to stare.

As well they might. A far-flung, complicated and astonishing prospect greeted them. Before them lay the Allan Water running broad and yellow and fast through grassy levels, with the baggage wagons of the Jacobite army drawn up just across from them, and the hamlet of Kinbuck a little way to the left. Beyond, the land lifted and lifted, out of the green of grassland into the dark brown of heather moor, up and up through rolling undulations to a long ridge more than two miles away, that was but the outlying rampart of the Ochil Hills. That ridge and its heather flanks was known as the Sheriff Muir, a lonely place of barren desolation. But today it was not desolate, not in its usual sense – though to many men undoubtedly it represented the ultimate desolation itself. It was in fact a battlefield, spread out before the newcomers like any stage backcloth, the steady lift of the land to the final ridge offering an almost unbroken prospect to the beholders.

But however clear the prospect visually, its interpretation was anything but clear. No battlefield, probably, is ever clear, during the actual fighting, even to the generals who seek to order it. But Sheriff Muir was in a category by itself for confusion. In the early afternoon of that frosty November day it represented chaos, widespread, comprehensive and appalling.

Men were moving everywhere over that extensive panorama. They moved in every direction, too, in large numbers and small – and many, it could be seen, did not move at all. There was nothing resembling a line anywhere to be seen, a front or any recognisable formation of either side. There seemed, at this stage, to be surprisingly little actual fighting going on – though that might be a misconception. Clouds of smoke lay heavily on the still air – but this appeared to emanate mainly from one or two points where the heather had been set on fire, rather than from artillery and gunfire. The sound of scattered and ragged musketry echoed across the strath, punctuating a more continuous sound that rose and fell like the sigh and sob of the tide on a distant sandbar, remote and impersonal – but which represented the voices of men, wailing, shouting, commanding, imploring, screaming and moaning; a peculiarly futile and weary sound, with less reality to it than the yittering of the curlews amongst the hillocks at the MacGregors' backs.

Rob gazed urgently, seeking to probe, distinguish, assess. The vivid scarlet uniforms of Argyll's regular troops at least ought to have been a guide to dispositions – but the scarlet was just as much scattered and dispersed over the scene as were the less outstanding colours of other men. Certainly there seemed to be a fairly large body of red-clad men up on the summit ridge to the right, stationary and seeming partly to block out from view an even larger nondescript mass of men further back and slightly to the north. But that was of little help. Groups of red-coats, mounted and foot, were moving hither and thither elsewhere over the wide vista, some hurrying, some not – but the same applied to other men; who were advancing and who retreating was impossible to tell. All that could be said for certain was that many of both sides lay fallen and unmoving.

Shaking his head in perplexity, Rob transferred his gaze from the wider scene to a vicinity closer at hand, where Gregor was pointing excitedly – to the left foreground, in fact. A continuous stream of men was coming down off the higher ground. Men were plunging into the rushing Allan Water at the Kinbuck ford and struggling across, many to cast themselves down on this side as though exhausted, others to hurry on, through the hamlet and beyond. These were almost all Highlanders, many of them wounded and bloody, others naked or nearly so, some without arms or targes. Not a few stumbled and staggered as they ran. They looked like defeated men.

'Campbells! Stewarts of Appin! Murrays of Atholl!' the keen-eyed Gregor cried. 'Dark tartans.'

'Aye,' his uncle nodded grimly. 'But what of these?' And he pointed, in his turn.

Coming upstream, from the Dunblane direction, were more men, many men, strung out down the valley as far as eye could see. These too were Highlanders, large numbers of them still wearing the Jacobite white cockade. There seemed to be few wounded amongst these, all were well armed, and any staggering and stumbling appeared to be occasioned by the heavy and miscellaneous burdens with which they cheerfully loaded themselves. There was no dejection in this stream, no falling down exhausted. Their fording of the river seemed, compared with the others, more in the nature of a frolic.

'Clan Donald,' Gregor observed, rubbing his chin. 'The Macleans. Glengarry's people. What means this?'

Rob shook his head. 'It behoves us to find out,' he said. 'Myself, I do not like it. Greg – go you down there to the ford, and bring me up two men, one of each sort, of each company. Intelligent men if it may be, who can answer questions.'

Gregor came back presently with three informants – a

young MacDonell who said that he was second son of Arasdale in Glengarry's country, and much pleased with himself; a brother of Campbell of Inverlyon, a Breadalbane man known to the MacGregors; and an unhorsed Lowland officer called Skene, one of the Earl of Panmure's corps, with a musket ball through his shoulder. The last two were less than cheerful.

'All is lost, Rob!' the Campbell declared without preamble, as he came up. 'We are cut to pieces. My brother is dead. As is Cononish and Ardmoine. Glendaruel himself is sore wounded. God knows how many others. The Robertsons are broke and Struan a prisoner. The Atholl men are scattered. The horse it was that failed us, damn them. . . .'

'You lie, fellow!' the Lowlander broke in. 'We failed nobody. We were transferred to the right. We but obeyed our orders. . . .'

'Orders to desert us – to abandon us to Argyll's cavalry, while you rode off after the MacDonalds, you Lowland scum!'

'Peace, gentlemen!' Rob commanded. 'Quiet you, Ewan – I want news, not bickering.'

'Och, you will be getting it from neither of these, whatever,' the MacDonell cried. 'They are poor creatures, who know not one side of a claymore from the other. Heed them not. *We* won the day for them. Clan Donald ate up the Sasunnachs like stubble, my God! Before our broadswords they fell like corn, just – like ripe corn, I tell you! Och, it was magnificent! All the way to Dunblane we chased them. . . .'

'And the accursed horse followed you, and left us naked!'

'We were *ordered* to the right, I tell you. "Horse to the right" we were ordered. We could not but follow them.'

'And left us dead men! The Greys rode through us and through us. . . .'

'We cut them down like thistles, just. We took their

225

banners. We spoiled them. The sons of Donald drank blood!'

'Strathmore fell. Huntly was dragged off his horse, and is a prisoner. My own beast was shot under me, and I have a ball in my shoulder . . .'

'The Mackenzies are slain! I saw Seaforth fall. The Chisholms are no more . . .'

'We smote them hip and thigh! We chased them off the field, whatever! They begged for mercy on their trousered knees. . . .'

'As Royal's my Race – *I* beg for mercy!' Rob Roy roared, slashing his hand down in a fierce cutting motion. 'Enough of this babble! Answer only my questions. Speak you only when I bid you. Men are dying while you deafen us. Now – you MacDonell. Tell me . . .'

By means of careful questioning and cross-questioning, Rob presently obtained what he hoped might be a reasonably clear picture of what undoubtedly was a highly confused battle. In effect, the right wings of both armies had triumphed. The Jacobite right, after winning the race for the ridge about an hour before noon, under the proud command of the impetuous Clanranald, had flung themselves into the attack first, before their left wing was in position.

Two battalions of his own MacDonalds, two of Glengarry's MacDonells, one of Mull Macleans and one of lesser clans. They had driven irresistibly through the Hanoverian left, smashing four of Argyll's best regular regiments of foot – the Royals, the Devons, The West Yorks and the Worcesters – and not only these but cavalry backing also, the 3rd and 7th Dragoons, chasing them all in headlong rout southwards right to Dunblane town. General Witham who commanded had last been seen spurring hard for Stirling and the south. They had, of course, found plenty of plunder in Dunblane – and that had been the end of the battle for many of the brave sons of Donald. Clanranald's fall at the height of the engagement had not helped in the bringing of his corps back under control. The second line, Mackenzies under Seaforth and Gordons under Glenbucket, had followed on, to turn Argyll's flank.

The left wing, Struan's Robertsons, young Locheil's Camerons and the Breadalbane Campbells, had had further to go to reach the ridge. They were forming up ready to charge in turn, when Argyll acted. Perceiving what was happening to his left, he did not wait for a similar fate to overtake his right. He had held back his infantry and flung in right away his main cavalry support – and the best cavalry in the world, at that, the Royal Scots Greys. Hundreds of them thundered down on the waiting mid-Highland clansmen. The clans stood firm. It had apparently been at this moment that Mar, seeing a situation that no infantry on earth could face successfully, had sent the urgent warning to his own supporting horse, hidden behind a fold of the moor – 'Cavalry on the right!' It had been a warning, yes, and a wise one – but it was not wisely worded. Cavalry on the right, the Angus and Fifeshire cavaliers had heard, and taken it as an order. And off to the right they had trotted forthwith, obediently, to go pounding after Clanranald's victorious warriors: And the left-wing clans were indeed left, abandoned, to face the avalanche of grey horses. They had been cut to pieces where they stood, as to and fro, backwards and forwards the troopers rode them down. No less than six times they turned and faced right-about. And after the Greys, Argyll had thrown in everything that he had left to command. The second line, the Atholl men, the Drummonds and the rest, could not hold them. The entire Jacobite left had collapsed.

After that, evidently, the Sheriff Muir belonged to anybody and nobody. Utter confusion had reigned. But whilst one disordered horde had had Red John of the Battles to command it, one of Marlborough's most experienced generals, the other had only Bobbing John, the agile politician.

That was the situation, so far as Rob Roy could unravel it. It left him in no little quandary and turmoil of mind.

Not so Gregor of Glengyle. He had no doubts. 'Lord!' he cried impatiently, as his uncle turned from his questioning. 'We wait here while others fight – as you said yourself, while good men are dying! Come – let us be doing, for God's sake!'

'Aye, lad,' Rob nodded, set-faced. 'But, where?'

'What do you mean?'

The older man waved his arm. 'There is the battlefield. Miles of it, man. Who do we fight? And where?'

'I care not – so long as fight we do, whatever!'

'Spoken like your own self, Greg! Myself, I prefer a more definite target! Mar had 15,000 men, and more. 10,000 of them must still be over there, somewhere. Our 300 will not . . .'

He paused. A more localised noise had been growing through the general hubbub for some little time. Now it attracted more attention, drawing the eyes to a point a little way upstream where a fold in the land created by a tributary burn opened on to the Allan Water. Out of this fold a trickle of men was issuing, a trickle that grew rapidly into a flood, that surged on down towards the ford also.

These were Highlanders, likewise. Soon they were identifiable as mainly Camerons. There were many wounded amongst them, too. But this contingent was different from either of the other two streams of men already straggling through Kinbuck. It did not straggle, for one thing; there was discipline here, command, control. Presently a banner came into sight torn and tattered but still fluttering proudly above the heads of marching men.

'The Arrows of Locheil!' Rob said. 'One flag that still flies.'

As the mass of the newcomers debouched into the main

valley, parties broke off to right and left quickly to take up defensive positions covering the line of retiral. On through these the pacing ranks came, the banner in their midst.

'*Dia* – Locheil is master of Clan Cameron yet!' Gregor exclaimed. 'But . . . think you that they are leaving the field?'

'Aye. It seems so. But, see you what they are at? The enemy must be close behind for them to act so.'

'Yes. Yes – we must go to their aid, then.'

'Wait you,' his uncle said. 'What is the river for?'

The Camerons came on, and presently, after a sizeable gap, another smaller tighter group of them came hurrying out of the side valley, broadswords drawn – the rearguard. They took over the positions of the defensive picket, who then came on.

'We can at least aid them at the ford,' Gregor urged.

'Do that,' Rob nodded. 'Take a score of men.' He himself remained in front of his serried ranks of MacGregors up on their vantage point.

It was there, presently, that John Cameron, Younger of Locheil, came to him wearily, his bannerman at his side. Blood dripped from a graze at his temple.

'Heaven's mercy, Rob,' he greeted. 'This is an ill day – and you with the best of it.'

'Aye, John – I believe you. An ill day. We are new come from the fords at Frew. And you – you have had enough of it?'

'By all the powers, I have!' Locheil's son and heir cried. 'I came to fight not to be made a fool of. This is not a battle – it is a fool's playground! We have not a general – only a posturing ape! I have not received one command, one order, this day!'

'Mar has lost his head?'

'Aye – if he ever had one, God's curse on him! We have suffered four hours of his folly, and I have lost four score of better men than he! I will hazard no more, for naught.'

'Is the King's crown naught?' Gregor demanded, but with less than his usual conviction.

'You were being followed?' Rob put in quickly, and waved his hand towards where the Cameron's rearguard crouched.

'Aye. By a regiment of Fusiliers, and others – a plague on them. We have had them on our heels this hour back. But we have kept them at arms length. They are little trouble – not like the Greys. Those ones are devils incarnate. All day they have haunted us. There is no peace from them. Without them I think Argyll would have achieved little.'

'And these others – the Fusiliers. Are they close?'

'They were. Och, but they have been the less keen as we neared this river. Now I think that they hang back. They may not wish to face the crossing. It may be that their scouts have seen you MacGregors waiting here, fresh.'

'It may be so. Where is General Gordon, John?'

'I know not, and I care not!' the younger man declared.

'And Mar?'

'They say that he is up there on the ridge, biting his nails. Waiting – for what, God above only knows! He has still many men up there, they say – most of the horse, and the Lowlanders and half the Gordons. But what difference does it make? He will not use them aright. . . .'

A new surge of men appearing now from one of the undulations across the river, downstream, drew their attention. It did not demand any very keen perception to see that these were actually fighting their way – indeed more and more of scarlet came into view behind them, until the lower valley on the far side was a mass of red. There was comparatively little musket-fire, though a great deal of other noise; no doubt both sides would be running very low in ammunition by this time. As yet it was not possible to identify the retiring force.

'We can advance to the aid of these, at the least,' the eager Gregor asserted.

'And throw away the strongest position in sight?' his uncle gave gack. 'No, lad – we can do better than that.' He turned to his waiting men, raising his voice, and gave the command for three volleys of musketry, aimed into the air above the approaching combatants, at the same time ordering the MacGregor banner to be raised aloft.

His strategem was highly effective. The three distinct and regular salvoes crashing out, orderly and disciplined and massive – for the MacGregors had had ample practice with their fine Government weapons, thanks to Montrose's lavish provision – gave new life to the retreating men and brought the pursuing red-coats to an abrupt halt. Here, obviously, were Jacobite reinforcements, fresh troops evidently with no shortage of ammunition. Perhaps someone even was able to identify the MacGregor banner. Caution could not have been more clearly indicated.

The newcomers proved to be the Robertsons, a badly decimated version of the fine body of men that Struan had put into the field, but still in good heart. With them were a fair sprinkling of Appin Stewarts – all, like the Camerons, part of the broken Jacobite left wing. Eager hands aided them across the ford.

The red-coats, keeping their distance beyond effective musket range, contented themselves with harrying the broken men who still thronged down all along that valley to reach the comparative safety of the far river bank.

Rob was surprised to see a lean and ascetic-seeming man of middle years limping at the head of the Robertsons. 'Struan!' he cried, 'Here at least is something to offer thanks for. I heard that you were captured.'

'Aye, and so I was, Rob. But they could not hold so aged and wily a campaigner.' Alexander Robertson. 17th of Struan, was a veteran of Dundee's campaigns and had served in exile with the French army. 'But I'll not say that I was not glad to see you here.'

'You were hard pressed?'

231

'Hard enough. I tried to rejoin Mar, but the enemy cavalry is everywhere. Those accursed Greys! And Mar keeps our own horse standing up yonder on the ridge like any royal bodyguard. Perhaps to support the honour of his new dukedom!'

'Dukedom . . . ?'

'Aye – heard you not? Just before the battle was joined, a courier from France arrived. King Jamie did not come himself – but turned Bobbing John into a duke instead! *Dia* – likely that is what has been on his mind this sorry day, instead of soldiering! God save us all, but it is a mad world! Ha – is that young Locheil? I heard that he was down. . . .'

More and more Government troops were converging now on the east bank of the Allan Water, cavalry as well as foot, the Greys' pale horses amongst them.

John Cameron, a fire-eater himself, if somewhat over-shadowed by the reputation of his fierce old father Sir Ewan, was staring back unhappily at the enemy. 'Think you, Rob,' he said, 'with your people and mine, and Struan's, as well as some of these broken men – think you we might not yet fall on the red-coats? If we crossed the river above and below them, we could turn their flank.'

'To what purpose, John?'

'We . . . we might rally this whole wing.'

'Again, to what purpose, at all? So long as Mar sits up there?'

'At the least we could kill some of the creatures!' Gregor broke in.

'Aye – kill and be killed. Without cavalry we cannot effectively fight theirs. We would still be a prey to the Greys.'

'We fought cavalry a while back, and had them running.'

'Only because we surprised them. There can be no surprise here. In morass or on a mountainside, foot may fight cavalry, and win maybe. But never on open ground such as this.'

'Rob is right I dare swear,' Struan Robertson said. 'There is no profit here. Myself I am tired, and my lads are tired. Many are wounded. With you it may be different. I am going back to Ardoch and the camp. Would it was to Struan itself! Shall we march in company, Rob?'

'God forbid . . .!' Gregor began, when Rob cut in swiftly.

'No. We wait. At the least, we can cover your retiral. And that of others.'

'As you will. For myself, I have seen enough madness and to spare for one day. . . .'

In the end, with a fair show of reluctance, young Locheil went with the Robertsons, lurching off on the arm of his brawny bannerman.

In compact martial array the MacGregors stood their ground on their hillock, like a stout rock in a flood of waters.

*   *   *

'I will stand here no longer, and see my honour spat upon by all who pass!' Gregor of Glengyle exclaimed hotly. 'I have borne it as long as I can, God forgive me!'

'Your honour, it is a great trouble to you,' his uncle declared heavily. 'I think that you would be well advised to take it in hand, Greg!'

'The clan's honour, then! Will you scoff at that?'

'The clan may have more to lose than honour on this field, lad. Are you wholly blind?'

'I see all to clearly, more's the pity! I see a battle lost for want of wit and want of courage and want of a man to take a decision. I little thought to see the MacGregors standing by these two hours, watching, their hands empty, their swords unblooded! The Gregorach!'

'You had rather that we had gone hot-foot in, and died uselessly?'

'I had rather only that we had acted as men!'

'Men,' Rob repeated. 'What is a man but his life, whatever? Is a corpse a man? How many MacGregors would you have die for a king who twiddles his thumbs in France, and a general who twiddles them up on yonder ridge?'

'But . . . but.' Shocked, the younger man eyed his former tutor and mentor.

'This from you, from Rob Roy MacGregor! This woman's talk!'

'Perhaps I have a thought for the women, this day,' the older man said sombrely. 'They are Clan Alpine also, are they not?'

'Lord – you will not fight for thinking of the women!' Gregor exploded. 'Upon my soul – what has come over you? A while back, at the Lodge Burn, you were not loth to fight. You had no ear for women's wails then. . . .'

'Then it was otherwise, Greg – as you must see. The die was not cast. We were still hastening to this battle – that is no longer a battle. That was but a local skirmish, where I had no fears but that we should triumph, and at little price. Even if we had failed, the price would have been small, in those circumstances. Now . . .' Rob shrugged heavy shoulders. 'We can *only* fail – and at a heavy price, a terrible price. The price of the future existence of our small and harried clan. A price that I am not prepared to pay, whatever. Look at these men at our backs, boy – look at them, I say,' The older man's voice quivered, but powerfully. 'They are all that malice and envy and strife have left of a once-great people. Clan Alpine, the sons of kings – there it is! Save for the boys, the dotards and the women. Would you squander it all on a lost battle, a dilatory king, and a timerous fool of a general? Would you?'

Before the pent-up emotion, almost the ferocity, of that demand, Gregor faltered. But only physically and momentarily. 'If . . . if it was my duty – yes.' he said thickly.

'Duty! Duty to whom, man? To James Stewart in France? To this new Bobbing Grace up on the hill there? Or to your own people whom you were born to serve? I thank God that *you* are not Captain of Clan Alpine this day! But *I* am – and I know *my* duty. It is to the clan first. Here we stand.'

For a full hour since the Robertsons and the Camerons had gone, the MacGregors had stood drawn up on their hillock, in solid silent ranks, plain for all to see, while the aftermath of battle eddied crazily around them. Cries, appeals and taunts had been directed at them, fists shaken. Only one or two of the broken lost rabble that streamed off blood-soaked Sheriff Muir had blessed them for standing there fast and firm in a disintegrating world and holding the ford of the Allan safe for all who could reach it. For their stand had been not altogether negative. The Government forces, wary and suspicious of that strongly placed threatening and uncommitted body of men, had kept their distance, and taken up defensive positions, out of range, to seek to contain them if they moved over. Even a detachment of the Greys had sheered off.

But none of this was enough for Gregor of Glengyle. As his uncle had pointed to the men at their backs, so did he. 'The clan! The clan!' he exclaimed. 'Always you name the clan. But there stands the clan – there! Ask them. The Gregorach are nothing if not fighting men. Think you that these feel as you do? Think you they have no minds of their own? They would fight, to a man!'

'They will do my bidding,' Rob said, without turning his head. 'So long as I am Captain, every man here will do my bidding. *Every* man!'

Gregor scanned all those faces behind him appealingly, hard strong faces. All stared directly ahead of them, grimly, fiercely, or blankly. None met his eye.

Only one man spoke, and he was no MacGregor, but one Alexander Macpherson, a burly drover from Laggan, in charge of the small party of Cluny's men attached to Rob's force.

'I am with Glengyle, Rob,' he declared, and his announcement was almost a shout, to bolster his resolve to oppose Rob Roy. 'I say that we can do no other than fight, whatever!'

'*You* say?' Rob turned now. '*You* say, Sandie?' The scorn was withering.

'Aye, I do.' Not liking the MacGregor's look, the man turned to his own Macphersons. 'Let us endure this no longer!' he cried. 'If he will not lead you, I will!'

There was a tense silence.

Rob broke it, his voice now, strangely, more pleasant. 'Were the question about driving Highland stots or kyloes, Sandie, I would yield to your superior skill.' These two had co-operated on many a cattle drive. 'But as it respects the leading of men, I must be allowed to be the better judge.'

'Did the matter respect driving Glen Angus stots, the question with Rob would not be which was to be last, but which was to be foremost, whatever!'

'Very good,' Rob nodded mildly. 'If you, Sandie – or any other man soever – would be foremost now, let him stand forward.' His hand slid down to the hilt of his broadsword. 'We shall settle the matter promptly, once and for all, I promise you.'

No man moved, no man spoke, almost it seemed that no man so much as breathed.

'Aye, then,' Rob almost sighed, and turned back to face the front, stocky, steady, firm-rooted as any tree.

Gregor all but groaned. 'There goes King Jamie's crown, then!' he said bitterly. 'Yonder sits Mar – and here stands MacGregor! And nothing achieved.'

'If they could not do it without me, they would not do it with me,' Rob Roy answered heavily, levelly, but finally. 'Peace, Greg.'

CHAPTER NINETEEN

Rob topped the long climb from Strathfillan to the pass, wearily, and drew rein at the summit to look down on the small fair oasis of Auchinchisallan, green amongst the sombre brown even in mid-December. And he sighed. He was alone; not even MacAlastair rode at his back. Better that way.

It was four weeks since Sheriff Muir, four sorry weeks for Scotland — and sorrier ones still for Rob Roy. The Jacobite cause was not so much defeated as suffering spontaneous disintegration. Sheriff Muir, despite all follies and failures, had not been a victory for Argyll; indeed, he had withdrawn from the field under cover of night, back beyond Dunblane, to lick his wounds, harder hit than anyone knew, leaving Mar still standing unmoving rather than immovable on the ridge where he had stood so stubbornly and unaccountably all afternoon. But in the morning, stiff and cold after another bitter night, instead of exploiting this residual advantage of being left in possession of the field, Mar had tamely retired back to Ardoch and Perth. And thereafter, since nothing more grievously disaffected Highlanders than retreat and indecision, the clans had begun to trickle off homewards into their mountains. One after another, under this pretext or that, or none at all, they had gone — MacDonalds, MacKenzies, Camerons, Macleans, Robertsons, Gordons, in large numbers and small they slipped away, having lost faith in their leaders and their cause.

A scapegoat inevitably had become necessary, for the cause in general and the army in particular. Mar himself did not suffice – for no one had held him in high opinion anyway, and criticism of Bobbing John was nothing new; moreover he still remained Commander-in-Chief, and so was unsuitable for open raillery. Others' reputations suffered likewise, of course – but then most of these were not sufficiently well known outside their own districts and spheres to fit the part.

But Rob Roy MacGregor was different. He was a hero, a paladin, an idol – now fallen. And there is nothing more satisfactory for angry and humiliated men to kick than a fallen idol. He had failed them, failed the army, failed the King. There were no doubts, no question about it. Everyone knew – whatever they themselves had done – what *he* had done, or not done. He had stood by while others fought and died. He had taken no part in the battle. He had held back his clan when they wished to fight. None, not even his own kith and kin, could deny it. Rob Roy was branded in the eyes of all men as rogue, craven – or worse, traitor.

Many things about Rob had been forgotten, then. But again, others were remembered. For instance, that he was a far-out connection of Argyll's, and that the Duke was said to have been notably gentle with him over his activities when outlawed. Might he not have been bribed to play the part that he did? And was his mother not a Campbell? Again, was he not famed for his fondness for other folks' goods? Had he not held his men back, perhaps, so that they might rob the baggage trains of whichever side lost? Was that not typical of the man? Certainly Mar's baggage down at Kinbuck, had been harried by somebody. . . .

And so Rob, after four grim weeks of it, had resigned his command to Gregor, turned his back on his fellows, and come home, more of an outcast than he had ever been in his outlawry. Why he came to Auch, the home that was no home to him, he might have found it hard to explain – save that it was Christmastide and his sons might possibly be looking for him. The fact was, of course, that he had nowhere else to go; his journey, even through a corner of his own clan country, had quickly demonstrated that.

He came down the hill to the cottage, snug under the remote snow-capped Beinn Dorain, and, though he did not realise it, his wide shoulders were bowed as though under a heavy load and a great tiredness. A few hundred yards from the house, the three boys emerged from the doorway and came running at their varying speeds to meet him – and his heart lifted a little. But their greetings were brief and perfunctory. Where was MacAlastair, they wanted to know? And Donald? And all the fine chiefs that had passed this way before? And how many men had their father killed in the battle? As they turned away disappointed, Rob saw himself as all but a stranger to them.

He walked his garron up to the cottage, bent of head. He perceived that Mary was standing in the doorway. He looked at her, and then looked quickly away. 'Well, Mary,' he said.

'Well, Rob,' she answered quietly, 'You have come, then.'

'Aye, I have come. You do not object to that, I hope?'

'No. No, Rob.'

'I am glad of that. I see you well, I hope?'

'Well enough, yes. And . . . and you?'

'I am tired,' he said.

She led him indoors, to the chair by the fire. She put before him whisky and cold venison and bannocks and honey. She spoke no more than he.

But she watched him, hunched there, staring into the fire, and presently she touched his shoulder lightly. 'Take them,' she urged. 'Eat and drink. It will help.'

He gave a single twitch of the head. 'Let be,' he said. 'I am tired, just.'

'Tired yes – but more than tired.'

Her tone turned him round to look at her. 'What mean you?' he asked.

239

'I mean that you need not carry your load in this house, Rob. Not here.'

He stared. 'Then . . . you *know*?' he said hoarsely.

'All the world knows,' she answered simply. 'Even I.'

The man swallowed, and his fist clenched. 'Then you know that your husband is a coward, a dastard and a traitor!' he exclaimed. 'In this very chair, one time, you named me no man. It seems that you were right, does it not?'

She shook her dark head wordlessly.

'You will know, since all the world knows, that I have cost King James his crown, lost a battle, sold my honour, failed the clans and tarnished the name of MacGregor for ever! That you know, also?'

'Should I know it, Rob?'

'Why not? No others doubt it.' Something in her voice made him look up, lost as he was in himself. 'But what has come over you, woman? It is nothing to you . . . now.'

She smiled at him, actually smiled, for the first time in what seemed an eternity – and though there was no mirth in that smile, neither was there bitterness. Indeed, there might have been a hint of warmth, of sympathy, of kindness there.

But the man if he saw it with his eyes, did not consciously perceive it with his understanding – though almost certainly it was the sub-conscious effect of that smile that broke down the tottering wall of his pride and self-esteem and hardihood. His red head dropped within his hands, and the pent-up hurt and misery was released on a flood of words.

'Did I do wrong, then? Did I fail?' he cried. 'Should I have sacrificed the clan for nothing, just? For some idea of honour? Was I wrong to be holding men's lives of more worth than that – the men who were mine to lead, whom I had brought out? Those same men, my God, who will not meet my eye now, and who turn away when they see me? Was it not to the clan that I owed first duty – the duty to use my head, my judgment? The battle was lost before ever we reached the field. Nothing that we could have done would have changed the issue, whatever. We could only have gone over and been broken. Died uselessly. Myself I would have gone, yes. But not to throw the clan away. Never! Never that! the clan that I have cherished and schemed and fought for all my days, that I would die a hundred deaths for – the clan that now turns its face from me! Aye, I care not for the rest – let other men point their fingers at me, spit at my back, say what they will. I care not. But my own people, the Gregorach . . . ! Gregor will scarce exchange a word with me, I tell you – Gregor whom I have loved as a son. Coiletter hides lest I see him. And Marchfield. And Bracklie. And young Roro. Donald will have none of me. All keep their distance. In our own country, women turn back in their doorways as I pass – the women whose men I saved! I am like a bearer of the plague, whatever – a leper! No man is my friend any more.'

It was a strange scene indeed, the great Rob Roy MacGregor, master of men, bugbear of authority, scourge of the Grahams, self-sufficient outlaw – brought low, broken, smitten to his knees, his potent armour pierced and penetrated in its one weakness, in his need for the esteem and worship of his own Gregorach. He did nothing by halfmeasures, did Rob Roy – and in his fall and abasement and hurt, the Celt in him reserved nothing. The woman, biting her lip, made as though to speak, but he went on, clenching and unclenching the fists that held his head.

'If I had not hastened from the fords of Frew, hoping yet that it might not be too late to save the folly and bloodshed of a frontal attack on Argyll, all would have been well . . . for me! Aye, even if I had turned back with Struan and young Locheil, retired with them, there would have been no outcry, I swear. God – if I had sat all day up there on the ridge with Mar, and never raised hand or voice, I would still be a man of honour and fame! But because I held the Allan Water to cover other men's retreat, because I stood my ground on the only spot that was worth the holding, because I did not throw live men after dead – because of this, I am a broken man this day! Because I was not a fool, I am a craven, a knave and a betrayer!' All but breathless, he raised a ravaged face that scarcely was to be recognised as that of the proud MacGregor. 'Was I wrong, Mary? Was I wrong?' he demanded.

And Mary MacGregor, lips parted and trembling, lovely eyes brimming with tears at last, raised open hands in a strange gesture at once surrendering, beckoning, enfolding and running forward flung herself bodily upon the man.

'Rob! Rob!' she cried, chokingly. 'My dear, my own dearest! My poor beloved Rob . . .' And her voice broke and failed her.

*   *   *

The man shook his head – but not so hard as to disturb the woman's head leaning against his neck and cheek. 'I cannot understand it, at all,' he declared. 'What has changed you, Mary?'

'You have, Rob. What else but yourself?'

'I have? How can that be? I have done you no kindness – been no other than I have always been.'

'You have needed me,' she said simply.

'Eh? Needed you? And have I not always needed you, Lass?'

'No, no, no!' She sat up within the circle of his arms, suddenly vehement, passionate. 'That you have not! Can you not see? For long you have not needed me. You were the great Rob Roy MacGregor – who needed no one but his own self. All men bowed to you. You were sufficient. You had need of none. . . .'

'*Dia*, Mary – what folly is this?' the man complained. 'You I always needed. . . .'

'A woman to keep your house, it may be! But you were

just as happy in a cave! The clan was your true love – not me! The heather was your home – not my fireside. . . .'

'Mercy upon us – what's this?' he gasped. 'You are not after telling me that *this* is what you have held against me all this time, Mary? That for such daftlike notion you have denied me your bed and kindness?'

Eyes blinking, lips tight pressed, she shook her head.

'I thought it was the Grahams,' he went on. 'Killearn – curse him! That you deemed me to have failed you, then. When they burned our house, and I was not there to be saving you. . . .'

Urgently, as with anguish, she turned to him. 'Do not say it, Rob,' she pleaded. 'That is past. I have put it from me, as well as I may. At a price. A nightmare – an evil dream! Leave it, I pray you, to time. And to God's mercy. Maybe that will be sufficient. This is otherwise. Now you have come back to me – to me truly, your wife. Needing me, as you never needed me before. Oh, Rob – *I* needed . . . just this. I am a wicked sinful woman, I think. I needed this – for all men's hands to turn against you. For you to be broken, scorned, lost. This I needed, to find you again. I have been far away, Rob – further than you, by far. Far, far, wandering, lost also. For so long. And cold – oh, so cold.' Her voice broke, but she recovered it. 'But now your need has guided me back to you, my dear . . . and I think that I will not go away again, God aiding me. Not ever. Will . . . will I serve, Rob? Now – in place of all the rest? Of fame and the regard of men? Of power, and a clan's acclaim? Will I serve?'

'As I hope for Heaven, you will!' Rob cried, his voice powerful and vibrant again. 'Lord – already you have made a new man of me, whatever! The clan may think what it will of me, and make do without me. It has Gregor, and Balhaldies – High Chief of Clan Alpine, forsooth! Inversnaid and Craigroyston may go to whomsoever can take them. Myself, I will bide here with you and the boys, Mary

a graidh. And we will let Scotland and the world go to the
devil in their own way. From now till the rim of time! And
be sorry for nothing but that I had not the wit to do the
same years before!'

The woman shook her head slowly. 'No Rob – that
would not serve. Not for you. You are too old to change
yourself into a different man – and too young to settle down
at any fireside, mine or other. Memories are short, in war,
and before long the clan will find that it needs you again.
Sooner or later you will go back to them – for you are Rob
Roy MacGregor still, and always will be, And James
Stewart is still your rightful king, no matter how weak.
But it may be that he, and the clan, will take second place
from now on . . . ?'

'Aye – by the Holy Powers, they will!' Rob cried.
'Nothing surer. I have learned my lesson, Mary my love.
You have raised me up and given me back my manhood.
One thing only I ask of you, now – and do not be lying to
me. Did I right at Sheriff Muir . . . or wrong?'

'I have never lied to you, Rob – and never shall, I hope.
I believe that you did right. Yes, right.'

'Thank you for that word, my heart's love – and thank
God! Thank God!'

EPILOGUE

THE night wind blew cold and gusty, with a hint of rain in it – though that was hardly noticeable in the spray that drifted inboard from the dark and angry waters of Loch Katrine. MacAlastair rowed the small boat, and in the stern, huddled in a plaid, sat Mary MacGregor.

'What is behind this folly?' she demanded, not for the first time. She was forced to shout, to counter the noise of the wind and water. 'Surely you must know, MacAlastair?'

The gillie shrugged his straining shoulders. 'Rob ordained it,' he declared briefly. 'He was after telling me nothing more than to bring yourself to Eilean Dhu, two hours after nightfall.'

'But why? Why?'

'I know no more than you, at all. Rob, these days, does not be honouring myself with his confidence!' That, from MacAlastair, was a remarkable statement, and the measure of the taciturn gillie's hurt. But it was not untrue. His master was a different man from former days, undoubtedly.

It was the November term again, Martinmas 1716, one year on from Sheriff Muir, eleven months from the reconciliation in the cottage of Auchinchisallan – the same cottage under Beinn Dorain that now stood a blackened and roofless shell, like the House of Inversnaid, mute witness to the zeal of General Cadogan in the cause of pacification.

Out of the squally dark loomed the blacker mass of the pine-clad islet of Eilean Dhu, in mid-loch. MacAlastair edged the boat into a point where undercut roots provided a landing-place of sorts, and aided his passenger ashore.

It required only a moment or two to establish the fact that, as yet, they had the island to themselves. It was a tiny rocky place, no more than an acre or two in extent, containing only the ruins of some ancient building against which a rude shelter of turf had been erected. Mary preferred even the gusty night to the black depths of this. In the angle between stone and turf walls, out of the wind, the gillie installed her, and lit a tiny fire, screened from all distant view, for what comfort it might offer. Here they waited, wordless.

Mary had been brought thus secretly from the small remote house of Portanellan on the rugged north shore of the loch, for Glengyle House, where she would always have found a welcome, like many another was now a burned-out ruin likewise; shelter for MacGregors had to be remote and well hidden indeed to escape the Teutonic thoroughness of the army of German, Dutch and Swiss mercenaries that King George had brought over and put at General Cadogan's disposal to teach the Highlands their lesson. Argyll was out of favour and superseded, as being too lenient and kindly disposed towards the traitorous clans, and his successor, General Carpenter, held no such views. He gave Cadogan a completely free hand. The latter could not avail much against the far and inner Highland fastnesses – but he could make an example of the fringes along the Highland Line. And with Montrose still Secretary of State and crowing louder than ever in Scotland now, official encouragement was readily forthcoming. The MacGregor country was occupied territory, for the first time in its history.

King James had come – and gone – spending a fantastic month in the North-east, holding reviews, levees and investitures, conferring honours, and then quietly departing for France again, taking Mar with him. The clearing-up process was now in full swing. So much for the cause.

They had fully an hour to wait on that island in the loch, under the sobbing pines, till the creak of oars sounded during a brief lull of the wind, followed by the sound of a powerful voice barking evident and imperative orders. There was no doubting whose voice that was.

Presently two men materialised out of the gloom. Rob Roy's figure was unmistakeable. His companion was smaller, though still a big man and heavily built.

'Ha, my dear,' Rob cried. 'You are here, then. See, my love – I am after bringing you a present.' And with a sudden explosive thrust, he hurled the other man, heavy as he was, headlong, to fall full length almost at the woman's feet.

Mary gasped – and then her exclamation changed into a choking scream as MacAlastair tossed a couple of pine branches on the fire, and it blazed up to reveal the fallen man beside her as John Graham of Killearn.

'Fear nothing, *a graidh* – he will not hurt you now.' Rob called out. 'That one's days for mischief are done. He is empty now – empty as his master's rent-box!' And he tossed down on the other side of the fire a heavy bulging leather bag that chinked musically.

Mary said nothing. Eyes wide, she stared at Killearn as he dragged himself slowly and unsteadily to his knees, panting – stared as though mesmerised in horror, but seeking, as it seemed without success, to draw back, away from him.

'Och, lass – look not so!' her husband cried, 'I thought that you wanted him? *Dia* – I have been at pains to get him for you! I vowed I'd have him, you'll mind – I vowed 'fore God he would die for what he did to you. It has taken time – but we have him now.'

The woman had managed to get to her feet, and had stepped back and back until brought up by the ruined walling. Her breath was coming in great gulps, and it seemed that she sought to hold it down with a hand across her breast, hysteria not far off. Killearn rose and stood swaying, shoulders hunched, wig askew.

Rob looked from one to the other in the flickering firelight, perplexed. 'Are you not well, my heart?' he wondered. 'What ails you? Was it the boat . . . on the loch?'

'That . . . that man!' she got out. 'Why . . . did you . . . bring him here?'

'The best place it was for him, whatever – where we could be sure to be undisturbed. Och, the country is infested, just, with these Germans. None will find him, or us, here on this island.' To give Mary time and opportunity to recover herself, he went on heartily. 'Aye – the bold fellow ventured out of his hole at last! He was after believing the tale that I set afoot that I was fled to Ireland. He conceived that it might be safe, now, with the soldiers thick as maggots, to risk showing his face to his master's tenants this Martinmas term. He chose Chapellaroch again, the man – as nearest to his bolt-hole at Buchanan Castle. But, och – not near enough, by God! Not with Rob Roy still above the sod! His fat Germans are chasing a dozen nimble gillies through the Flanders Moss – and he is here, to face his end! Montrose will be after needing a new factor from this night on, whatever!'

Mary, despite her husband's thought for her, did not seem to be listening. She did not appear to be able to take her eyes off John Graham. That unhappy individual's glance was not similarly drawn to her. He looked indeed everywhere but at the woman.

'MacGregor,' he blurted, 'You canna do this! In sweet Jesu's name o' mercy. . . .'

'Quiet you, cur! Did that name of mercy prevail with you at Inversnaid two years back? Mary – the choice is yours. How shall we reward him?'

'No,' the woman whispered, head shaking. 'No, Rob. . . .'

'Come, lass – this is not like yourself. You are a MacGregor, daughter of kings. . . .'

'I want nothing of this man. Only, never to see him again. Never!'

'That I can promise you, *a graidh*. But the manner of his end is surely of concern to you? Your vengeance. . . .'

'I want no vengeance.'

'But, *Dia* – did you not charge me to avenge you? That day at Corrycharmaig. Would that he should die, you said, as *you* had died those nights before!'

'I . . . I was beside myself, just. I spoke wildly, sinfully.'

'You spoke justly. You asked how he should suffer sufficiently. What was just a little pain, before the end, you asked? A little fear? Did I think that would serve, you said? And I swore that I would make it sufficient – I swore it before the throne of God Almighty, that he should pay in full. Now it is time to redeem my vow, Mary.'

'No! No, Rob. I will not have it. I want none of it.'

'But why, in the name of Heaven? Why?'

'Because . . . because I have put it from me. At great cost. I have fought and fought this thing, Rob. I thought . . . I thought that I had won. Now, I cannot be sure, any more. But this I know – that this man's hurt will not help me. Let him go in peace, Rob.'

'No!' It was her husband's turn to cry out. 'That I will not, by the Powers! Your soft heart may melt, your woman's will may flag and fail – but I am made otherwise. This is not a man – it is a murderous animal! While yet he lives, men will suffer. And women and bairns. Such as he are not to be spared.'

'If *I* can forgive him – as I pray God's aid to do – cannot you, Rob?'

'Forgive, is it? Do you forgive a snake that has bitten you? A wolf that has savaged a child? This animal mishandled *our* children, burned our roof over their heads, and cast them out into a winter's night. He even struck yourself, you said, my God! For that, there is no forgiveness in *me*!'

Mary MacGregor and John Graham actually looked at each other then, exchanged glances – an exchange that was as brief, furtive and strange as it was almost guilty. The woman had never told Rob the full enormity of what had been done to her that November night – had told no living

249

soul, indeed. Now, suddenly, it dawned upon Killearn that that must be so – otherwise Rob Roy would scarcely have emphasised this mere striking of his wife as the major injury. The man's abrupt tenseness betokened the first gleam of hope.

Rob, in the uncertain light of the fire, perceived nothing of all this. He went on. 'I will not forgive him – but I will do for him a deal better than he deserves. I will not kill an unarmed man, however evil. He shall even have the choice by which means he shall die – have the means to defend himself, whatever. None shall say that Rob Roy makes war on the helpless. By sword, dirk, pistol, or bare hands, we shall fight, here and now. And the choice shall be Graham's.'

'No, Rob. . . .'

'But, yes. Can I do more than that? When all that he deserves is to be cut down like any dog?'

'Pay heed to her, MacGregor,' Killearn put in, urgently. 'It would be murder, just the same. I am no fighting man. . . .'

'You were fighting man enough that night at Inversnaid, when it was women and bairns to be fought!'

'It was but my duty, man. As Sheriff.' Again that swift glance at Mary. 'In law, your goods and gear were forfeit. As an outlaw avoiding arrest. . . .'

'*Diabhol* – enough!' Rob roared. 'Would you hide behind the law now, you snivelling whelp? Choose you your weapon!'

'No – I tell you, I will not fight. Kill me, defenceless, if you will. But MacGregor – what value is my death to you? Killing me would result only in reprisals against your people. His Grace would avenge me, I assure you. But alive, I could serve you well. I am the Duke's instrument, and I could carry out his orders but gently, interpret his will towards the MacGregors more kindly. I swear that I will do this, if you spare my life. . . .'

'Faugh! Think you that I will bargain with you?' Rob

cried. 'What you have done is no more to be chaffered over than forgiven. Save you your breath, Graham.'

'Rob – heed *me*, at least!' Mary interposed, stepping forward from her wall. 'If you will not think of this man, think of ourselves. If you kill him, his death will be between us all our days. I know it. He will be like a shadow over our lives. Do you wish that? Have we not had sufficient of shadows? Oh Rob – do you not see? If you kill him, his blood is on *my* hands! And that is a thing that I could not live with.'

'Och, lassie – wheesht! Here is nonsense. You are distrait. . . .'

'Distrait, yes – and like to remain so, if you do this thing. I vowed, Rob, that nothing would again come between us. But *this* would – I know it, I swear it! Is that nothing to you? Nothing, whatever?'

'Dear God, Mary – you cannot mean this? It cannot be so.' For the first time uncertainty, indecision, sounded in the man's voice.

Quick to perceive it, Mary slipped to the ground on her knees before him. 'Look, Rob – I kneel to you!' she exclaimed. 'To ask, to beg of you, that you do not do this thing. I have never knelt to you before. . . .'

'Lord! Get up, woman – get up!' he cried hoarsely, striding forward to her. 'Never do that. Never kneel – you must not! And for this worthless cur!'

'It is not for him – it for myself. For us,' she answered, as he lifted her up. 'It is our future, our happiness, that I beg for. Will you not heed me, Rob?'

He stared at her, so close now, this strange new Mary, humble, pleading. He had never known her thus, all their days together. And he shook his head. 'I do not think . . . that I can deny . . . anything that you ask, lass,' he muttered.

'Then – you will spare him?'

'If I must.'

'Oh, Rob – thank you! Thank you! She clung to him

251

tightly in her relief and emotion. 'You will not regret it, Rob, ever. The other would have been unworthy of you. And it will be for the best, too.' She was whispering now, in his ear, held close. 'For the clan. For all of us,' she went on eagerly. 'Make him swear to treat the Gregorach kindly ever, as he promised – on pain of fullest retribution. Even have him write it down. He will do it – he will do anything for his life. Then let him go. Ourselves we will go, too. Away from here, right away. West into Argyll. To where MacCailean Mhor has offered us refuge, deep in his country. None will dare seek us there. Argyll is still king in the Campbell country. We shall be safe, and live at peace, Rob. There is nothing here for us, any more. Nothing. Let us go there, to Glen Shira, and have done with hatred and fighting. We have had more than enough. Let him, let this man that is no man, go his way, Rob, and us ours.'

He nodded slowly, to her breathless anxious spate of words. 'And my vow?' he asked.

'You swore another vow, once – before an altar. In my presence, Rob. It takes the precedence, I think!'

'Aye, lass, you have the rights of it – as ever.' He turned, one arm still around her, to Killearn. 'You owe your life to this woman whom you have wronged,' he said, flatly, evenly. 'I trust that you will value it accordingly. You will write me a paper, swearing by all that you hold sacred that you will deal kindly at all times with all of the name and race of MacGregor in acknowledgment of this life of yours. Break that bond, and I will seek you out, wheresoever you may be – and no pleading of even this woman shall save you then. Is it understood?'

'Aye. It is understood.'

'Good. And tell you James Graham of Montrose, from me, that our account is not yet closed, whatever. I think that it will not be closed while he and I still live. You will tell him that?'

'Aye.'

'MacAlastair – paper, inkhorn and quill. And more wood for the fire.' He turned to his wife, ruefully. 'As Royal's my Race – I had not thought to end this night with a quill!'

She pressed his arm. 'The night is not ended yet, Rob,' she said gently. 'Indeed, it has hardly begun!'

NIGEL TRANTER

MacGregor's Gathering

Gregor of Glengyle
– a fierce young Highlander, loyal to the cause

This was the time when the famous Rob Roy MacGregor and his swaggering nephew Gregor led the landless clan of the MacGregors. Their very name was proscribed and outlawed, but they still clung to Glengyle, one small remaining corner of their ancient territories, and held fast in their loyalty to the King over the water.

Both Rob Roy and his nephew opposed the plan to unite the English and Scottish Parliaments, a scheme that would send any self-respecting MacGregor reaching for his dirk. But in the midst of the political struggle young Gregor still managed to find time to pay court to Mary Hamilton, a lovely girl from the Lowlands who at first rejected his rough Highland ways . . .

NIGEL TRANTER

The Patriot

The year is 1678 and Scotland lies under the dark threat of union with England. In an era of intrigue and bloodshed, it is Andrew Fletcher, laird of Saltoun, who shines out as one man of ideals and integrity. His fearless and dogged opposition to the Treaty is a thirty-year campaign fought in Europe as well as his native land. His defeat is the defeat of a hero and of a cause so dear to his people that his name is glorified in Scottish history.

NIGEL TRANTER IN CORONET

All these books are available at your local bookshop or newsagent, or can be ordered direct from the publisher. Just tick the titles you want and fill in the form below.

Prices and availability subject to change without notice.

CORONET BOOKS, P.O. Box 11, Falmouth, Cornwall.

Please send cheque or postal order, and allow the following for postage and packing:

U.K. – 55p for one book, plus 22p for the second book, and 14p for each additional book ordered up to a £1.75 maximum.

B.F.P.O. and EIRE – 55p for the first book, plus 22p for the second book, and 14p per copy for the next 7 books, 8p per book thereafter.

OTHER OVERSEAS CUSTOMERS – £1.00 for the first book, plus 25p per copy for each additional book.

Name ....

Address...

....